*She* smiled. Who
so confident in his
ridicule or criticism
*her*? Or at least, let her be?

He'd certainly proven to be a friend. He had witnessed her lose all sense and control, and he'd acted as if everything was as it should be. He'd even apologized for his own poor behavior.

Had a man ever apologized to her before? She thought not.

"Thank you." The words flowed out of her.

He pulled a face, the black eye she'd given him darker than the other in the evening shadows. "For what?"

"For being—" She paused. What was the right word? "Trustworthy." She'd believed in Michael, and yet he'd proven she shouldn't have. He had never been completely honest with her, and that had been part of her discontent and frustration with living under his roof. He'd certainly never apologized for leading her on.

But this man . . .

Silvery eyes studied her a moment. She wished she could read his thoughts. He'd become quiet.

He shifted. That was when she realized their legs were practically intertwined. Her breasts rested on his chest. Her nipples were hard, and her hip rested on his—

Kit sat up, changing their position. It put some space between the two of them, and she wished he hadn't moved.

**Also by Cathy Maxwell**

# One Dangerous Night

*A Gambler's Daughters Novel*

—◦❦◦—

# CATHY MAXWELL

A V O N

*An Imprint of HarperCollinsPublishers*

This is a work of fiction. Names, characters, places, and incidents are products of the author's imagination or are used fictitiously and are not to be construed as real. Any resemblance to actual events, locales, organizations, or persons, living or dead, is entirely coincidental.

First Avon Books mass market printing: March 2024

Print Edition ISBN: 978-0-06-324121-3
Digital Edition ISBN: 978-0-06-324122-0

*Cover design by Amy Halperin*
*Cover illustration by Juliana Kolesova*

Avon, Avon & logo, and Avon Books & logo are registered trademarks of HarperCollins Publishers in the United States of America and other countries.

HarperCollins is a registered trademark of HarperCollins Publishers in the United States of America and other countries.

FIRST EDITION

24 25 26 27 28  BVGM  10 9 8 7 6 5 4 3 2

# One
# Dangerous
# Night

# CHAPTER ONE

*Talk of the devil and he will appear.*
IRISH PROVERB

This was not a night for running away.

Rain pounded against the mail coach, pelting painted wood, man, and beasts while a hard wind threatened to push them off the road. Despite the oilcloth covering over the windows, water splashed inside around the edges, puddling on the floor and dampening the wool cloak Miss Elise Lanscarr wore. She gripped the passenger strap tighter, her stomach queasy from the vehicle's wild swaying.

She was very thankful to be inside the coach. When she had set off on this adventure in the wee hours of the morning, the only passage she could afford was one of those on the roof of the Mail. She'd not been worried about the weather then. Her thoughts had been about escape.

Elise was going *home*—to Ireland and County Wicklow, to the stately Wiltham where everything in her life had once made sense. The headiness of taking action for herself was thrilling. She was bolting from London and all its nonsense, including sisters who no longer seemed to understand her.

The driver was a crude, boisterous man who yelled at his horses more than she thought he should, but she hadn't minded the open air on the roof. In fact, it had been rather pleasant considering how some of the other passengers smelled.

She had kept to herself, the hood of the black cloak she had filched from her great-aunt Tweedie pulled up over her wide-brimmed straw hat. Her blond curls were ruthlessly pulled back away from her face to keep them hidden since they were her most identifying feature.

Of course, that hadn't stopped the driver from attempting to roughly flirt with her. She was traveling alone and she was young. Apparently, that made her fair game, a completely rude and ridiculous male attitude.

Elise ignored him. She pretended she was a pious churchwoman. She kept her eyes downcast as if in prayer, murmuring a "Dear Lord" here or a "Thank you, Brother," there, as warranted.

This was not an easy role for her. She was the most outgoing of the three Lanscarr sisters; however, running away was daring. Bold. Unconventional. Even though she was taking secret pride in her independence, she didn't wish to be ruined. One person recognizing the "Belle of London" could create a scandal. Or lead her family to her before she was ready to speak to any of them.

Of course, as the day had worn on, the weather had turned. The air had grown heavy while dark, rain-laden clouds had gathered as if to declare war.

The driving also became increasingly erratic. The coachman drank without apology. The passengers all complained, and even the armed Mail Guard spoke up, not that any of it did a speck of good.

At the last coaching inn, in the face of what anyone could see promised to be a wicked storm, most of the travelers had disembarked with no intention of returning in time to leave. Apparently, they thought their lives were worth more than staying with this coach.

Not Elise. No storm, or drunken coachman, would stop her from going home, especially since she didn't have enough money squirreled away deep in the pocket of her cloak for her trip to suffer a delay.

It was to be a long journey. Her first destination was to reach Liverpool. From there, she'd cross the Irish Sea. But for now, her purpose was to get as far away from London as this coach would carry her.

Of course, that hadn't meant that she wanted to continue to sit on top, exposed to the weather. She had some sense, and if everyone was leaving, why shouldn't she invite herself to sit in the coach?

While the driver had been busy with the changing of the horses, she had scrambled down from her perch and climbed inside.

The driver had objected to her move. He'd wanted to toss her back up onto the roof next to him unless she paid the fare for the better seat. When she had tried to appeal to his goodwill, he had suggested there was one way a lass could earn her fare—and that was when Elise met her current traveling companion, who sat less than a foot from her on the hard leather seat.

He was a complete ruffian. He wore a wide-brimmed hat pulled low over his eyes and a greatcoat made of oilskin, and sported what must have been several days' growth of beard. His boots were dusty and worn as if he had already traveled a good distance and had even farther to go. He certainly didn't appear to be anyone's champion, except, he had become hers.

The driver's coarse suggestion had shocked Elise, and she shouldn't have been. Wasn't this the reason gently reared young ladies needed to be chaperoned? To keep them from men's unsavory lust?

Except Elise had always believed that if any rude fellow dared to make a disrespectful comment to her, she would *crush him* with one *cool* look. She'd even practiced it in her looking glass.

However, in that moment, instead of being disdainful, she had been so astonished by what he had suggested—and she wasn't completely certain that women actually did that to men? It sounded rather distasteful—that she'd frozen. *Her*. The one who was never at a loss for words. The *worldly* Lanscarr sister.

That was the moment the ruffian had interfered and entered her life.

He had approached the vehicle just as the driver had made his demand. Upon hearing it, or perhaps upon seeing the shock on her face, the newcomer had clapped a heavy hand on the driver's shoulder. In a low, gravelly voice, he had said to Elise, "Climb inside the coach."

She'd hesitated.

"*Go on*," he'd barked.

This time, Elise had obeyed.

The door had shut behind her, and then there was a thump as if something, or more like, *someone*, was shoved against the coach. Words were spoken but the ruffian's voice was so low, Elise couldn't make out what was being said.

Then, the door had abruptly been yanked open as if the ruffian didn't realize his own strength. He'd climbed aboard without comment, the coach leaning in his direction. He'd settled himself heavily on the seat as if exhausted. His long legs took up most of the space between them, sending Elise scooting as far away from him as she could, literally squeezing herself in a corner.

She covertly studied him. He'd removed his hat and rubbed his leather-gloved hands over his jaw as if tired. His hair was dark and in need of a barber. He didn't even glance in her direction. Instead, he slapped the hat back on his head and closed his eyes, dismissing her completely.

Elise didn't wish to talk to him. She would prefer to ignore him. Except, there was something too, well, *large* about him. With those broad shoulders, it had probably been effortless for him to toss the burly coachman around.

He also smelled of gin or perhaps rum . . . and manliness. His scent. It swirled in the air around him.

Still, she knew her manners. "Thank you," she had whispered.

In response, he'd pulled the brim of his hat lower over his eyes.

Elise gathered the hood of her cloak around her face. She could be aloof, too.

And then the driver had shouted at the horses, the Mail Guard had blown his horn, and they had been off—leaving Elise alone with her thoughts . . . and her doubts.

In truth, she needed to guard against her fears. Any wavering of her intentions to reach Ireland would see her back to her sisters, Gwendolyn and Dara, and her great-aunt Tweedie. She didn't think they'd learned she had run away yet. Last night, when Elise had slipped the money for her trip from the carved wood box where Gwendolyn kept the sisters' personal funds, she'd left a note promising she would pay back every penny. She wasn't certain how yet, but she would honor her word. She'd also asked them to not worry. She would be fine. Since they all now lived with Dara and her new husband, Michael Brogan, a week could possibly go by before the box was touched. As to her absence, she had been spending so much time as her friend Lady Whitby's guest, they would assume she was there.

Elise also worried about her reception at Wiltham. It might not be a welcoming one. After her father had been declared dead, her cousin Richard had inherited the house and grounds. Richard was not fond of any of the Lanscarr sisters. He thought them a burden and they thought him a ninny.

However, in this moment, Richard and his mealy-mouthed wife, Caroline, were preferable to staying in London, where Elise had been expected to swallow her pride and live under Dara and Michael's roof. One huge happy family—except they weren't. Elise loved Michael. *Fervently.*

She had from the moment she'd laid eyes on him at Lady Whitby's salon several months ago. In fact, she had been the *first* of the Lanscarrs to notice him. He was handsome, quick-witted, and cared about issues that mattered. As an Irish Member of Parliament, he used his position to speak out for those who were too often ignored.

Out of *all* the gentlemen who had courted

Elise, and there had been many, Michael had been the only one to capture her interest. He was perfect for her. She could see herself as his wife, standing by his side as he battled against the greedy and the arrogant.

She had also believed that he had fallen in love with her. After all, he'd always been attentive to her and had never once made a disparaging comment when she spoke her opinions. Instead, *he'd listened*.

For that alone, she would have given everything to him—her mind, her body, it could have all been his. This wasn't some small gift. Everyone claimed she was the beauty of the family. She was the most well-read. She was the one who admired great ideas, especially *his* ideas.

However, instead of Elise, he had chosen Dara. Worse, he acted happy with his decision. He even behaved as if he *loved* her.

And here is the part that hurt Elise the most in this small tragedy—Dara, her closest sister, had known the intensity of Elise's feelings for him. She'd *known*, and had married him anyway.

Now, as the only male, because society was so ridiculously silly about gender, Michael was legally considered the head of their little family. He was expected to care for his unmarried sisters-by-marriage, and Michael was the sort of man who honored obligations. He'd rented a large house close to Mayfair and had moved Gwendolyn, Elise, and Tweedie in to live with him and Dara.

That meant Elise had been forced to watch the newlyweds cooing at each other like turtledoves, day in and day out, until she just couldn't any longer. She wouldn't. She had pride. *And*, she had choices.

She would rather be beholden to her lug-headed cousin Richard than watch Michael and Dara build the life together she should have had. At least Richard and his wife, Caroline, could barely abide each other. She wouldn't have to listen to them coo. They argued constantly—

A clap of thunder was the only warning before a bolt of lightning struck close to them. Even the rain and wind seemed to stop. Light electrified the night. A tree could be heard splintering. The horses screamed. The driver swore fiercely, but his commands didn't stop the coach from jerking as the team lost stride. They seemed to swerve from one side of the road to the other—and then the guard's gun went off.

The sound sent the coach lurching forward, and then the wheels seemed to leave the ground. The horses had gone wild. No number of curses were going to control them.

Elise reached to grab the strap with both hands. She missed as the vehicle heeled up on two wheels. The force of movement sent her flying across the coach into the ruffian's hard body. Strong arms banded around her a second before the coach crashed to the ground and then rolled, up, down, over. Wood splintered all around her.

Elise's mouth opened to scream, but whatever cry she'd had was caught in her throat by the suddenness of the moment.

The coach came to an abrupt, muddy halt. Hooves pounded away as if the horses were running free of the coach.

And then—silence . . . save for the rain.

Elise held herself still, uncertain. Was it done? Was she alive?

Paradoxically, above her, one of the outside oil coach lamps still burned in the wet night. That is when she realized what she thought was the floor of the vehicle was actually a side. The door close to where she'd been sitting was missing. The opening allowed the lamp's weak light to shine inside the coach.

She'd never been so close to death. Her face was wet, whether from tears or rain she did not know. She swallowed.

Certain she must have broken something, she wiggled the toes of one foot experimentally, then the other. All good. Even her gloved fingers moved. Her rough companion had protected her fall. Once again, he had saved her, this time by his own sacrifice. She lay upon his motionless body.

Gingerly, Elise moved off him. He was like a granite boulder, practically unmovable. Her skirts and cloak were caught under his hip. She patiently tugged them free before reaching for a handhold to sit up or even stand, avoiding splintered wood.

Finally, gaining her balance, she asked, "Sir? Are you all right?"

There was no response.

He could be unconscious.

He could also be—

Elise couldn't take the thought any further. She leaned toward his face. Against all odds, the hat was still on his head. She listened for the sounds of breathing. He was turned away from her, and to be honest, if his eyes were wide open in death, she had no desire to see them. Or to touch his skin to check for a pulse.

"Let me fetch the driver," she said as if he had spoken.

He couldn't be dead. He mustn't be.

*"Sir?"* She shouted the word at him. Still no response.

He'd just saved her life. And she didn't even know his name.

Tears stung her eyes. She willed them back. A Lanscarr never cried, not when there was work to be done, or so her papa had said.

She had her bearings now. She moved, trying to avoid stepping on Mr. Ruffian's body. Yes, she could think of him that way. Someone who had rescued her on more than one occasion deserved a bit of a title out of respect.

Elise grabbed each side of the open door, placed a foot on the edge of the seat, and lifted her body out of the coach. She was tall for a woman. Not as tall as Gwendolyn, but she was strong and managed to sit herself on the open door's edge. The rain made every movement more challenging than it should be. Water ran in rivulets down her face. Her cloak felt heavy from it.

Elise pulled off her hat—it was ruined. She tossed it aside. It landed in the mud. She pulled the hood over her head.

The rain slowed, becoming a light mist. Even the wind went quiet. Elise released a shaky breath. In the oil lamp's wavering light, she surveyed the scene.

The road was lined with the dark shadows of trees in the twilight.

Her suspicion that the singletree attaching the horses to the coach had broken appeared correct. It was a blessing the animals were alive. They had run off still hooked together in their harnesses. Poor beasts. She prayed they weren't tripped up in them.

She did not see the driver or guard. "Hello? Coachman? Guard? Will you help us?" She waited for an answer. The wet air deadened sound. All was silent until she shouted, "*We need help.*"

Then, just beyond the flickering circle of coach light that reached the edge of the road, she saw a pair of boots attached to legs bent at an unusual angle. The rest of his body was a darker shape in the trees' shadows. Her heart almost stopped in distress. The heaviness of death weighed her down.

She turned away, toward the road behind them, and saw the guard. He lay crumpled in the mud as if he'd been tossed by a giant hand. Even at this distance, she knew—

No, she couldn't think on it. The thought was too terrible.

And she realized she was completely alone.

Alone and stranded someplace on the road to Liverpool. She had no idea where she was or when, or even if, help would come.

Nor was the storm finished. She could sense it marshaling its forces to come at her again.

She shouldn't have run away. Dara was right. Gently reared women were not supposed to venture out into the world. Perhaps her defiance was the reason this had happened. She may have caused these men's deaths with her willfulness.

In this moment, Elise wished nothing more than to be back in her bed in London, where her only complaint was spending another day watching the happily married couple—

A strong hand wrapped around her ankle.

It pulled on her, threatening to jerk her down. Horrified, Elise grabbed whatever she could reach to hold on to and resisted being tugged into the dark hole of the coach.

# CHAPTER TWO

*There are three creatures beyond ruling—a pig, a mule, and a woman.*

IRISH PROVERB

Consciousness came to Christopher Fitzhugh-Cox, Duke of Winderton, with a gasping start.

He lay a moment, disoriented. It hurt to breathe, it hurt to move, and he didn't understand why.

He first believed he was in his bed at Smythson—except he wasn't lying on a cotton-stuffed mattress. There were no fine sheets, no fire in the hearth. Interesting. It had been some time since he'd woken with that confusion. Of late, he'd always known exactly where he was—in a hell of his own making. No soft sheets there.

But this time, he'd apparently outdone himself. The question was: Was he sober?

That was always the first question he asked himself in the morning.

This wasn't morning.

All was wet and gray. His head pounded, the rhythm echoing in the pumping of his own veins.

Something ran down his temple, tickling him. He attempted to raise a leather-gloved hand to check it, and realized he was wedged into a tight space. He lay on his side. Apparently, water was everywhere, soaking into his clothes where his oilcloth greatcoat didn't protect him.

His wits began to return, a sign that his brain wasn't completely addled. Kit took stock of his situation. First, he hadn't been to Smythson in close to a year. Nor could he recall the last time he'd slept peacefully in a bed. And he obviously wasn't going to do so this night.

Instead, he was surrounded by an eerie silence.

Where the devil was he?

He attempted to move and discovered more aches and pains—

*The lightning strike.*

Memory returned: the wildly swerving coach, the crash, and the feeling that he would die here . . .

Kit forced himself to swallow, to draw one full, deep breath. His ribs pressed back, sending a sharp twinge through his side. If he'd questioned whether he was alive a moment ago, pain gave him the answer. Blessedly, and painfully, alive.

And sore ribs and bruises were the price he paid for tempting Fate. And for climbing into a coach everyone else was deserting, because there was a group of men on his trail and he had no desire to let them catch him. Besting them had become a source of pride.

But actually, Kit had not been in a good mood when he'd decided to take this stage of the Mail, going wherever it was going. His horse had taken lame. The beast was little better than a nag, but he'd liked the rascally thing. He'd left the gelding with the stable master and thought he might come back for him.

He also might not.

Such had been his life for the past year.

Kit had run away—from expectations, from women who rejected him, from women who gave too much of themselves to him. He'd started off this trip with some drunken idea to emulate the stories of Prince Hal. It had sounded like good fun and Kit had needed to do something. He was a complete disgrace to his family and his title. He'd gone from being a shallow but obedient duke to somewhat of a rake, but without any of the questionable redeeming qualities of one.

A year ago, when he'd found himself in a fistfight with the local doctor *and had lost*, Kit knew he'd reached the bottom. The only woman he'd ever loved had married his uncle, he had started drinking too much, he played cards as badly as his father, and he had been deserted by anyone he could call a friend. Worst of all, the only person he mattered to was his blessed mother, and she deserved better.

So, Kit had come up with a plan to save himself.

Prince Hal had not been a bad idea. The tale was his favorite as a schoolboy. They said before Prince Hal had become King Henry V, he'd lived in disguise among the commoners. He'd consorted with petty thieves and criminals. He'd seen firsthand how the classes differed. *And*, he'd enjoyed himself.

As had Kit.

He rather liked living by his wits. He'd changed his name from the weighty Christopher to Kit and followed one rule—he could not use his title or its money. If he was going to do this, he was going to do it right.

Would this experience be the making of him? Kit wasn't certain. He'd always felt inadequate. Inheriting a dukedom at a young age hadn't helped.

Over the years, he'd been told he was too inexperienced, too old, too young, not his father, too much like his father, featherheaded, too serious—the list of criticisms was tiring.

However, tramping around the country, he'd come to learn that most people, whether of the highest of the upper classes or lowest of the lower, were very much the same. There might be a difference of education, but they were all motivated by self-interest. Greed ruled mankind, he had decided, and felt both soiled and worldly for the knowledge.

Suddenly, Kit remembered The Girl.

They had been in the coach together. Where was she?

She probably was some farmer's wife or daughter or even a maid. What the devil, she could have been a nun. Cloaked from head to toe, she'd burrowed herself into a corner as far away from him as she could even though he had rescued her from the damn bastard who had been driving the coach.

Yes, she had thanked him, but in a wee voice as if he frightened her more than the lecher. Wasn't that the way it always was?

To be honest, Kit knew he wasn't a hero. He hadn't interfered because the coachman was vulgar. *All* coachmen were vulgar. Come to think of it, men were vulgar. Kit had even been vulgar more than he cared to admit.

No, he had stepped in because he was bloody tired of bastards and no longer in the mood to look the other way. The chit had the right to go wherever she wished without having to worry about rape.

Should she be under the protection of menfolk? Absolutely, but she wasn't.

So, he'd ordered her into the coach, closed the door, and grabbed the driver by the neck until the man had changed his mind about charging her extra fare. It was a simple meeting of the minds. Far from a ducal action, but vastly more effective.

Come to think on it, Christopher the duke wouldn't have even noticed a coachman making a foul suggestion to an innocent . . . so maybe Kit *was* becoming a better man?

Doubtful.

Especially if the bellwether was his antics over the last month. He was exhausted. He had those bastards from Moorcock hunting him and a host of regrets and fears he couldn't seem to shake. He'd been ready for a fight this afternoon. The coachman had provided it.

Afterwards, he'd climbed into the vehicle, ignored the chit staring at him as if he was Beelzebub, and tried to sleep despite the splashes of rain flying in his face around the edges of the window flap.

Then they had crashed.

Kit remembered the woman landing against him. He'd wrapped his arms around her, as much for his sake as hers. The weight of two bodies might manage to keep them from being thrown from the vehicle. He'd had no desire to see his neck broken.

Apparently, his plan had worked. His neck was fine, but here he was, stuck between the seats of the coach, half on his back and half on his side. The floor was wet with rain and, he imagined, the filth from who knew how many passengers.

That thought alone served as impetus to right himself.

Putting his weight on one hand, he pushed and freed his other arm. Awkwardly, he tried to unwedge himself, his ribs complaining sharply with even the smallest movement . . . but he could breathe. That was something.

He reached up for a handhold. His fingers found a dangling object, and he wrapped them around it.

At first, there was give, and then the thing pulled back. He gripped harder.

*"Let go, let go.* What are you doing?" a cross female voice said. That is when he realized he held the chit's ankle.

Good to know she was alive, too—but where was she?

He released his hold, and the leg disappeared through *the door of the coach.* The vehicle rested on its side. Of course. Now he understood the lay of it.

She had been sitting in the open doorway. He'd been so caught up in his own thoughts, he'd been oblivious to what was over his head. He heard her body scramble across the side of the coach, and then a sound, as if a weight had dropped to the ground, followed by a feminine "Oompf."

Kit found his footing and stood. His height meant his head and shoulders poked out the open doorway. *No bones broken—well, perhaps a rib,* he thought triumphantly.

Soft, misty rain struck his face. Thunder rumbled in the distance. He removed his glove and pressed the back of his left hand against his temple. The stickiness *was* blood. He had a cut, but he no longer felt disoriented. Instead, he had an urge to curse his present circumstances—which he did fluently and with great gusto. So much for adventure.

And then he realized he didn't hear sounds. Not from the horses, or the guardsman and driver, or the maid.

Where in Hades's name had she gone? Or was she on the ground with something broken? Had that "oompf" meant she was in trouble?

The concern gave him strength. He gripped the edges of the door and started to heave himself up and out when something hard and wet stirred the air around his head. Instinct helped him duck back down in the coach just in time, saving him from having his head lopped off.

He poked his head up again. "What are you doing?"

"Protecting myself." The maid sounded desperate. She was standing near the boot of the coach, on a step or something. She held the dark shape of a broken branch up as if ready to swing at him again.

Fortunately, his arms were longer. He snatched her awkward club out of her hand and threw it to the other side of the coach. "You don't need protection from me," he answered. "I'm in the middle of this like you are."

She made an exclamation of alarm before jumping from her perch and out of his view.

There had been a time when Kit had believed women were the most delicate of creatures. He'd been trained to shield them from life, to handle them with the utmost care. He was over that.

He now philosophized that the feminine sex

had a will of their own, one that rivaled cats. They did what they wanted, when they wanted, and no amount of coaxing or common sense could move them. He didn't trust cats and he didn't trust women.

Here he'd been nothing but kindness to this chit and she wanted to bash his brains in.

As he pulled himself up to perch on the coach edge she had vacated, his feet dangling in the open doorway, he immediately spied the body on the ground. With grim practicality, he surmised the man was dead. The other coachman probably hadn't survived either. There were no cries for help.

It was just Kit and the maid.

"What a bloody mess," he grumbled before looking around. "The horses are gone."

He was stating an observation, speaking aloud.

The maid's voice came from a different point than before, another side of the coach as if she hid from him. "The front of the coach is destroyed. The singletree is smashed. They must have bolted. Who knows where they are now?"

She was *Irish*.

The realization was a surprise, although Kit didn't know why it should be. Many households had Irish servants. He liked her accent. It gave her report of desperation and mayhem a musical lilt. He could appreciate that—

A wave of dizziness washed over him. He

paused, placed a hand on the side of the coach to hold himself steady, waiting for it to subside.

"Is something the matter?" she asked. Her voice came from the right front of the coach now. Apparently, she was circling him as if on the prowl.

He grunted a response.

Her head popped up again by the boot. *"Are you all right?"* She sounded frantic.

He was tempted to make a sarcastic response about worrying about him after her attempt at clubbing him. Unfortunately, he suspected she would rattle on to justify her contradictions. That is what women did. "Haven't been better."

His words sounded garbled even to his own ears. Wanting to prove his point, he pulled his legs out of the coach, thankful they still worked. Well, his ribs weren't happy, but he could live with that. A man needed his legs more than ribs.

As if deciding to offer a benediction upon them, rapidly moving clouds parted to reveal the last of a setting sun. Now Kit had a full view of the destruction around them. He was shocked they were still alive. It was as if the seats in the coach had protected them.

"The Mail Guard is behind us," the maid said. This time, her voice came from the back corner of the coach. She paused, hummed a moment, and then whispered, "He is very still."

"Oh, he's dead," Kit said, sounding a touch cheerier than the occasion warranted. "And will you stay in one place? You are as annoying as a black fly the way you buzz here and there."

She climbed onto her perch by the boot again, her expression a fierce scowl. "We have a crashed coach, we have dead people, and *I'm* annoying?"

"More than a little," he assured her. Kit slid down off the broken vehicle. He landed heavily in the mud but kept his balance. Still, his *knees*.

Leaning against the coach, she watched him warily. She looked like some specter in her long black cloak. She stood on a broken plank of wood from the boot and appeared drenched to the skin. Her hood had fallen back and her hair was plastered to her head. He probably didn't look any better.

Having firm earth beneath his boots seemed to help his equilibrium. The dizziness stopped. He walked to where the driver lay. His boots squished into the mud. Water seeped into the seams. He wished he didn't have a hole in one of his socks. Right over the big toe of his left foot, and then he silently laughed. Some duke he was. There had been a time when his valet would have never allowed even so much as a stray thread to mar his sleeve.

"You have blood running down the side of your face," she offered.

He waved off her concern.

Along the heavy forest lining the road, a hint of fog was starting to rise like wraiths from the ground. Kit was also certain the rain wasn't finished. The distant rolling thunder bothered him. It sounded as if it was moving toward them. There wouldn't be much time to do what needed to be done.

He knelt to inspect the body. The driver's neck was broken.

The other was just as dead, although Kit couldn't tell from this distance the exact cause, and he really didn't care.

"What can we do for them?" she asked.

Kit scowled. "Do?" He shook his head. Did she think they could return to life? Women. So impractical. "Say a prayer," he answered and lifted the driver. Kit's ribs on his right side complained, but not as sharply as he had first feared. Possibly, they were just bruised. He would manage. He settled the body over his shoulders and walked to the coach.

The maid made a sound of impatience. She had apparently heard the condescension in his voice. "I mean, do we bury them?"

"Too wet for that. And soon it will be too dark." Kit lifted the body up onto the coach and climbed up beside it. "I'll store them inside until we can report what happened." He gently lowered the man into the vehicle. "Sorry, man. Wish we could do better." The coachman had been a proper ass, but he hadn't deserved this death.

Kit had also best hurry with this grim task. The storm was rapidly rebuilding. The clouds were gathering to block out what little of the fading day was left. He jumped down from the coach and walked to the guard's body.

"What of us?" the maid asked. "Where will we go?" She paused, and then, as if admitting a great failing, confessed, "I don't know if I want to weather the storm inside the coach with dead men."

"I know I don't." Kit boosted the guard onto his shoulders. "Especially since more rain is coming. We need to find somewhere drier."

He'd managed not to look at the dead men's faces. This was grisly work. A year ago, he would have been too fastidious to do it.

Reaching the coach, he climbed onto it with his second burden. He was about to lower the guard inside when, in the oil lamp's weakening flame, he caught sight of his hat. It had fallen off when he'd stood up and now rested precariously on the edge of the seat.

Kit had grown fond of the wide-brimmed hat. It made him feel like a man of the people.

Rolling the guard's body aside, he reached until he could catch the leather brim between two fingers. It gave him great satisfaction to slap it on his head. He then eased the second body into the coach. One man lay on the other. It couldn't be helped. Tomorrow, when he had light and, hopefully, more help, he would see to giving them the dignity they deserved.

He straightened. The mist was rapidly changing to rain. "I suggest we seek shelter."

The maid stood to the side of the vehicle. "And how shall we do that?"

"We are on a main road. There must be a cottage or a manor close by."

"I don't know," she answered, her voice worried.

"I do," he replied with confidence. This was England. Certainly, there would be someone living close to the road.

"Maybe we should stay here?" she suggested.

"With the bodies?" he reminded her.

Her face was a white oval tight with concern in the gathering darkness. "Which direction shall we take?" she asked at last.

"Does it make a difference?" He hopped down. The bottoms of his socks were thoroughly soaked now and it was damn uncomfortable. "Come," he said. "We shouldn't have to walk far." He offered a gloved hand. "Are you dry beneath that cloak?" He was thankful for his oilcloth coat.

"Dry enough," she answered, ignoring his hand. She started walking back in the direction the coach had traveled.

So much for friendliness. With a shrug, Kit followed, a bit relieved to not have made the decision on direction. Hauling bodies was not only unsavory work, but a reminder of how close Kit and the maid had come to death. He was more than willing to put distance between him and the accident. He hoped they could find a safe haven quickly. A friendly fire and a warm toddy would mellow the hard edges of this day.

He began scanning the forest for any sign of civilization.

He was so taken with that task, he almost walked right over her.

"Would you watch yourself?" she demanded.

"Would you move a little faster?" he snapped back. "I'd like to find shelter before we receive another drenching."

Her response was a huff. She pulled ahead of him, head up, shoulders back. A queen couldn't hold her nose so high in the air. Her feet made sloppy sounds in the mud.

Kit grinned. Wasn't it said Irish lasses were too headstrong for their own good? His companion was giving truth to the statement.

Except at that moment, the skies opened. Rain poured down and from off in the distance came a crack of lightning.

Enough of games. Kit reached for the maid, grabbed her arm, and dragged her into the shelter of the forest.

# CHAPTER THREE

*Any man can lose his hat in a fairy wind.*
IRISH PROVERB

"*W*hat are you doing?" Elise snapped as she dug in her heels and yanked her arm away from Mr. Ruffian.

He released his hold. "Nothing vile," he informed her. "Just trying to keep both of us as dry as possible."

There was that. It bothered Elise to think he might be right. She took a step closer to the trunk of a very large tree, thankful for what shelter the leafy branches could afford her from the heavy rain.

However, it wasn't much.

"We need to keep moving," Mr. Ruffian said. "There has to be shelter somewhere."

She wasn't certain his assumption was correct. She had also decided this was a miserable trip. And while her act of running away was to let her sisters know she could not, would not, live under Dara and Michael's roof . . . right now, the thought was small comfort.

In fact, she felt completely foolish. What if she perished out here? Or was swept away in flooding—

"Why were you traveling alone on the Mail? Don't you have any family?" His gruff voice stopped the strident trajectory of her thoughts.

She had plenty of family. And they would be horrified by her actions.

But she wasn't about to share that with him. He was nobody . . . and exactly the sort of male who could ruin her if word got back to London of them traipsing around together. Elise had enemies. The other debutantes of the Season envied what they perceived as her social success. Whether she stayed in Ireland or returned to London, no one must ever learn anything about this terrible night.

Without answering, Elise pushed away from the tree, pulling the damp hood of her cloak over her head. "We aren't finding shelter standing here." She took a step in the direction of the road and stopped as the rain suddenly whooshed down in curtains. She jumped back, right into Mr. Ruffian. Her shoulder blades bumped into his chest. She teetered slightly, her balance giving in the soft earth under her feet. His arm, strong and solid, came around to steady her.

Elise's first instinct was alarm. She hadn't expected him to be this close. Her heel had almost stepped on his foot.

And then came awareness. A *dangerous* awareness. At how tall he was. How muscular. How he'd stopped her movement as if he were a brick wall.

A brick wall that caused a tightening response inside her. Surprisingly, *deep* inside her. In her most intimate places.

The jolt of awareness catapulted Elise into a new confusion. She was in no mood to deal with men. Her heart had been broken, never to be repaired. And yet, something inside of her was stirring, and it wasn't anyplace close to her heart.

In that moment, she had clarity: she'd made a mistake. She *shouldn't* have run away. She shouldn't be alone with such a rough man whose presence unsettled her. She needed to return to London. *Now.*

As if the hounds of hell nipped at her heels, Elise charged into the rain. She didn't completely understand her momentary unasked-for attraction to Mr. Ruffian, but she was not going to cater to it—

Her foot slid on mud and wet grass. She lurched forward. Her hands reached out to catch her, but then something pulled on her cloak, setting her back on her feet.

Mr. Ruffian. *Again.*

"Careful," he warned, rain sluicing off the

brim of his hat. "It is growing too dark to go racing off."

These were not romantic words. Certainly not the flowery phrases of her London suitors who would have thrown down their coats for her to walk over. He hadn't even offered his oilskin for her protection.

Could it be that he didn't find her attractive? This was a confusing thought. Granted, she didn't appear at her best but men had catered to her. Sometimes, just for her youth alone. Apparently, Mr. Ruffian had no reaction to her. He acted as if she was being silly.

Elise picked up her cloak and her skirts and tried to march on, vowing to be more circumspect in the future. She didn't care what he thought. He meant nothing to her. She moved into the forest, keeping to where a leafy ceiling of branches offered some protection from the weather.

"Yes, princess," he muttered, following her.

*Princess?* What was he talking about?

Men were so annoying. She kept moving.

And he kept it up. As she pushed her way along the forest edge, the rain impeding her progress, he walked behind her, sarcastically grumbling, "Thank you, princess. I only live to serve, princess. Is there anything else you need of me, princess—"

Elise whirled around and punched a finger into his chest. *"Stop this.* I didn't ask you to help me. You don't even have to follow me—"

Lightning cracked the sky, electrifying a tree in the distance. For a brief moment, the flash of light emphasized just how dark it was in the forest.

His manner changed. "We need to get out of this," he shouted. Before she could respond, he threw an arm over her shoulder and started to drag her into the almost total darkness of sheltering trees.

He practically carried her several feet into the forest before Elise had the wherewithal to balk. She threw her arm back so that she could twist away. "I don't need—" she started when her gloved outstretched hand hit something.

There was a loud, hurt yelp.

Now Elise practically jumped into Mr. Ruffian's arms. Her mind scrambled with fear. What had she touched that could make such a sound? Her first thought was of a story about a lion that had escaped from a traveling menagerie in Exeter and had attacked a coach's horses. Could a lion be out and about with them?

"*What?*" he shouted at her through the rain. "What is the matter?"

A bark, a snarl sounded close to them. "*That's* what," she answered. Couldn't the oaf see? *Something* was there.

He turned so that his body shielded her from this unseen menace and took a step forward. Thunder rolled overhead, a herald that another crack of lightning could not be far behind.

There was a whimpering sound.

"What the—?" Mr. Ruffian whispered and then knelt. "It's a dog." Lightning flashed a hair's breadth before the sky crackled with it, highlighting the animal's wet nose, inches from Mr. Ruffian's offered hand. The dog cowered from the sound. Mr. Ruffian said gently, "It is all right, boy. It can't harm you."

"Actually, it can," Elise had to point out. "Especially if it hits that tree."

As if he agreed, the dog barked.

Mr. Ruffian stood. "He wants us to follow him."

"You don't know that," Elise answered. She liked dogs and missed the ones at Wiltham, but she couldn't commune with them. And she wouldn't follow any of them in a storm. "Dogs don't do well in storms."

Instead of listening, he started chasing the dog who had already taken off . . . almost as if he understood what Mr. Ruffian had said.

Elise waited a moment, the darkness all around, and then there was a series of lightning flashes. She didn't know if she was safer standing where she was or following the dog. A particularly nasty crack like a tree branch toppling close to her settled the matter. She wasn't safe here. She might not be safe with Mr. Ruffian, but at least she wouldn't be alone.

She took off after her disagreeable companion.

He wasn't hard to follow. She just had to tag after the crashing sounds and the grunt of pain as Mr. Ruffian tripped over something on the forest floor.

Then, just as she reached man and dog, they stepped into a clearing.

Lightning lit the area, revealing a small, wayward-looking hut. The dog didn't waste a moment but ran inside the door that was barely hanging on leather hinges.

Mr. Ruffian and Elise both followed. Anything to get out of this horrid weather. Elise practically threw herself into the room. A shadow blocked the door as the ruffian joined them.

They stood in the dark, dripping wet and catching their breaths.

"You are a good boy," Mr. Ruffian whispered to the panting dog. "Thank you." He'd bent down, his movement silhouetted by the doorway.

"Do you imagine he speaks English?" Confusion, fear, and frustration made her sound sharper than she wished. This was not how she'd planned her trip to go. She should have almost been to Liverpool by now.

"Someone is in a foul mood."

She ignored him and tamped down all the doubts swirling inside her. She moved a few steps into the space surrounding them, her arms outstretched. Her hand felt a wall. She turned, moving slowly in another direction. Seven steps and another wall. There was some wetness in the air, as if the roof leaked. That would not be surprising, and she remembered the stories her Gram had told her about how fairies and sprites lived in the trunks of trees and inside moss-covered and rotting logs. Elise had imagined their homes as little cottages, and that is exactly what this place seemed. A full-sized fairy home.

Her Gram would have also admonished her to keep her chin up and make the best of what was happening. The storm, the bolting horses, none of it was her fault.

They also weren't *his.*

She could almost hear Gram's voice point out how difficult she had been behaving.

Whether Elise liked it or not, they were going to be sharing this shelter until the storm let up and they could reasonably seek help. Some of the tension inside her released. She glanced in the direction of the still half-open door where he stood.

He was holding a hand up as if to ward off something. "Wait, boy—don't shake. *No.*" But his admonishment didn't stop the dog from letting all the drops of rain fly from his fur. They whisked through the air, hitting everything in the small space.

Elise was so wet, she couldn't tell if she'd been struck. "I doubt if he is a dog at all," she said.

"You don't? He smells like one."

"Dogs don't need shelter. Or appear at the right moment when needed."

"Then what is he?"

She almost smiled at the suspicion in his voice

before saying lightly, "He is probably a wizard in disguise."

There was a moment of startled silence, and then her companion gave a sharp sound that might have been laughter. "You Irish," he muttered.

Yes, *we* Irish. A wave of homesickness overtook her. She yearned for the past, her life at Wiltham, hearing her Gram's teasing about fairies and the little people who lived in the meadows. Or telling her she was a "lazybones" and best be up and about her chores.

She also missed the way she and her sisters had been back then, so close it was said one couldn't slide a sheet of foolscap between them. Or how she and Dara would lie in bed and whisper secrets about the day. They had always shared a room . . . until Elise's jealousy about Michael had boiled over.

Her throat tightened. She squeezed her eyes, willing back tears. This was not the time to fall apart—

The sound of metal striking flint caught her attention.

Her gaze was pulled to a flame. In the wee light, she watched Mr. Ruffian blow on the tinder, urging it to nourish the flame.

While she had been feeling sorry for herself, he had been practical. He had gathered everything dry that he could find and had set about to start a fire. In the growing light, she could see a small pile of sticks.

Elise reached out around her, finding what felt like wood bits and the like. She gathered them up and leaned forward to offer them to the fire.

He nodded at her, smiling. "Not so bad now, is it?"

"It is terrible," she replied honestly. "The smoke will fill the hut."

"A bit. That's why I started it by the door."

"Wet air won't draw smoke."

He sat back. "We can only do what we can do. This won't last long anyway, but it is nice for the moment."

She frowned, knowing he was right and, for some reason, not liking it. She wasn't comfortable with him. Perhaps if he'd been shorter, thinner, less *present*, she could relax.

"You sound like a vicar," she managed. "Platitudes won't help us."

He shrugged, not taking offense. "Platitudes are all I can offer." He sat back against the wall, one knee up, his other leg stretched out, careful of her space.

The dog lay down. He was a shepherd's dog, a little collie, with an intelligent look to his eyes. He behaved as if his work was done and he was glad for it. He was a shaggy thing. His coat was black, his legs white. A mask of brown covered his eyes and nose. He rested his head on crossed paws.

Outside, the rain wasn't showing any sign of letting up, although the thunder and lightning seem to have passed. That's when Elise realized how fast her heart had been beating, how high-strung she'd felt since the crash—no, since the very early hours of the morning when she'd snuck out of the house on her mission—

"Are you hungry?"

Elise glanced at him blankly, needing a moment to register his words. Hungry? Dear God, *yes*, she was starving. She'd taken two buns and a piece of cheese from her family's larder, but that was long since gone.

Still, she needed to be wary. A lone woman must be careful. He'd not acted as if he would harm her, however men were funny creatures. They assumed rights. Wise women were cautious.

He didn't wait for her answer. Instead, he pulled a cloth bag from the pocket of his coat and opened it. "I don't have much. Just some salted meat, but it will do us some good, I think, to have something to eat."

Salted meat. Elise detested the stuff and yet her stomach gave her away. It rumbled in the most unbecoming fashion.

"Here," he offered, holding out the bag. "We have plenty of water to go with it." He nodded to the door.

She hesitated. The more distance between them, the better. Except, she *was* hungry. She took the bag. It was almost empty. She pulled out a piece of the beef, murmuring a doubtful thank-you to acknowledge his willingness to share with her.

He removed his leather hat and ran a hand

through his hair before taking the bag back. He pulled out two pieces and tossed one to the dog, who had been watching the transaction with eager eyes. The pup snapped at the meat while it was still midair.

Elise nibbled on her beef stick before sinking her teeth into it, her appetite springing to life.

Mr. Ruffian didn't waste time chewing on his piece. He closed his eyes and leaned his head back against the wall as if savoring the finest dinner. Elise studied him. She'd not lie. She was grateful for the company and for his help in this terrible adventure. Nor was he hard on the eyes, even in his ungroomed state . . . or perhaps because of it?

And then there was the dog. After finishing his beef, he'd laid his head on Mr. Ruffian's leg and fallen into a snoring sleep. Didn't dogs have some ability to sense out the motives of people? Elise had always thought they did. The dogs at Wiltham knew the difference between a guest and a stranger. They'd even been smart enough to growl at Richard when he'd made his first appearance.

Mr. Ruffian absently patted the dog's head. Elise took in every movement as if they were a cypher to the man—

"So, who are you?" His deep voice interrupted her thoughts. "What is your name? And why are you traveling England alone on a night like this?" He hadn't opened his eyes but spoke in staccato notes as if she owed him an answer.

She didn't. The world must never know that Miss Elise Lanscarr spent a night with the likes of him, even in these circumstances. Even if nothing untoward happened, which it wouldn't. She knew how to take care of herself.

"I'm going to sleep," she replied, taking her cue from the dog. But first, she needed to . . . have a moment of privacy. She also realized she was very thirsty after the salted meat. That meant going outside.

Elise stood. She would have to step around him to reach the door. Reasoning that she needn't explain herself to him, she started moving in that direction.

He turned so that his legs, crossed at the ankles, blocked her way.

"Where are you going?" he asked. His eyes were open now.

"Excuse me?" she said pointedly, frowning at his legs in her path.

He lifted a brow. No duke, she thought, could have had a better brow lift. Then he raised a hand as if silently divining what she planned. Slowly, as if with great effort, he stood. "Here, you will do better wearing my coat in that mess out there."

"I don't—"

"Take it." He had already shrugged out of it. He was wearing a deep marine jacket over what had once been a white shirt, the neckcloth tied in a loose knot as if he couldn't be bothered with any formality. He held the oilskin out to her. "Go on. The one you are wearing is all but soaked through. You'd be best to leave it here."

He was right. Still, she hung back. All the money she owned was in the pocket of the cloak.

Mr. Ruffian shook his head as if she annoyed him. "You needn't be afraid of me, lass. You don't even tempt me."

*Not tempt him?* Elise had never heard those words. She attracted most men, and then she realized that she probably resembled a drowned rat more than a pampered debutante.

He shook the coat he held in his hand.

Outside, the rain kept its steady beat. She took his coat.

"You might wish to remove your cloak. Let it dry," he repeated.

Elise hesitated, but then decided that if she returned and the money hidden in its deep pocket was missing, she would wait until he was asleep and lash into him in such a way he'd never thieve again.

Decision made, Elise removed Tweedie's cloak, folded it once, and set it on the ground.

"What in deuces are you wearing?" he asked in astonishment. "Is this some new fashion? Can't say I admire it."

Elise felt her cheeks heat up. She wore three of her best dresses. One on top of the other. Her elegant muslin gown was beneath a sensible walking dress, which was beneath a sprigged muslin day dress. It made for an odd pattern.

The reason she had on three of her best dresses was that she had not wanted to be caught sneaking away from the house with a valise. She also hadn't wanted to carry the heavy leather bag on a Mail Coach. It would become tiresome. Besides, in her anger over the marriage and living arrangements, she'd been spending a great deal of time at her friend Lady Whitby's house. She reasoned that her sisters would see the valise stuffed under her wardrobe and assume she could not have run off far if it was still there.

Still, she'd needed something to wear in Ireland, and wearing three frocks had seemed the best solution.

She threw his oilskin around her. The greatcoat engulfed her. That didn't matter. She wanted to block his critical gaze, and her needs had been growing since they had started sparring over the coat. She wrapped it around her, lifting the collar to cover her head, and, without a word in his direction, moved out into the night.

It didn't take long to see to her business. She didn't even have to travel far because it was dark and somewhat scary to be out here alone. Relieved, she splashed rainwater in her hands before cupping them to catch what she could and taking a drink.

For a moment, she considered staying out in the night. The rain was soft and gentle now. There was no more thunder or lightning. Still, it was wet. Muddy wet. She was also tired. Now that she had let herself relax, exhaustion was taking over.

Elise looked toward the hut with the warm glow of a fading fire coming through the doorway. Mr. Ruffian had sat back down again. She could see his long leg stretched out. The dog waited on his haunches in the doorway as if concerned for her return.

It was not the ruffian's fault the coach had crashed. Or hers. She didn't need to be so suspicious. All would be fine. She'd be back on the road to Ireland on the morrow. This night would soon become the past. She just had to be brave and see her way through it.

The dog stood and wagged his tail in welcome as she entered the hut. Mr. Ruffian glanced up. Was it her imagination that he seemed peeved with her?

Should she care?

"Elise," she heard herself say. "My name is Elise." That was all he needed to know. Nothing more. She removed the coat, shook it off, and offered it to him.

He took it from her. "And here I had you pegged for a Molly."

Elise frowned. "Molly?"

"A good name for a maid."

The Lanscarrs had a maid named Molly. It was on the tip of Elise's tongue to let him know she was no maid, and then she realized that it did not matter. Let him think her a maid. Then he wouldn't expect to find her in a London drawing room or a County Wicklow cotillion. She returned to her place on the other side of the narrow hut.

"Why are you wearing everything you own?" he asked.

"Convenience," Elise said and sat on the dry dirt floor. She gathered Tweedie's damp wool cloak around her, checking the pocket. Her money was there. The inside of the cloak was still a bit dry. That was the value of good thick wool.

Mr. Ruffian grunted a response and then asked, "Would you like my name?"

"I'm fine with thinking of you as Mr. Ruffian."

"What?" His shock echoed in the hut, and then he started laughing.

Elise burrowed down into the cloak, scooting herself comfortably into a corner.

"Did I hear you correctly?" he demanded. "Did you call me a ruffian?"

She had, but she didn't need to tell him that. Instead, she curled herself into a ball, and surprised herself by falling asleep. She was so weary. So very weary.

✦✦✦✦✦

KIT WATCHED ELISE shut him out and fall into what appeared to be a deep sleep. She had a powerful will.

*Mr. Ruffian.*

Now that was one he would not forget.

Her hair was still wet from her trip out into the rain. Dark blond hairs curled around her face. He eyed the dog, who watched him with intent golden-brown eyes. "She is a lovely lass. I hadn't noticed till now. Young, too."

The dog didn't answer.

Kit scratched the dog's neck. The animal had saved them this evening. With his other hand, he reached for some more of the pieces of dry twigs and leaves and threw them on the fire. It wouldn't last until morning. However, he had needed the bit of light and warmth, and he suspected Elise had as well.

There was a story to the girl. Over his last year of travels, he'd met more than his share of fellow wanderers with their own tales. He wondered about hers. He wouldn't have thought twice about a maid sent out alone, but not one wearing everything she owned.

What could her story be? A broken heart? A disappointment in love? Perhaps she was running from a cruel master. Mayhap the master's son had tried to take terrible advantage of her. Yes, that was the story. A servant on the run. Or a cousin of some family that didn't want her any longer because, after all, Elise was not a servant's name.

She was heading home, he decided. Her direction was Ireland.

And what did it matter to him? He had his own demons.

Since she didn't want his coat, he huddled under it himself, and sleep quickly found him.

⬦━✦━⬦

ELISE SLOWLY WOKE, her head on her arm. The shepherd's dog curled next to her. Her dresses would be ruined by sleeping on the ground. There was nothing she could do about it.

Outside, the rain kept its relentless pace, a watery light coming in through the windows, and that is when she realized she was at Wiltham, her family's Irish estate. She'd slept on its hard floor. She stood and found herself in the upstairs hallway. She could feel the worn carpet beneath her bare feet. The dog had vanished. Poof. Gone. She must have dreamed it, and she was now awake?

Gram was here. Somewhere. She knew it.

Elise hurried her step, anxious to find Gram and let her know what Dara had done to her. How she had ruined Elise's life. How she had expected Elise to pretend her heart hadn't been destroyed by her sister's selfishness—

There were voices.

Elise stopped, turning as she tried to hear what was being said. The voices came from one of the bedrooms. So many bedrooms up and down the corridor. The hallway had never been this long before.

*The voices were clearer now, and to Elise's horror, she heard Dara's voice. Then Gwendolyn's. They were talking about her. She couldn't make out the words. Were they speaking to Gram? Elise hurried her step, frantic to reach her grandmother before Dara and Gwendolyn could persuade her that Elise should not have run away.*

*And then she heard inarticulate cries.*

*Where were the sounds coming from? The cries sounded like mewing cats, or were they the voices of her sisters? Of Tweedie?*

*She shouldn't have left London. Shouldn't have.*

*Desperate now, Elise opened the first door she could reach. The handle dissolved in her grip. She ran to another door. That handle, too, evaporated at her touch.*

*The cries grew more frantic. She tried another door, and this time the handle stayed solid. She opened it—and spiders rained down on her. Brown, hairy, angry spiders the size of her hand. One landed on her shoulder and Elise screamed—*

"Elise. *Elise.*"

Her eyes opened. She stared up into a man's face. She didn't know him, and yet, he was familiar? But not in a safe way. Her heart lurched in fear.

Elise balled her hand into a fist, and she struck him in the face with everything she had.

# CHAPTER FOUR

*If a cat had a dowry, she would often be kissed.*
IRISH PROVERB

The last thing Kit had expected was a blow to the eye that would have made even the most hardened, bare-knuckled brawler proud. The power behind her punch rattled the inside of his brain.

He fell back, the dog giving a sharp bark of alarm. Kit covered his eye with a palm, waiting for the wave of pain to subside. With the good eye he had left, he watched as Elise looked around dazed as if she was coming from another place and time.

Instead of apologies or even anger, she sat up straight like the most proper of young ladies. She touched her hair, her shoulder, and then the rough floor, obviously attempting to regain her balance or sense of place . . . and then her gaze settled on him.

The fire had long ago died out. What light they

had flowed through the door. Outside, the morning air was cool and moisture-laden.

He shifted or she shifted—Kit wasn't certain which—but the movement allowed a thin ray of sun to catch on the loose, gleaming gold of her hair. The light intensified the jewellike blue color of almond-shaped eyes, the pink of perfectly formed lips, and robbed him of speech.

Even when she'd been soaking wet, there had been no denying her youth or the perfect oval of her face and the clarity of her skin. But he had been busy trying to survive a crash and a storm. He'd had little time for ogling.

He found the time now, and all he could do was gape . . . because this didn't make sense.

No man in his right mind, even the master of a household with a thousand servants, would let such a beauty wander around without an escort. The English countryside was not safe. Kit knew. He'd just spent months meeting the very best rascals and scoundrels of England. A fresh beauty like hers would be bait for every scheming villain. Ones much worse than last night's hapless coachman.

A concerned line formed between her brows. "What were you doing over me?" she demanded, dark suspicion in her voice.

His momentary admiration for her beauty evaporated. Damn it all, he'd been nothing but bloody gallant to her and she treated him as if he was some reprobate. The notion offended Kit.

He lowered his hand to let her see the damage she had caused. He had no doubt his eye was already turning bruised. She'd landed a good one. "You were having a nightmare. You were screaming. I thought to wake you. Even the dog was upset," he added churlishly.

Her response was not one of remorse or contrition. Instead, as if she was the bloody queen, she looked away.

And that was it. No words of gratitude or apology. Just a silent dismissal.

Kit rose. His boots were still wet, his clothes felt plastered on him, and he smelled of dirt and woodsmoke. He dragged open the door on its leather hinges and stomped out into the world, his oilskin greatcoat flapping behind him.

He made his way through the trees. The ground was soaked and muddy beneath the leaves and pine needles. The dog had chosen to follow him and now charged into the woods as if he, too, wished for his own company.

The cool air was exactly what Kit needed to restore his equilibrium. What the bloody hell had come over him?

The lass meant nothing to him. She'd had a bad dream. He'd sought to help. In turn, she had just made it clear she didn't want anything from him. Very well. This was not his first black eye. It probably wouldn't be his last.

However, why did *he* feel as if he'd failed? Why was he so anxious to please? Especially when it came to women? And why was he attracted to the most independent of their sex?

Just once, he would like to be gallant and have a female do more than act as if his attention was expected. Well, that wasn't true. Many women had fawned over him . . . but they were never the ones who sparked his interest.

He stopped by a stalwart oak, taking a moment to himself, before recognizing another unexplained emotion—the chit irritated him.

Yes, she did. Kit wasn't certain why . . . but she made him edgy and . . . uncertain?

He hadn't felt this particular stew of feelings since Kate Addison.

Now he *knew* he was on dangerous ground. The thought of Kate stirred up uncomfortable regrets and a host of unresolved grievances. Her rejection was what had sent him spiraling out of control. Because of her, he'd felt the need to say bloody good riddance to London, and to all the rest—the responsibilities, the gossip, the constant watching, the jaded attitudes.

And it had been fun to escape, at first. He'd experienced unbridled joy in doing exactly as he felt, saying whatever he wished, being unrecognized. If he behaved like an ass, it was Kit who had done it, not the duke. If he lost money gaming, no one raised eyebrows and shook their heads. No one suggested that the "duke" suffered from his father's misdeeds.

He did miss his mother and the staff at Smythson who had been more family than servants to him. He'd also started to realize that Kate had been a rite of passage in a young man's life instead of some great love. The older woman and the younger man. His memories of her had grown less bitter as time had passed . . . or perhaps he'd matured a bit.

But that had been a hard-fought maturity. Kit had no desire to come under a woman's thumb again.

He scratched his whiskers. They annoyed him, but he was too lazy to pull out the kit in his coat's pocket to shave. He started back to the hut. The early glow of a July sun was working its way through the trees.

He stepped over a small brook and then knelt for a drink. The rainwater had an earthy taste. It was not unpleasant.

The bushes close to him quivered and shook as the dog came crawling out, his expression one of wolfish delight. This morning's run through the woods must have been good. He loped over to Kit as if they were the closest of partners and started drinking.

"Not ready to give up on us yet, eh, lad?" Kit asked, pleased the dog had returned.

The dog looked up, panted with his red tongue lolling out, and then returned to the stream.

Kit took what was left of the salted meat from his pocket. There wasn't much. He gave the dog a piece.

One stick left. He wrapped it back up. The chit would need it. He'd find something to satisfy his appetite later. He knew how to go hungry.

Rising, he said, "Come, let's see if the princess is ready to return to the road." He wanted to be at the coach when it was discovered. People jumped to conclusions, especially around dead bodies. He wanted to tell his story before one could be made up. Also, another Mail should be coming through, and he planned to be on board.

Having gulped down the meat, the dog was happy to dance at his heels as Kit walked back to the hut. He ducked in, and then stopped. The hut was empty.

The dog's bark made him look outside—the chit was leaving. He could see Elise's cloaked figure tramping off hurriedly through the forest.

After all he'd done to see her safe, she was just marching away without even a farewell?

He looked at the dog. "Some people are never grateful."

The dog didn't comment but observed Elise work her way through the trees.

"Do you believe we should tell her that if her goal is the road, she is going in the wrong direction?"

A tail wagged.

Kit shook his head. "I'm tempted to let her discover for herself." He watched her. The damp, heavy cloak weighed her down. She stumbled, and his view was blocked by some shrubbery. He heard her make a frustrated sound. Her head popped up into view as she righted herself. She trudged on.

Elise was *not* his responsibility.

A wet nose nudged his hand. He looked down into anxious brown eyes. "You go tell her," he said to the dog. "She won't appreciate it from me. She's labeled me a bounder."

His canine companion didn't act mollified.

Nor was Kit's conscience.

*God in His Heaven.* He marched to the hut and retrieved his hat. It had been with him from almost the beginning of his journey. Since donning this hat, Kit had learned some very hard lessons. The hat seemed sometimes to be the only thing holding him together.

And that is when he realized what it was about Elise that had captured his attention—well, his attention *beyond* those startlingly beautiful eyes.

She was angry.

Kit recognized it because that same anger burned bright and deep within him. He hadn't even known it had existed until Kate had rejected his love and chosen his uncle instead. Then, that anger had exploded. After all, dukes weren't supposed to come in second best.

And if they did, what did it say about them?

That question still haunted Kit. He'd made a muck of everything . . . betrayed everyone who had cared for him. He didn't even know if he could return to his former life, not without appearing a damn fool.

Whether Elise knew it or not, she was traveling the same road. He recognized the tightness in her and that fierce fury that was always ready to erupt.

He didn't know her story. But he felt her confusion.

Suddenly, he understood. His task was to protect her until she could take care of herself. And the first order of business was to point out to her that she was *physically* going in the wrong direction.

"Come, dog."

He set off after Elise.

HER GRAM AND aunt Tweedie had agreed that Elise was the most obstinate of the sisters. Many had believed Dara was the one who had to have her way in every matter. Or Gwendolyn, who always seemed to do exactly as she wished whether her sisters supported her or not.

But Gram and Tweedie were right. Once Elise set her mind to a task, there was no stopping her.

Right now, she was using her stubbornness to keep going.

She had paid her fare to the next posting inn. The Mail should honor it. All she had to do was reach the road and wave down the next coach.

Perhaps she could still make Liverpool before tomorrow evening. Perhaps she could pay her way onto a boat and sleep there for the night. After a dream of spiders, she wanted to focus on outcomes that gave her hope. Elise could thrive on hope—

Footsteps behind her interrupted her thoughts. *He* was coming.

Of course he was. The man was a sticky burr.

He was also guilty of that trait Elise had seen in every male of her acquaintance from the village oaf to a noble lord—overconfidence. They naturally believed themselves to be superior beings whose commands should be instantly obeyed. They couldn't stand for anyone, especially a woman, to take action for herself.

She and Lady Whitby had discussed the matter thoroughly. Lady Whitby ran a political salon that was a favorite of London's governing set. She was as independent-minded as Elise.

The laws of England were woefully unfair to women. Why, the whole reason she and her sisters had been forced to venture to London to find husbands was because the law had handed their ancestral home, the home of *their* childhoods, to a cousin *who had never, ever lived there*. And the reasoning—he was *male*.

Every time Elise thought on it, she became incensed. Richard didn't deserve Wiltham. It wasn't a part of his blood the way it was hers.

And now she would have to throw herself on

Richard's mercy to live in the only true home she'd ever known. So, so unfair.

This march through the forest in wet shoes and with damp skirts did nothing to calm her outrage. She was rubbing a blister on the side of her foot. Maybe more than one blister.

She stepped over a group of tree limbs the storm had knocked down. Her cloak became entangled in them. She would have fallen if not for a gloved hand reaching out to steady her—

Elise spun on him, the branches forming a sort of cage around her legs. *"Will you leave me alone?"*

She didn't know who was more startled by her ferocity, herself, or him.

The ruffian held up his gloved hands as if to show he had no tricks to play.

Elise felt tears scratch the backs of her eyeballs. "I don't need your help." This time, she sounded more composed, but as unyielding.

He shrugged and glanced down at the dog. They seemed to exchange a look, and then Mr. Ruffian did something that truly startled her. He turned and began walking away. He didn't hurry, but he wasn't lingering either.

Good. She wanted him gone.

Elise reached down to untangle her cloak from the branches. She stepped on one to hold it down while pulling another to release the cloak. The challenge was that she dealt with several branches, seemingly laced together. She tugged on what she considered the stem of one. It didn't give as readily as she had hoped. After several minutes of battling the branches, she was in a worse position than when she'd started.

She shot a look in the direction Mr. Ruffian had gone. His tall body in its buff oilskin coat was no longer to be seen through the trees.

"The dog didn't even wait for me," she muttered, before taking a deep breath, releasing it, and attempting a different tactic—

"If you don't untangle yourself soon, we may miss the Mail when it comes rolling by."

His voice from behind her startled Elise. She straightened like a shot.

Her nemesis leaned against the trunk of a large tree. The dog was with him but not paying attention to her. Instead, he had plopped down on the ground and started scratching behind his ear with a diligence that was admirable.

"What—?" she started, confused. "I saw you leave."

He considered her gravely a moment and then stated the obvious. "I walked in a circle, so I wasn't over there, because I was here. Do you need help?"

Such a reasonable offer.

Elise wished she could stuff it in his mouth. "I'm fine," she informed him and tried to step out, only to lose her balance. Her hands went out to break her fall, but she was too late. Her chin hit the muddy ground, and she could feel it cake on her face.

The incident infuriated her because it had happened in front of *him*. Elise rolled onto her back and then began kicking her feet like a child having a tantrum, trying to free herself of the annoying branches. She accompanied her actions with a growl of frustration as if she was some bear given to outrage.

The dog stopped scratching and leaped to his feet.

Mr. Ruffian watched unperturbed, and that made her all the angrier. She gave another kick, and one foot freed itself. The action also sent her skirts all the way up to her knees.

Elise didn't care if her stockings were showing. She needed to be free, and she wanted to do it herself. She put her hands on the ground behind her and tried to scoot out of the branches, most of which were held in place by her body weight. At last, she escaped the puzzle of branches, but in the most undignified way possible.

However, she felt exhilarated. She'd never before given in so openly to her temper. She'd always had to keep it at a genteel and respectable level. Gentlewomen weren't supposed to be angry.

Mr. Ruffian offered a gloved hand. "Excellent work. Now, shall we head to the road?" He didn't stare at her legs, exposed almost to the top of her stocking ties. Or her hair, which had come loose from the braid she'd made. She'd had nothing to use to tie it off, so it was really just the hint of a braid. Instead, he behaved as if her looks were of no consequence.

Who was this foreign creature disguised as a man?

He sighed, the sound that of Atlas with the weight of the world on his shoulders. "Elise, we must go."

She took his gloved hand, and he lifted her up in the air to set her on her feet as if she weighed nothing, which was not true. Elise wasn't one of those debutantes who were waiflike or even willowy. He pulled a kerchief out of the pocket of his greatcoat and offered it to her.

"Mud," he said, pointing to his own chin and nose to show her where.

She wiped her face. The mud smudged.

"Not a problem," he said. "There will be water along the way." They came to a brook. She dampened the cloth and washed her face.

Then he offered her the last of the salted beef. She gratefully accepted the gift and was almost finished with it before she thought to ask, "Did you eat?"

"The dog and I did," he responded.

Now with him guiding her, they quickly found the road. Guiltily, she realized she *had* been walking the wrong way. Mr. Ruffian didn't mention her mistake. She appreciated his restraint.

There was some traffic on this fine morning. Not much. A farmer with a full cart and what seemed a dozen children. A rider who was too intent on his own journey to even glance at them.

The wrecked Mail Coach was closer in distance than Elise had supposed. The blisters on her feet hurt, but she managed to walk with some semblance of grace. Of course, it called for all of her concentration. Pride would not let her show the pain she experienced.

"What do we do now?" Elise asked as they approached the wreckage.

"Wait," he answered.

"How long?"

"I don't know." He frowned. "We wait until the Mail comes or word reaches someone about the wreck."

Elise walked over to where a piece of the wooden boot of the coach jutted out, and sat.

She no longer worried about covering her head with the cloak. The morning air felt good. It was clean and fresh after the storm.

He leaned against the side of the coach and looked down the road as if willing the Mail to come. That is when Elise noticed his eyes. Gray. A light, silvery gray, one with a very purple bruise around it. And he had dimples, deep lines bracketing the corners of his mouth beneath the scruffiness of his whiskered jaw.

Those attributes along with a strong nose and broad shoulders that appeared as if they could handle any difficulty made him a rather impressive specimen of a man. She was surprised she hadn't noticed earlier.

Or perhaps she had. Hadn't her body reacted to how solid he was? How completely masculine?

She reminded herself that she could trust he knew his worth. Most men did. They truly believed women should prostrate themselves at their feet. Even the barrel-shaped, the lisping, and the smelly ones. She and her sisters had marveled over their confidence. Males seemed to be born with it. Perhaps that was why men thought they should lead.

The dog jumped up on the wood beside her. She reached over and stroked his coat. "You are a handsome beast," she cooed softly. "And you saved us." She received a nudge on her hand, a signal the dog wished her to keep telling him how wonderful he was.

Mr. Ruffian removed his leather hat and ran a hand through his hair. It was a dark brown, a rich color. She didn't want to trust him. Or to like him—

"So, what is your name?" she heard herself ask.

He looked over as if surprised she was speaking to him. "Oh? You are finally interested?"

"Well, I can't keep thinking of you as Mr. Ruffian." And then she said, because she should, "I'm sorry I struck you. I was asleep. There were spiders."

"Hmm, spiders."

"Dozens of them," she assured him. "Maybe hundreds." She paused. "Does your eye hurt?"

"Unrelentingly," he answered, catching her off guard—once again. She'd assumed he would say something polite such as, *No, my lady, it doesn't bother me at all.* He didn't.

Seeing her surprise, he shook his head. "Don't fret. It will serve as a reminder to not startle you awake."

He would not have an opportunity in the future. Their time together would soon be at an end and they would go their separate ways, as they should. The realization made her feel almost warm toward him.

"So, your name?" she pressed.

"Kit."

"What of your surname?"

"Kit is fine, Elise." Hadn't that been the way she'd answered him?

She wished she'd given him another name. Perhaps Mary or Jane. Something common.

Like Molly?

He'd teased her with the name Molly and it had worked. She'd told him the truth of her identity. She'd best be more wary. He was proving to be sharper than she had expected.

Frustrated with herself, Elise pulled the hood up over her head. That is when she noticed what was left of her straw bonnet. It was matted into the mud. The sight made her sad. She'd spent hours over the past few years refashioning it with ribbons and feathers, wearing it almost every day. It had been important to her.

They fell into silence. She kept her arm around the dog's neck. His presence comforted her, especially since Kit seemed to be growing increasingly distant as they waited. He also winced a time or two, and not just because of the bruise around his eye.

When he did it the third time, Elise said, "I noticed that you seem to hold your side from time to time. Are you all right?"

"I'm fine," he replied without looking at her. Instead, he watched the road.

"You could have been grievously injured last night." *Protecting me,* she remembered guiltily.

"We both could have."

He might dismiss the danger of the accident, but the wreckage spoke volumes. The splintered wood, destroyed wheels, and mangled seats bore home that they could have ended up like the coachmen.

She tried to change her thinking. "Where were you traveling?"

His gaze swung to meet hers. His brows beneath his hat brim lifted. He studied her before he answered, "No place of importance."

"You were just traveling?" The idea puzzled her.

"One direction is as any other." He turned away.

Elise fell quiet, done attempting to be polite.

A few other travelers came their way. They asked questions about the wreck, shook their heads over the deaths, and marveled over how lucky anyone was to be alive. Elise left the conversation to Kit.

Instead, she talked to the dog. "You will have to return home," she told him gently. "We appreciate your help, but I can't take you to Ireland."

The dog acted as if her words were hurtful. "Oh, please," she whispered. "Don't look at me that way."

"He's skinny. Can't you see?" Kit said. "He is as stranded as we are. He doesn't have a home."

But before more could be said, she heard the rumbling of a team of horses.

*The Mail.* Elise jumped up. Kit walked over beside her. The dog sat up but did not join them.

They watched the red-and-yellow Mail Coach come charging into view. Elise had never been so happy to see a vehicle in her life. She waved her arms for it to stop.

The guard blew his horn. The coachman slowed the horses and brought them to a halt. Passengers sat on the roof. A few of them Elise thought she recognized from the night before.

"What happened here?" the driver said in alarm, setting his brake.

"There was a wreck," Kit replied, approaching him. "The coachman and guard are dead."

"Morris, dead?" the driver echoed.

He looked back to the guard who muttered, "Sad business."

"Well, then here, let us look at this." The driver

climbed down while the passengers craned their necks or leaned out of the windows to see what had happened.

Kit handled the matter of the bodies. Male passengers helped lift them out of the wreckage. Elise looked away. A tarpaulin was found, and the bodies were bound in it.

The driver was obviously upset. He sobbed nosily, his nose turning red with his grief. Apparently he and Morris had been good friends. He personally transported a small strongbox and the mail over to his vehicle.

Elise petted the dog, appreciating the animal's presence while others dealt with the sadness of the wreckage.

Kit even aided the driver and guard in tying the bodies to the top of the roof. Several passengers sitting up there made a protest, but the driver would not hear of it. "Gave his life to this road. You can just button it up," he said.

When all was done, the driver held out a gloved hand to Kit. "Thank you, man, for your help."

"It was the least I could do. Now, where can we pack ourselves? I must take the dog." He said this as if it were established fact. "I'll sit on the roof. Even by the bodies."

The driver frowned. "We are full up, man. You will have to make your way to the George. That is the next coaching inn. You'll pay your fare from there."

"What?" Kit said in surprise.

Elise spoke up. "We paid yesterday."

"Aye, you probably did," the driver said, swinging up into his box. "However, we are full up, especially with the bodies. There was a storm last night, and passengers were waiting—"

"We are *most* aware of the storm," Kit cut in angrily, and then he paused. He drew a breath as if steadying himself. "Take this young woman," he ordered. "I'll stay with the dog."

"I said I can't," was the answer. "I've got the Mail to run. There isn't a smidgeon of space for her."

"Then bump one of these male passengers off," Kit demanded.

The driver didn't answer. He picked up the reins and released the brake.

"What? You are leaving? You blackguard—"

The driver flicked his whip toward the ear of the lead horse, and they were off.

Elise stared in mute disbelief.

Not Kit. He scooped up a hunk of mud with his gloved hand and threw it after the coach.

It landed wide of its mark, but that didn't stop the barrage of Kit's very choice language.

# CHAPTER FIVE

*Beware the anger of a patient man.*
IRISH PROVERB

*The* bloody pox-ridden scoundrel—

Kit picked up a rock this time and tossed it even as the coach disappeared around a curve in the road, too far away for any of his missiles to be effective. The bastard driving the vehicle had known he was full up before he'd had Kit help lift and carry bodies. He'd used Kit's strength and then left him and Elise behind—

"It makes sense, you know."

He turned in surprise at Elise's statement. "Makes sense? He left us behind."

That tiny worry line appeared between her brows. "Some of those passengers were from last night. The coach *was* overcrowded." She paused and then said as if trying to have a positive outlook, "There will be another along."

Kit scowled at the thought. "Excuse me? Are

you not the one who was whining on about needing to reach Liverpool as quickly as possible?"

Her chin lifted as if she was greatly affronted. "I don't whine. But I see no purpose in throwing things. *I'm* trying to be calm."

"Are you saying I'm not calm?" he challenged, knowing full well he wasn't. He was beyond annoyed and damn *hungry*—because he'd chivalrously given her the last of his salted beef.

He had assumed that by now they would be on the Mail and off on their separate travels. He would be able to find something to satisfy his hunger that was better than salted beef at the next posting inn. He'd been *waiting* to eat, *counting* upon it, and now, it appeared as if he'd have to wait *more*.

And, to cap it all off, he was still stranded on the most isolated stretch of English road he'd ever encountered. Meanwhile, she acted like some chirpy governess who believed she had the right to tell him what to do. *Him*. The Duke of Winderton.

While he didn't wish to inform her or anyone of his identity until he decided to return to his former life, he also didn't want to listen to her criticize him for doing nothing more than being rightfully angry.

"I don't know why you aren't just as incensed," he said. "They could have put off one of the male passengers for you. They should have."

"But they didn't. Let me assure you, I'm not

happy about the matter either. I just believe there
are more productive solutions than flinging mud.
Another Mail will come along."

"Yes. *Tomorrow.* The vehicle you were on yesterday had been running late. That is why the driver
had insisted on heading into the storm. What just
left was the one coach for the day going in our
direction. Fancy returning to the hut?"

Her lips formed a perfect "oh" of surprise. The
worry line reappeared, and she pulled her hood
over her head to hide her face, a face that could
make angels weep, he realized, what with her
glorious halo of golden curls—

That is when Kit realized he might be a touch
mad—the little maid was starting to appear like
Helen of Troy to him.

Hunger apparently made him delusional.

He turned on his heel and went stomping toward the woods. He needed either a moment of
peace or to find a few trees to uproot and throw.

The dog started after him, his eyes worried. Kit
snapped his gloved fingers. "Stay with her." The
animal proved his intelligence by returning to
Elise's side.

Kit stormed into the forest. Slowly, his temper
subsided.

Once again, life was not going the way he
wished, and that was when Kit recognized the
true source of his anger. He was actually ready to
return home. To Smythson, his seat in the village
of Maidenshop.

The thought caught him off guard. But once he evaluated it, he realized it was true.

He longed to see his mother, to share a laugh with her over the breakfast table the way they once had before he'd gotten himself all tied into knots over women and defending who he was. He wanted to sleep in his bed. The longing for that haven had been appearing with increasing frequency in his thoughts. He wished to connect with friends he'd ignored with his wild ways.

Most of all, Kit wanted to be right with himself, and he wasn't.

He was also clueless about how to go about discovering what was wrong. The more he tried to make the best of things, the deeper he seemed to sink. Who the devil was he? Why did he matter?

Why was he not ready to return to the life he'd left?

He reached for a sapling and attempted to pull it up in his muddied, gloved hands. His palms slid on the smooth bark. He heaved with all his might. The damned tree held on to the earth. The ground was still muddy and soaked, but the tree would not give—

"What are you doing?"

Elise. Of course.

Kit straightened. He attempted to ease the tension from his shoulders and faced her.

She watched him with the shepherd's dog at her side. The dog had his head cocked, as if to be asking the same question she had. What *was* he doing?

A ray of morning sun shot its way through the trees to land directly upon her. The light caught the glints of gold in her hair. Her jewel-bright eyes appraised him as if he was some sort of strange specimen she should understand and didn't. The little worry line still lingered between her brows.

And she was waiting for an answer.

He looked down at his gloves. It would take hours for the mud to dry and flake off. He raised his gaze to meet hers. "I was having a fit of temper."

Her mouth, a generous mouth, quirked to one side as if he'd just confirmed her suspicions.

How old was she? Last night, he'd thought she could be as young as five and ten. Now, she appeared older than his own three and twenty—wait, was that his age? Right now, he felt ancient.

It was the world-weariness. There were times he wondered if anything mattered.

Then she said, "When you are done, let us know and we'll be on our way. Come, Tamsyn." She turned away, but he stopped her.

"Tamsyn?"

Her fingers found the top of the dog's head. "Yes. Do you like the name I choose?"

"Tamsyn sounds like a female name."

"I know," she answered. "Apparently, Tamsyn had us fooled about her sex. Or we had jumped to conclusions. Now I know why she has been so openhearted about helping us."

She paused, letting that mild barb against his

gender sink in. She might look like a goddess, but he'd wager she was a scold at heart. To prove his point, she added, "Come join us when you are finished with tantrums. Apparently, we have a bit of walking ahead of us. I think it wise we make our way to the next posting house."

And then she strode off, Tamsyn, her newly designated sister-in-arms, trotting at her heels.

Elise returned to the wreckage to wait, hoping Kit didn't take long to come to his senses.

His behavior had been alarming, although he'd not lashed out at her or blamed her. That was what most men did when they were angry.

To be candid, Elise found men a mystery. She'd grown up in a household of women. Her father had made an appearance from time to time, but he hadn't been necessary to the smooth workings of Wiltham. He'd breezed in with good humor and gifts and then, after a few days or even as much as a week, he'd be gone. He wouldn't even mention he was leaving. Gram had said it was because his feet were itchy. Some men couldn't stay in one place long. Gram had always assured Elise and her sisters that their father loved and valued them—and they had believed her.

But it would have been nice if he'd spent more time with them.

It would have been nice to know him better.

A wave of homesickness swept over her, just as it had the night before. She shoved it aside. She had to be strong. But the burn of tears was becoming too familiar to her.

She tried to distract herself by giving Tamsyn a good scratch. It was possible that, back in London, Gwendolyn may have discovered the note she had left in the wooden money box. Then again, she might not . . . and Elise realized the hard part was not knowing.

"I'm too far into it now," she told the dog. "Whatever happens, they can't change it."

Tamsyn answered with a look of adoration.

At that moment, Kit came striding out of the forest. He held an uprooted sapling in his hands.

Elise stood. Tamsyn jumped down from her perch and trotted over to greet him. "What are you going to do with a tree?"

"I had to prove to myself I could do it."

Men were so strange.

Kit seemed stranger than most since the black eye she'd given him made him appear a touch sinister.

"And?" she prodded.

"Well, now that I have a witness, I shall replant it and we'll be on our way. However, one thing." He walked up to her, set his sapling aside, took off his gloves, and pulled a folded length of material from the deep pockets of his greatcoat. He offered it to her.

"What is this?"

"Binding. For your feet," he prompted when she looked blankly at him. "You need to wrap them. I noticed you were limping slightly. I imagine you have blisters. They will grow worse if you don't take care."

"Where did you find the material, or is there a peddler's cart of goods in those pockets of yours?"

He grinned at her. "I like when your accent has the best of you, Irish."

Elise frowned. "I speak English better than you."

He ignored the comment. "Wrap your feet while I plant this tree, and we shall be on our way. I feel a bit sorry for this little sapling being the brunt of my temper and all."

"Tamsyn and I were the brunt of your temper as well," she reminded him.

He gave a start as if to argue, and then he agreed with a nod. "I was churlish. Wrap your feet. I'm a better man when my belly is full, and I am determined to find food soon."

Elise understood how cranky hunger could make one. A few of her doubts about Kit dissolved. She turned the strip of material over. "Where did you find this?" she asked.

"It's the hem of my shirt."

Elise was startled. Was it proper that she should share his personal clothing with him? She could even feel heat rise to her cheeks. "I—I . . . This is rather personal, isn't it?"

"It is material. What is personal about material?"

"It came off your *person*."

"Don't use it then," he replied almost cheerily as he turned and started toward the forest. "But if you start limping, I won't carry you." Tamsyn leaped from the seat and joyfully went tearing after him.

And then they both disappeared, swallowed up by the woods.

Elise debated her next actions for only a moment. She didn't know how far they would have to walk before they caught a ride or reached the next posting house.

She might also find herself doing more walking than she'd planned over the next few days because, yes, it could take her that long to reach Ireland. Wrapping her feet seemed a wise course of action.

Elise went around to the side of the wreckage where she could sit but be somewhat hidden from any traffic coming down the road from either way. She removed her shoe, glanced in all directions, and then lifted her skirts and untied the ribbons holding up her stockings. She rolled them down.

Kit's shirt material was soft. Not fine lawn but good cotton and not at all scratchy. Elise made her own clothing, so she had an appreciation for different fabrics. She also knew how to use her teeth to rip the fabric. Dara was horrified by the practice, but Elise and Gwendolyn had done it all the time.

Careful to keep her feet out of the mud, she wrapped the binding around the ball of her foot and around her toes, covering a raw blister there, and then put on her stocking. It was almost a pleasure to slip her foot into her shoe. She quickly set to work on the other foot. She even had enough of the material to braid her hair and tie it off securely.

Her tail wagging, Tamsyn found Elise in her hiding spot. She pushed the muddy dog to the side and realized Kit stood not more than five feet from her. With his superior height, he could easily see over the barrier she had placed between herself and the world.

Elise rose from her seat. "How long have you been watching me?" Her feet felt much better.

He picked up a stick and threw it. Tamsyn went bounding after it. "Elise, you are a comely lass, but your blisters are not that exciting."

"I didn't suggest they were," she shot back. "Shall we go? And you'd best watch yourself. You will grow attached to that dog."

"I already am," he admitted. "She's a good one."

True.

"Shall we?" he asked, already moving down the road.

She watched his tall form a moment. Tamsyn proudly carried the stick in her mouth as if hoping Kit would notice and throw it again.

Her traveling companions. For better or worse.

Elise half skipped her steps to catch up with them.

# CHAPTER SIX

*May the roof above you never fall in, and those
gathered beneath it never fall out.*

IRISH PROVERB

*London*

Dara had not expected to see Lady Whitby at
Harding Howell and Company.

The shop was fairly busy. Word had gone out
that gloves of the finest dove-gray leather imag-
inable were offered for sale at a reasonable cost,
and many had come to see what they thought.

It dawned on Dara that there had been a time
when she and her sisters had crossed paths with
Lady Whitby quite often. Then the troubles had
started with Elise.

Her ladyship was definitely on Elise's side. She
considered herself a mentor to their younger sister and even allowed Elise to be a welcome guest
in her home for days without end whenever she
was upset with Dara and Michael.

Yes, her youngest sister was not happy about living under Michael's roof. After all, Dara and Elise had the closest of bonds. They had slept in the same room since birth. Dara knew Elise had not accepted her marriage. Her feelings were hurt. And while Dara could not make matters right because she loved Michael, fully and completely, this estrangement with her youngest sister was a heavy weight.

In the crush of other glove customers, Lady Whitby had not noticed Dara yet. Dara turned, expecting Gwendolyn to be beside her. Instead, her tall, elegant sister was in a conversation with Mrs. Hastings, their vicar's wife. Mrs. Hastings was a chatterbox, and Gwendolyn was too kind to excuse herself.

Therefore, it was up to Dara alone to deal with Lady Whitby. She wanted to know what her youngest sister was doing. She longed to have a conversation with Elise, a peaceful one, where Dara could attempt to talk sense into her sister, because Elise should not keep running to Lady Whitby's every time her nose was out of joint.

Aunt Tweedie had advised Dara to stop being embarrassed over the matter. Sisters fought, Tweedie said. She had fought with their Gram when they were Dara's and Elise's age. Her advice was to give it time. "Elise will eventually realize she is being petty. She'll overcome this upset. It is all part of becoming mature."

Dara wasn't so certain. She loved her husband. He loved her. But here was the truth—if Dara could have prevented herself from falling in love with Michael, she would have. Her first loyalty had always been to her sisters. However, there were some things in life that couldn't be controlled. Michael had been one of them. Dara was very proud to be his wife.

She also wished to heal the rift with her sister. To do that, they must speak. Certainly, Elise could understand that.

Lady Whitby turned as if ready to make her way to the door. Dara did not hesitate in seizing the moment. She moved as if also intent on leaving and feigned practically stumbling into Lady Whitby's path and almost knocking her over.

"Oh, dear," Dara said in alarm. "I'm so sorry. Please excuse me." And then she acted surprised to see whom she had almost run over. "Why, Lady Whitby, I'm doubly sorry to you for my clumsiness."

Her ladyship was some years older than Dara with an unfortunately long face and large nostrils that flared at the unexpected intrusion. "*Mrs.* Brogan—" The emphasis on the salutation was an implied insult. "Not a problem at all. Now, if you will excuse me—"

"I was leaving as well. Let me accompany you out of the store—"

"You need not go to the trouble—"

"It is not a task at all, my lady." With those words, Dara followed the woman out of the shop.

She would explain her disappearance later to Gwendolyn. Nor would she be gone long.

Out on the busy street, Lady Whitby looked up the road and down. It was difficult to find places for vehicles to wait, especially early on a fine afternoon like this one. Her driver was probably circling the square until she signaled she was ready to depart.

Dara knew she had perhaps three minutes to speak her piece. She plunged in. "How is Elise?"

Lady Whitby pulled back as if Dara had attacked her. "You are very blunt." Her disapproval for Dara was etched in each word. Then, she saw her driver in the distance and took a step as if to meet him halfway.

Again, Dara stepped into her path. "You are correct, I am, especially where my sister is concerned. Please, my lady, I love Elise. I—" She paused, groping for the right words. Lady Whitby appeared to not be paying any attention at all to her heartfelt entreaty.

But Dara was nothing if not bold. She had never backed off when she felt a cause was just. "I miss Elise. Please tell her that I long to make amends. But I can't do so when she refuses to speak to me."

"You may tell her that yourself," Lady Whitby answered crisply. "I do not direct Elise." She took a step around Dara and would have charged off to meet her coachmen except for Dara's next statement.

"You *are* directing Elise if you make it easy for her to avoid us."

Lady Whitby stopped. She turned and frowned at Dara. "Avoid you?" She sounded confused.

"You are keeping her from us," Dara said, moving closer to her ladyship lest this very private discussion be overheard by someone in the public.

"I'm doing no such thing."

"As long as you repeatedly allow her to be a guest under your roof, Elise does not have to confront us. I know she is upset. My heart breaks over it—"

"Truly? It seems to me you overrode your sister's heart quite effectively, Mrs. Brogan."

"That was not my intention. *Ever.* Please, I wish to speak to my sister." There. Dara had sounded almost calm.

"Then speak to her," Lady Whitby shot back. "I'm not stopping you."

"May I call on you later today to see Elise?"

Her ladyship's coach had almost reached her. She'd been about to hurry toward it when she paused. She looked to Dara. "Call on me to see Elise?"

"If I am to talk to her, I must go to where she is."

Lady Whitby held up a finger to her driver, a signal she would be right there. She faced Dara. "Your sister is not with me."

If the ground had opened up beneath Dara's

feet, she could not have been more surprised. "We assumed . . ." She stopped, confused.

"Is she not with you?"

Dara dumbly shook her head.

It was a testimony to Lady Whitby's regard for Elise that she genuinely looked concerned. "Mrs. Brogan, she is not my guest. I haven't seen her since, well, the Norwards' musicale. When was that? Last Monday?"

"We thought she went to you. She hasn't been home. We haven't seen her for the good part of two days."

Lady Whitby's voice dropped as if she realized the import of this conversation. "I do not know where she is." She took a cautious glance around. It would not do for word of the missing Elise to spread through the *ton*, and half of the most rabid gossips were inside Harding Howell's looking at gloves.

"When we talked at the musicale," Lady Whitby confided, "I told her she needed to repair matters between the two of you. I have my own thoughts about what happened. I understand why Elise would find her circumstances difficult. However, sometimes in life, we must accept what we do not like. That is what I told her when she asked if she could count upon my hospitality again."

"We did talk a bit," Dara said. "Michael and I both thought that matters were repaired between us." Or had they assumed they were because, well, there was nothing that could be done? As a young unmarried woman, Elise needed to live with her family.

"Obviously she did not agree." Her ladyship narrowed her eyes. "Therefore, the question is, where is she? And is she merely hiding—which, given Elise's strong nature, could be possible? Or is she in *danger*?"

Dara felt her heart clutch in her chest. She had been certain that Elise was with Lady Whitby, that she had been nurturing her anger, and that all would eventually be well.

But danger?

She desperately searched her mind, trying to remember exactly when she had noticed Elise missing. "She said she was going to a salon you were holding Monday . . . the afternoon she didn't come home." However, had Dara seen her that morning? Life had been so busy lately.

"That was almost two full days ago." Lady Whitby clucked her disapproval. Her coach pulled up beside them. A footman jumped down to open the door, heedless that the vehicle was blocking traffic. He ignored the shouts of those trying to pass by. However, Lady Whitby did not climb in. "We must find her. Where would she have gone?"

Where indeed?

"I need to speak to Gwendolyn." Now it was Dara who wished to be away. She took a step toward the shop but paused to say, "Thank you for giving me a moment of your time, my lady.

I—" She stopped, her throat closing as her mind leaped to all the evils that could have befallen her sister. Elise was the family's golden beauty. Men coveted her. Gwendolyn and Dara had always warned her to be careful. "I must speak to my husband."

"Please, let me know if there is anything I may do to help," Lady Whitby said.

Dara mutely turned and walked into the shop. Gwendolyn had found a pair of gloves she liked. She was the tallest of the sisters with black hair and golden brown eyes that seemed to look right into the heart of a person. The clerk was fawning all over her. "I shall have them delivered to you later. I will bring them myself," he assured her.

"How kind of you."

The clerk blushed at the simple compliment.

Dara touched Gwendolyn's elbow and whispered, "We need to leave." Gwennie was absolutely the sweetest soul Dara knew. The news about Elise would distress her.

"Do we? I had hopes of stopping . . ." Gwendolyn's voice trailed off. "Is everything well with you?"

Of course Gwendolyn would notice that Dara was upset.

But the idea of being ill was a good one. "I'm not feeling quite the thing. Shall we depart?"

"Yes, yes." Gwendolyn gave the clerk one last smile and they were out the door.

On the street, Dara began telling Gwendolyn of her alarming conversation with Lady Whitby. Both of the sisters had assumed Elise had been with her friend. Now they experienced terrible guilt.

Less than fifteen minutes later, they were crowded into the room Michael used for his study, telling him of their concerns.

He was equally alarmed. "Let us search her room for clues."

But they found nothing. Even her valise was stored away where she kept it. It was as if Elise had disappeared, and Dara was distraught.

Their butler, Herald, informed them that a clerk from Harding Howell and Company had arrived with a package. Gwendolyn was annoyed, but she understood her obligation.

"I need to give him a few coins for his effort," she said apologetically to Michael and Dara. "You two, keep thinking. One of us must remember something Elise said or what she could be about." She left the room.

"If she isn't kidnapped," Dara tagged on darkly, speaking her fears aloud to her husband.

"I'll send for a runner," he announced. "We must make inquiries outside of our household."

Dara's stomach knotted in worry and fear. She had heard mention that there were slavers who stole white women and sold them to far-off lands. Was Elise trapped in the belly of some moldy ship on her way to be basely used—

"Dara." Michael's voice cut through her fretting. "Don't leap to conclusions. Not yet."

"I'm just so afraid. Michael, and it's my fault—"

*"She ran away,"* Gwendolyn shouted, running into the room. In one hand she held the carved money box where she kept the sisters' funds. In another, she waved a piece of paper. "She left a note. She's returning to Ireland."

And then Gwendolyn said something that put a chill down Dara's spine. "We need Mr. Steele. *Now.*"

# CHAPTER SEVEN

*Many a ship is lost within sight of the harbor.*
IRISH PROVERB

The traffic on the still wet road was lighter than Kit had expected, perhaps because of the storm the night before.

A few carts and wagons passed them by, but there was no room to take on two more passengers. Kit asked anyway . . . because after the first fifteen minutes of walking, Elise began to limp again. The bindings were not a solution.

To her credit, she didn't complain. She lopsidedly muddled along, her jaw tight and her gaze stoic. When he suggested they might rest a moment, she shook her head and charged on without him—even though there were snails who moved faster than she could.

Pride. Stubborn pride. She seemed full of it. However, it was something he understood all too well.

Still, he had no desire to see the chit crippled.

He grew excited when, after an hour of walking, a hired coach came rolling upon them, moving at a quick pace through puddles and slowly drying mud. Noticing there was only one passenger, Kit began running beside it, calling up to the driver, "Sir? Sir, would you please offer us a ride? It is for a woman. She needs help, sir."

The driver didn't respond. Instead, he slapped the horses forward and the passenger—the *sole* passenger—lowered the shade so he could pretend he hadn't heard Kit's request.

*What the devil was the matter with people?*

Or would he have done the same? He liked to believe he wouldn't have been so namby-pamby as to ride in a vehicle on such a fine day. He would have been on horseback, preferably Dodger, the blood bay gelding he had raised from a colt.

Then again, if he had been in a vehicle, the old Kit, Kit the Duke, might have driven on. He had rarely looked at the passing countryside or considered the plight of others even when he was on horseback and he could see the people plainly in front of him. No, he'd focused on himself and reaching his destination as quickly as possible, just like this passenger.

Seeing that the coach wasn't going to slow, he came to a halt with a few choice words and then turned to Elise and Tamsyn. Ever since Elise had started limping, the dog had steadfastly walked by her side.

"He wouldn't stop. Self-righteous old codger," Kit complained.

"I wouldn't stop for you either," Elise answered.

"What?"

She had reached him and now determinedly limped past him but not before giving him a cool look. "You attacked the driver. You chased him."

*On her behalf.* Kit fell into step beside her. "Attack? I merely asked him for a ride. We could have sat on the tailboard and not been a bother to him."

"*That* would have been enjoyable," she murmured, meaning the exact opposite.

Kit shook his head. "It would have been better than hobbling your way to the next posting inn."

"You needn't worry about me. I'm *fine*."

There it was—the "I'm fine."

In the female vocabulary, no two words could ever be icier.

"I'm sorry I tried to help," he muttered. "You can crawl your way to—where are you going? Oh, yes, Liverpool—if that is your preference."

She did not like the sound of that. Now her gaze was as icy as her words. "I don't *need* your help," she said. "I *didn't* ask for it." She paused to loosen the ties of her cloak, throwing the edges over her shoulders.

The day was growing warmer. Her cheeks looked flush. He realized he was sweating as well. He took off his coat. "Very well. Hobble on."

"It is better I do that than you trying to accost coaches."

"I know of no other way to ask for a ride," he protested in his defense. "I have to use words. I need their attention—"

She came to a halt, her eyes snapping with frustration. "Have you taken a look at yourself? You look—" She paused as if for a loss of words, then found them. "You look like a brigand."

"A brigand? Now that is a word one doesn't hear every day—"

"*Stop it.* I'm trying to tell you something."

"Yes, governess," he shot back, and began walking. He was hungry. He hadn't slept well. He didn't want to listen to the chidings of some impudent little housemaid who should have stayed home—

"You *reek.*"

Kit stopped, one foot caught in the air in the action of moving forward. He set it down, faced her. "*What* did you say?"

She didn't even bat an eye as she repeated, "You reek. You smell. You are—"

"*I know* what reek means," he almost roared.

"Do you?" she questioned, fearless in the face of his outrage. She began limping past him.

"You are saying I smell."

"That is what reek means," she tossed off in a tone that made him want to grab her braid and yank her back to him.

Except, she was probably right.

Kit couldn't smell himself. Well, that wasn't true. There had been a time or two when he'd noticed he was a bit ripe. But he was traveling. He was living like the common people did. Yesterday, he'd had quite a bit of ale waiting for the Mail and the scent of that could come through one's skin . . .

He paused the thought, reconsidering.

Perhaps he had fallen into a terrible rut, one of his own making.

It was the drink. He'd been imbibing too much. It made a man careless. Then his horse had gone lame, he'd been walking, there was the storm—he had a long list of excuses.

And now he reeked.

He scratched the growth of whiskers covering his jaw and became aware of how they'd grown. He couldn't contest Elise's verdict, and Kit hated that. Especially when he realized that he found himself rather foul as well.

Abruptly, he turned and walked off the road, heading into the woods.

"Where are you going?" Elise asked.

He paused his march. "Stay here," he replied. "Rest. Put your feet up."

"But *where* are you going?" she insisted, and even Tamsyn gave a worried bark.

What a great dog. Sharp as they came.

"Stay with her," Kit ordered Tamsyn. "Don't let her out of your sight. I'll be back." What he had in mind shouldn't take him long.

Tamsyn wagged her tail as if she understood her assignment and was rather pleased with it.

"We may not be here when you return," Elise threatened.

"Then I will catch up to you." Even if he was gone an hour, she'd wouldn't be that far up the road. Not limping the way she was.

"Not likely," she declared.

He didn't answer. What he was about was his business. She had made a complaint; he had realized she was right—he was a proper mess; he would find a solution.

It was simple.

Kit tramped through the woods. There were always streams around. He would find one. The rain-damp forest floor was covered with ferns and thickets and years of twigs and leaves. Squirrels scattered at the sound of his booted steps, and birds heralded him. He noticed a path. It was narrow and muddy. He followed it and after several minutes of walking, came to a pool of water.

Sunlight filtered through the trees. Kit moved toward the edge. It didn't look deep. There were tracks all around marking it as a watering hole.

It would serve his purposes. He reached into the deep pockets of his greatcoat and felt a dry sliver of soap. It had been there a while. Not too long ago, he'd been more fastidious. What had happened?

He knew the answer. He'd let his role of Prince

Hal go a bit too far. Men had that talent, he'd come to realize. They could become so wrapped up in their own motives, they forgot themselves. He'd seen that truism played out repeatedly as school friends had gone out into the world. They'd changed. They became ambitious. Some ruthless.

And what was he? That was the question.

Kit had never had a titled father to guide him. His uncle, who had been his guardian until he came of age, was a self-made man, and a busy one. He wasn't one for garden parties or balls or mentoring. Yes, he had rebuilt the Winderton fortune that Kit's father had almost lost . . . but he didn't understand the nobility. He expected Kit to be productive. To work.

Meanwhile, tutors had never pressed Kit on his studies. His mother had spoiled him. His friends had turned to him for favors that he could not deliver, and then he had created his own problems . . . and soon, Kit had been convinced he was the worst duke in the world.

Leaving had forced him to be himself.

He still wasn't certain what his *role* should be, except he wanted to be more than a title. Exactly what that was kept eluding him.

Right now, his "self" needed a good wash.

Kit took little time to strip down. He set his still damp boots under a tree, the socks with a hole draped over the side to dry. He placed his folded clothes with his beloved hat on top of them and then waded into the pool with the sliver of soap.

His eye ached, reminding him it was bruised. No wonder the coach driver hadn't wished to stop. The fresh water would feel good on it.

With a whoop, Kit dove under. The bottom was shallow but he managed to swim a few strong strokes before popping his head up. For a long moment, he drank in the perfection of nature, of being surrounded by the green beauty that was England, and he felt rich in a way few of his acquaintance could appreciate.

Since he'd begun his travels, he'd had many moments like this one. He'd come to value his freedom and enjoy the simple pleasure of just being. He chafed at rules and restrictions. He liked living as he pleased, until his drinking had led him astray.

And that is when Kit realized something that should have been quite obvious . . . if he'd only stopped to think: The problem was not with the world. It was with himself. He was the problem.

He brought his feet to the bottom of the pool. The water gently lapped around his waist. The muddy bottom was soft and silky between his toes. He stood there in the ring of sunlight and allowed himself to just be while he turned this new awareness over in his mind.

Kit had been furious when he'd left London. Kate's rejection had humiliated him. He'd not behaved in his best manner. He'd done everything

expected of him . . . and it hadn't been enough—
not to win Kate's heart, or earn him respect, or
be comfortable in his own skin and feel as if he
mattered in this world.

Now, in this pool, with barely a shilling to his
name, a calm settled over him.

What if life wasn't about striving and achiev-
ing? Or deadening emotions that were uncomfortable? Why couldn't it always be like it was
now, when he savored the moment? He enjoyed
the warmth of the air around him and the crisp-
ness of the rain-cooled water. He had a clear head
and no obligations. None.

If he wished to disappear, he could. He could
wander forever.

And Kit didn't know what he thought of that.
Because there were things he did miss. His
mother was one. She'd always been his champion, perhaps too much of one at times. Smythson, the sprawling home that was his ancestral
seat, was another. He'd once imagined raising his
children there, teaching them to ride, to care for
the livestock and the land, to value their family
history.

What he didn't miss was believing *he* could do
no wrong.

The soap in his hand was melting. Kit looked
down at it. There wasn't much left. He'd best put
it to good use. For months he'd been living by
doing the next thing in front of him. What he
wanted now was to be clean. To not *reek*.

The rest would sort itself out in time.

With that decision, Kit began scrubbing. The little maid was correct. He had not taken care of himself.

He marveled at how lean he'd grown through his travels, gaunt even. His muscles were long and hard. His hair was in need of a barber. He could almost pull it back in a short queue.

His beard was the worst. He had been snipping at it from time to time with a small pair of scissors he carried. However, rubbing his hand over it, he realized its patchiness and unevenness made him look as if he had gone to seed. Time to be done with it.

He lathered the beard with the very last bit of soap in his hand. Then he waded to shore, going to his greatcoat to search the pocket where he carried a small leather traveling case—scissors on one side, a razor on the other. He picked up the coat and was startled by the sound of Elise's sharp gasp of surprised alarm . . . even as Tamsyn came panting up to him, happily wagging her tail.

Elise was not so friendly.

Kit's immediate thought was that there were two ways this could go. Elise might see him in all his glory and be tempted to strip down and join him in the pool. That would be a delightful outcome.

Or—and this was, unfortunately, what happened—her features froze in scandalized horror.

She reminded him of his aunt Lady Benson, whose drawn-on eyebrows made her always appear offended.

And that was just her reaction looking at Kit's chest and legs. What would she do if he dropped the coat he held in front of himself? Because his reaction to her was immediate and very hard.

How could it not be? With the deep green of the forest bringing out the gold in her hair, the jewel brightness of her eyes, and the pouty fullness of her outraged mouth, even an octogenarian would have gone erect. Her beauty had that power, and he was no eunuch.

Slowly, Kit straightened his shoulders. He kept the coat as a shield, but he met her shock with a cool gaze. He had nothing of which to be ashamed—

She whirled and took off running back toward the road.

No hobble there. Her feet barely touched the ground.

Kit sighed. His little maid could be so dreary. She was as squeamish as a debutante. She'd only seen his chest, after all. Since he was holding his coat, she'd not had a chance to see anything interesting.

Besides, she was the one who came upon him. He would have to remind her of that fact.

Then he remembered he hadn't actually said where he was going when he'd left her on the road. He'd been so annoyed, he'd just wanted to put distance between them. So, she had been caught off guard.

*Still*, she was not his responsibility. Being on the same ill-fated coach didn't mean that he had to nurse her all the way to Ireland . . . although he didn't wish to see anything bad happen to her. Of course, she'd just acted so scandalized, she'd probably wish him to the devil than to accept his help.

That was the way of it for him. He always wanted to do what was right, and it always went wrong.

The best thing to do would be to finish up here and find her. She would prattle on about how he had offended her. He would listen with one ear, let it out the other, but at least she couldn't claim he reeked any longer.

He dropped his coat and waded back into the pond, razor in hand. The soap on his face was quickly drying. He wet it as best he could and began shaving. Tamsyn had not run after Elise. She'd stayed with him, and she acted as if the pool was a great discovery. She jumped in, splashing water everywhere, and swam great circles around him as he gently scraped the whiskers from his face.

When he was done, he tried to look in the pool at his reflection. He couldn't see anything. Apparently seeing one's reflection in water only happened in myths. He washed off all the soap and climbed out. He dried his body with his shirt, because it was all he had, and dressed.

Tamsyn happily bounded out of the pool, her tongue hanging wildly out of one side of her mouth. She shook hard, sending water flying.

"You had better be careful, too. She won't be happy you didn't follow," Kit warned the pup as he pulled on his breeches. His skin was still damp and the buff leather didn't glide smoothly up his legs. He buttoned them and threw his shirt on over his head. He quickly knotted his neckcloth.

He was tempted to not wear his jacket. The day was warm. However, at heart, he was a gentleman, and a gentleman always wore a jacket. He slapped the hat on top of his head and then rolled up his oilskin. He tied it over one shoulder to wear across his chest as if it was a pack.

"Come along, Tamsyn," he said after he'd tugged on his boots. "Let's go hear what lecture Elise has been preparing to deliver."

The two of them headed toward the road, where he expected to find an angry little maid ready to give him a scolding.

But she had a surprise for him. She wasn't there.

# CHAPTER EIGHT

*If you dig a grave for others, you might fall into it yourself.*
IRISH PROVERB

Elise was furious.

She couldn't walk fast enough away from Kit and his nonsense. He'd *left* her *alone* on the road without a word. He'd just sauntered off.

Elise had assumed he had needed a *moment* of privacy. She had *expected* him to return. She'd waited. After all, to this point, they had been in this disastrous situation together.

When he hadn't appeared in a few minutes, she had paced until she realized his suggestion she rest her feet was a good one. She had chosen a relatively dry, high part of the banking beside the road to sit. Her feet were overjoyed for the respite, and she would have stayed there except for an oncoming group of laborers walking their way down the road toward her. Their clothes were dirty and their shoes worn.

They had been approximately Elise's age, maybe younger. They were loud and in high spirits. Their steps had slowed as they noticed her. They'd whispered to themselves.

She'd yanked the hood of her cloak over her head and stood, moving closer to the tree line. She pretended to be occupied studying the grass around her. She could not hear their words, but she did catch the tenor of their conversation. She told herself not to worry. If she didn't pay attention to them, they would let her be.

Or perhaps another traveler would come this way, disturbing whatever they might be plotting.

*Or*, and here was a radical idea, Kit would return from wherever he'd gone? Was that an unreasonable expectation?

It had annoyed her that she had to depend on him for a bodyguard. A woman alone should never be a target . . . but she was. She could tell just by the way they started moving toward her, a sidling walk, the predators spotting a treat.

"Hello, miss," one of them had called out. He was short with straw-colored hair under a much-abused tricorne. The others, the older ones, had pushed him forward with snickering suggestions. "You are a fetching sight."

"Go away," Elise had ordered. Beside her, Tamsyn had growled, the hair on her neck rising.

"Whoa, there. Call off your dog. We are just being friendly," said one. "Can't we talk to a pretty girl on such a fine day?"

"Or invite her to travel with us for a spell. Especially since we are all as lonely as you seem to be," another chimed in with a smile that warned Elise to run—which is exactly what she decided to do.

"Come, let us find *my husband*," she'd announced to Tamsyn, wanting these louts to know she wasn't alone. Of course, the hard part was turning her back on them. What if they rushed after her?

What if Kit had abandoned her and he wasn't close by to help?

Then she would pretend. She must. She had no other option.

However, to her surprise, Tamsyn had confronted the pack of men. She'd barked and snapped at them, revealing rows of sharp teeth, and they'd backed off, giving Elise a chance to escape.

She had charged into the woods. Behind her, she heard someone shout, "*Damn dog.*"

Elise had not stopped. She had worried about Tamsyn, about what might happen to both of them—and then, to her relief, the wily shepherd's dog had come running to join her.

Glancing behind, she saw there were no pursuers. Elise stopped, her breathing heavy. She threw her arms around Tamsyn. "You are so brave. So very, very brave."

Tamsyn had basked in the adoration.

But of course, the big question had been, where was Kit?

Again, she turned to Tamsyn. "Find him."

The dog understood. She was as smart as they came. She had sniffed the ground, trotted several feet, and then stopped, her body alert before she went off again.

Elise had followed as best she could because Tamsyn had been practically racing through the trees—and then they had found Kit.

Oh, yes, they had.

Elise's cheeks burned with the memory of what she'd seen.

It wasn't as if she didn't know what a man's chest looked like. There wasn't anything special about them. Elise was a country girl, and men were never modest. She just hadn't expected *him* to be naked all over. Even his feet. *Naked.* Out in the everywhere.

But what had really taken her aback was how he looked naked. He wasn't like any of the yeomen, stable lads, or crofters she'd glimpsed without their shirts on. They had appeared pasty and ridiculous.

In contrast, Kit's body had been a work of art, one that could rival any Greek statue.

He hadn't been shy either. He'd met her eye, even while she'd struggled to breathe, or even to think. Coming upon him that way had been a shock.

And now the image of him standing in the forest like some proud *naked* warrior was burned in her mind, never to be forgotten, even as she put as much distance between herself and Kit as possible.

There she'd been, almost attacked waiting for him while he'd been seeing to his—what? Toilette? Or something she didn't wish to think about? Because men were odd creatures. Lady Whitby had assured her the majority of them were quite disgusting in their habits. She'd shared with Elise rumors of some of the unsavory things that even the most genteel of them had done. One that had shocked Elise was the story of a well-known lord who had consummated his marriage on the sitting room settee *while* his guests were in the next room enjoying the wedding breakfast.

"Everyone could hear them," Lady Whitby had proclaimed.

Elise shook her head as if wanting to dislodge such a distasteful piece of gossip.

She also reminded herself that behavior like embarrassing one's wife or parading naked in the woods was the reason her heart had gone to Michael Brogan. There was nothing unsuitable about Michael. He was the model of a true gentleman. Whereas Kit was a nobody, she reminded herself. A self-professed *wanderer*, whatever that meant. A *naked* wanderer.

No matter how awe-inspiring his physique— and the hard planes of Kit's torso were a wonder— she must never forget Michael. She'd run away because of her devotion to him. This whole escapade with the crash and being stranded and seeing a remarkable naked man had been because of Michael—

A sharp pain brutally reminded Elise of the blisters. Their number was growing. She'd been so wrapped up in turmoil over Kit's naked defection that she hadn't felt them until now.

For a second, she thought about stopping, untying her still damp walking shoes, which was a challenge, and adjusting the cloth bindings. If she did, Kit might catch up with her.

He couldn't be far behind her now.

Elise glanced back.

No one was there, and that made her angrier.

Granted he didn't owe her anything. They were two strangers thrown together by circumstance.

But the fact was, everyone in her life had let her down—her sisters, her aunt Tweedie, Michael . . . why not Kit and Tamsyn, too? And she told herself they didn't matter. None of them mattered. She would go on. She would reach Wiltham.

Determination spurred her forward. All she had to do was show up at the next posting inn.

Ruggedly limping along, she acknowledged that Tamsyn's defection hurt most. The dog had been so protective of her that Elise had believed they had a bond.

"And, once again, you are wrong." Elise spoke the words aloud. She told herself that it was best Tamsyn had chosen Kit. What if the next coach didn't let Elise keep the dog with her? She'd hate to leave the animal behind. Let Kit worry about her.

The problem, she decided, was that although Fate had thrown them together, Kit was not a good traveling companion. He was too—

Her mind struggled for a word and decided on *manly*. He was too manly. Any sensible person would realize that he would be naked around her sooner or later. Was that not the nature of men?

Cataloging the many sins of the opposite sex bolstered her resolve to see this trip through, although Elise wished Lady Whitby was walking with her. The two of them could shred this topic to pieces. Society was unfair to females. Men refused to allow women to have any say when it came to government even when the laws they made affected them.

And all the unfairness in her mind was punctuated by blistered feet that screamed for relief—

The sound of slowly rolling wheels caught her attention. Elise turned to look as she walked. She pulled up her hood.

Two lean oxen pulled a cart carrying a cutting of hay.

The driver walking beside the team was an older man, a grandfatherly one. Because of her blisters, the oxen team, as slow as it was, had no trouble catching up with her.

As the driver came closer, Elise smiled. He was very much of the same age as her father would have been if he was alive. Beneath a straw wide-brimmed hat, the portly man had a shaft of snowy white hair and a round nose.

His eyes were kind, the sort a person could trust.

He halted his oxen as they reached her. "I say, girl, what are you doing out here on the road by yourself?" Then his voice turned concerned. "You're hurt. I saw you limping."

She was silent.

He shook his head. "Comely lass like you out here all alone. It isn't safe."

"It isn't," she agreed, finding her voice in appreciation of his acknowledgment of the fact.

He pulled the pipe he'd been chewing on from his mouth. "If you need a ride, lass, you can sit in the back of the wagon. How far are you going?"

She glanced at the sweet-smelling freshly mown hay. His offer was tempting. Still, a woman must be cautious. "I'm traveling to the next posting inn. Tell me, do you know how much farther up the road it is?"

"Couple hours' walk. I won't be going all the way there. However, I can take you some half that way."

"That would be lovely," Elise had to admit. She hesitated, studied him a moment. He seemed a good sort . . . and her feet begged for relief. Her father's eyes had been blue, with just the same friendly twinkle. That small resemblance, and her aching feet, settled the matter. "I would like to take you up on your kind offer."

As she'd spoken, her hood had fallen back. The driver's eyes widened. "You are a beauty."

Elise felt herself blush. She pulled the hood up again. "Thank you."

"What are you doing out here by yourself? Don't you have family?"

She thought of her sisters, of Michael. "No, I'm alone." The sooner she thought of herself that way, the better. She must be brave in the face of her life's circumstances. She also felt safe enough around him to be blunt.

"A sad thing to be by oneself in life," he said, commiserating. "Well, climb in the back and I'll take you as far as I can."

"Thank you, thank you," she gushed, moving to the rear of the cart to hop aboard before he changed his mind.

"I'm Simon," he called to her.

Simon, such a lovely name. No one who was dangerous could ever be called Simon.

"You are?" he prodded.

She hesitated. She wished she'd not given Kit her true name. She would not make that mistake twice. "Dara," she said, tickled to think how annoyed her sister would be to know she'd used her name.

It also reminded her that her family may have found her note by now.

She wondered what Tweedie and her sisters thought. Were they angry? Worried? Might there be a hint of understanding?

Did she truly care what they thought? They needed to understand that she had pride.

They always trampled on her feelings, on her wants and desires. They expected her to fall in line. Well, now they knew she couldn't. She wouldn't.

The moment she settled in the freshly mowed hay, her feet seemed to thank her for the relief. The scent of summer surrounded her and she let herself relax. She was safe.

Simon called "Haw" to his team, and they were traveling.

Elise untied the ribbons of her cloak and lay back on the hay. The sky above was a deep blue with a few lazy clouds.

A yawn caught her. She wanted to stay awake except the movement of the wagon and the afternoon warmth conspired against her. It had been a difficult night. She was still traumatized by the coach accident and the bodies—

She tried not to think about them. Instead, she closed her eyes, giving them a momentary rest, and just like that, she fell asleep, but for what only seemed a second.

Did she dream? She could not remember.

Instead, she abruptly came awake and lay there a moment, uncertain as to where she was. This was not her bed—not in Wiltham and not in London. She moved and felt the shifting beneath her. She was riding in the hay wagon. Yes, that was it. Simon was taking her toward the posting inn.

Elise sat up, expecting to see the road.

They were not on the road. Instead, they were

coming to a halt in front of an aged stone cottage surrounded by tall grasses and broken pots and furniture. Some puny chickens pecked around the front door. There was a stone lean-to close to the house and an overgrown garden off to the side. Black smoke drifted from the chimney, and the air smelled of manure.

She twisted her body toward the front of the cart. "Simon?"

He didn't answer. Instead, he called, "Tommy, come out here. See what I have for you."

Elise didn't understand.

"What is it, Pa?" a high-pitched voice called out.

"Go check the back of the wagon," Simon said.

Elise wasn't certain what was happening, but her every instinct warned her to *run*. She climbed out of the wagon, her cloak still on the hay where she'd slept. She started to reach for it, but then Simon was right there in front of her. She hadn't heard him move.

She gave a sharp gasp of surprise.

Simon grinned. This time the expression was not grandfatherly. "You can't leave, lass. Not yet."

"Why, she is lovely," the high-pitched voice said from behind her.

Elise reeled, and met Tommy. He was no child or woman but a giant of a man with gray at his temples. He had long arms and appeared strong in spite of a belly that hung down over his breeches. His nose had obviously been bro-ken several times. He reached for her hair with a hand that seemed to be the size of a serving platter.

"Don't touch me," she warned, stepping back.

"Stop it, girl," Simon answered. "Her name is Dara," he told his son. "Don't abuse her like you did the last one."

"Simon?" a woman's voice said from the house.

"That is my wife, Tommy's mother. You won't have to mind her much," Simon said as if Elise had asked. He raised his voice. "We're busy," he stated bluntly. "I brought Tommy another girl."

Elise caught a glance of a woman hovering just inside the door. Simon's wife was a gray thing, thin and pale like a ghost. She didn't show a sign of curiosity. Elise had seen that in a woman before. There had been a gamekeeper at Wiltham who had been cruel to his wife to the point that the woman had no spirit. Gram had let him go. She'd offered to take in the wife, but the woman had left with her husband.

There was no mettle left in Simon's wife. Her only reply to his rude words was, "Let me know when you want dinner."

Simon looked up at his son. "Don't be cruel to this one. Word has gotten around. It's harder to find you girls."

"Dara." Tommy tested out her name. He smiled. His teeth were brown.

And Elise decided the time had come to leave. Without warning, she lifted her skirts and took off as fast as she could.

There was a whoop behind her. Simon said with a laugh, "Go after her, Tommy. Give her a chase. But remember, not too rough."

Once again, Elise found herself running. Did her feet hurt now? She had no idea. Fear drove her. The rowdy laborers appeared tame compared to this danger. She reached the woods.

"Dara, you can't run from me," Tommy called. "I know this land better than you."

She kept going, believing she could escape him—

He shocked her by jumping right into her path, launching himself off a pile of trees and debris.

Elise screamed. *How did he get there?* She'd thought he was behind her and she'd been terribly wrong.

She pivoted, ready to race away, but he reached out with his long arms and grabbed her braid.

Her head jerked back. Pain shot through her. With a laugh, he began wrapping her braid around his meaty hand, bringing her toward him.

*But a Lanscarr did not give up.*

In a fit of pure rage, she spun around and, clasping both of her hands into a fist, whacked him hard right between the legs.

Tommy released his hold with a howl of pain. He doubled over and Elise was off again. However, she had not gone more than ten steps when he caught the left shoulder of her dress and tackled her to the ground.

He rolled her over. "You bitch," he growled, placing a hand around her throat.

Elise felt his grip, felt her air being closed off. He didn't even need both hands to choke her. She pleaded with her eyes for him to let go, and that is when she saw him poised with a fist raised in the air, ready to bring it down on her—

A figure slammed full force into Tommy.

His grip on her neck released as he lost his balance. Crying out in outrage, Tommy confronted his new attacker.

*It was Kit. He was here.*

He'd thrown himself at Tommy only to bounce off the giant and land heavily on the ground, the wind knocked out of him.

Tamsyn came rushing forward, as brave as she was with the laborers. She snapped and snarled, but this was a different adversary.

Tommy rose, forgetting Elise, who was busy taking great gulps of sweet, blessed air. He picked up a good-sized branch from the ground and swung it at the dog. He struck Tamsyn's hindquarters. She gave a yelp and backed away. Tommy then started for Kit, who had finally rolled over but was still weak.

"This will be fun," he gloated, and Elise knew she must stop him.

# CHAPTER NINE

*God is good, but never dance in a small boat.*
IRISH PROVERB

Elise struggled to her feet. The sleeves of all three dresses had been torn down her left shoulder. She wobbled a moment and then, as Tommy lifted his branch to club Kit, she launched herself for his arm. She grabbed hold as tight as she could, feeling quite ineffectual considering the man's size and strength. He threw her off.

However, Elise was not alone. As Tommy swore and tried to elbow her away, Tamsyn attacked, sinking her teeth into the man's calf. Tommy howled in pain. He turned, ready to use his weapon on the dog, but Kit was up now.

"Tommy," he said.

Confused by pain, the giant spun toward the sound of his name, and Kit punched him a good one right in the nose.

Tommy screamed in outrage. This gave the

very excited Tamsyn the chance to circle around and bite his other calf.

Nor did Kit let up. He struck Tommy in the jaw, and he kept punching until Tommy's head snapped back with enough force Elise could imagine it flying off. His eyes closed. For a second, Tommy teetered, and then his legs buckled, and the big man went down. And there he lay.

Elise stared in wonder. "Is he—?" She paused before finishing, "Alive?"

"I'm certain he is," Kit answered. He stood ready to fight if Tommy moved. "That bastard is a tough one."

It was Tamsyn who sniffed their opponent. She looked up at them and wagged her tail as if to say they were safe.

Unfortunately, footsteps could be heard running through the woods toward them. Panicked, Elise copied Tommy and picked up a branch from the ground. Kit took a protective position in front of her just as Simon stomped upon the scene.

His gaze went right to his son. "*Tommy.*" He flew to his son and bent over the still body. Elise stepped forward and whacked him in the head with all her might. He dropped, landing right on top of Tommy.

Kit did not waste a moment. He swept his hat up from the ground. "Come," he said, throwing his arm around her. "We're leaving."

"My cloak?" She tried to go toward the cottage. He pulled her back.

"We *must* leave, Elise."

"But my money." All she had, the coins that were to pay her way to Ireland, was in the pocket of that cloak.

"*Elise.*"

This time, she didn't argue. He was right. They might not be able to defeat Tommy and Simon a second time. Together, with Tamsyn running ahead of them, they raced from the scene of their battle.

It was obvious Kit was hurt. His jaw was tight as if he clenched against pain. Elise understood. Her shoulder ached where she'd fallen, and she feared she would have a bruise on the morrow. Even Tamsyn seemed to favor her right leg.

However, the three of them managed to make good progress. Elise and Kit didn't speak. It took all of their energy to breathe. She put one blistered foot in front of the other, focusing on Kit and allowing him to lead her—until she realized they were traveling deeper into the woods. She slowed her step. "Shouldn't we go to the road?"

"That is where they will expect us to go," was the terse reply.

"But where are we?"

"Safe."

Did she agree? She didn't know. She was hungry, thirsty, and, now that her excitement was wearing off, exhausted. It was all she could do to keep moving.

When they reached a stream, Kit allowed them to stop. "We can rest here. Have a drink."

A drink. She fell to her knees on the mossy bank without a thought to staining her skirt.

Tamsyn was already lapping away. Elise realized that through everything, she still wore her gloves. She almost laughed at the absurdity of it.

"Drink," Kit ordered. He'd removed his own gloves and was cupping water up to his mouth—that is when she noticed he'd shaved.

She stared, shocked by the change. He was *handsome*. Oh, he'd been good-looking before in a rough way, but this was . . . different. Kit appeared younger than she had supposed. The hard clean-shaven jaw also made him seem a tad more dangerous. Here was a man who commanded attention, who could have whatever he wanted.

He must have felt her staring because his head turned to look at her. Their gazes held. Did he know what she was thinking? That she found him attractive?

And then, in a quiet but very angry tone, he said, "The next time you try to see yourself raped, Elise, please pick someone who isn't bigger than I am by *five stone*."

*Raped?*

He thought she had encouraged what had happened?

For one long second, Elise couldn't breathe.

Simon's treachery and Tommy's assault mingled

with years of being thought of as nothing more than the "pretty" Lanscarr sister. Men doted on her without a care to her opinions or even her dreams. The most boorish of them thought she should be honored by their attention. And she was not fooled—if not for Society's "rules" many of her aristocratic suitors would have acted like Tommy.

And Kit believed her at fault?

Her hand went to the water, and she scooped it right up into his face. "You contemptible, self-centered, *low*, no account, *English*—" Words failed as her mind scrambled to express exactly what she thought of his statement. Instead, she splashed another handful of water in his face just as he was recovering from the last one.

Elise leaped to her feet. "You are *despicable,*" she hissed, and marched away. He called her name but she kept going. She had never been so insulted. Her *trying* to be *raped*? He was mad. *Insensitive*—

His hand grabbed her arm. *"Elise."*

She snatched it back, turning as she did so. "That was the *vilest*, most *horrid* thing anyone has ever said—"

"You are right. You're right," Kit interjected, holding his hands out as if wishing to keep the peace. "I was wrong. *Wrong,*" he repeated. "It was an irrational thing to say."

"Especially since my being in those circumstances was all *your* fault." She was not going to let this go.

"How was this my fault? You took off without me—"

"*Because you weren't there.* You were walking in the woods naked—"

"I was bathing. You told me I reeked."

"You *left* me," she answered. "Just left. Not a word. *Nothing.* And there were these rude farm workers and—"

"Farm workers?"

"Yes, and they made me uncomfortable because of how they acted, so I thought I would find you, and Tamsyn growled at them—"

"Elise, I'm sorry," he said, cutting her off. "I didn't know. I thought you were fine for the moment."

"Fine—?" She shook her head in disbelief. There were no words. She wanted nothing to do with him. She charged off.

"Elise? *Elise.*"

She kept going and would have walked her way to the coast except his arms came around her waist. Lifting her off her feet, he swung her back, planting her on the ground in front of him—and she exploded in fury.

How dare he manhandle her as if she was his to direct—and a low simmering anger that had been building long before Dara and Michael's marriage exploded into unabashed rage.

Elise slapped out at him, her palm hitting his chest, the first place she could reach. He was solid muscle. Her blow had no impact on him so she gave him a hard shove.

Kit stepped back as if catching his balance and she launched herself at him, pushing and hitting, her hands curling into fists.

"You *left* me," she said through the onslaught. "You didn't say anything about where you were going or what you were doing. But isn't that the way men are? Always blaming women for whatever happens? Treating us as if *we don't matter*. Then stealing our inheritance and robbing us of *what is ours*. And thinking you can get away with it—"

Kit kept backing away, trying to protect himself from her flying fists. Did she hurt him? She didn't know, but she was so *bloody* angry she had to try. Men had everything, didn't they? They ruled the world.

"And the *scurviest* of you think that you have the right to any woman's person. That just because my looks catch your eye you can grab me and *basely use me*?"

"Elise," he tried again, almost falling into the stream until he shifted to stay on the bank. "Stop this. Please."

She ignored him—because months, even *years* of pent-up anger had finally found release, and release it she did. "*You left me*, you left me, you left me," she repeated over and over until she realized she didn't know if she was talking to Kit—or her father?

The startling insight frightened her.

*What was she doing? What was she saying—?*

Her mind reeled, right as her legs collapsed beneath her, and she would have crumpled to the ground except Kit caught her weight and lowered her with him. They were beneath an old oak with far-reaching roots. His back rested against the trunk.

She attempted to elbow her way free of him. "I don't need *anyone*." She didn't need sisters who expected her to swallow her pride or a father whom she had rarely seen. Or London's judgmental Society matrons, or its bitter, jealous debutantes.

And she certainly didn't need men.

Instead of letting her go, Kit tightened his hold. "Elise, I'm sorry. I'm so very sorry." Regret, true emotion, etched every word.

That was when she became completely undone. Hot tears of frustration, of belonging nowhere and having nothing, poured out of her and she couldn't have stopped them if she'd tried. Her fingers gripped the material of his jacket. She turned her face into his chest and cried as if her very soul was being ripped from her.

Kit held her. One hand smoothed her hair back as one would a child's. "It's all right, Elise," he murmured soothingly. "I'm sorry. It will all be well."

He didn't understand. Her life hadn't been right since her father had been pronounced dead. Everything had changed then. Gram had died. Richard had taken over. Everyone in the county had looked at Elise with a melty-eyed pity that she'd despised.

Then there was the family betrayal. How could Dara have done that to her? How could Gwendolyn and Tweedie side with Dara? Why was Elise the one who must always sacrifice? To do as the others wished?

She cried for each of them, for those who were gone, for all she couldn't change. She cried in anger and regret.

But one can't cry forever.

At last, eventually, she was spent. Her face felt hot and wet. Her body boneless. She lay still for several long moments . . . and then she drew a long, shaky breath. She released it, and shame washed over her. *A Lanscarr should never lose control.* That is what her father had always told his daughters. It wasn't done. It made one too vulnerable.

Kit didn't move, not even to shift his weight. Her head was under his chin, her cheek against his chest. She could hear his heartbeat. It was steady and strong, comforting.

A sense of calm returned.

There was a rustle of twigs and grass as Tamsyn crawled forward with worry in her brown eyes. Their argument must have looked confusing to her. Elise pried her fingers off Kit's jacket and reached out so that she could pet the dog and reassure her. Above their heads, a bird sang, and there was the buzzing of an insect accompanied by the stream's gentle burble.

Elise let the hand petting Tamsyn drop to the ground. She pressed down, shifting to move. Her weight couldn't be comfortable for Kit, not after all the two of them had experienced since the crash.

Instead of letting go, his hold tightened slightly. "Not yet," he whispered, and because she really didn't know if she had the strength to rise, she stayed where she was.

He still stroked her hair, wrapping a stray lock around his finger from time to time.

"I was overwrought," she whispered.

"*I* was out of line."

"You were."

He made a sound as if her frank agreement was what he had expected. Elise felt herself smile.

"I was worried when I came out of the forest and you were gone," Kit said.

"You made me angry."

"I should have told you where I was going."

"True." She paused. "I shouldn't have just walked off." If she had been with Kit, Simon wouldn't have spoken to her.

He hummed his thoughts and then said, "Anger was flowing both ways. We have had a challenging night and day." There was a pause. "You were also right that I 'reeked.'"

*That* conversation. It seemed like it had taken place weeks ago instead of a few hours.

Elise took in the greenery around them. The day was winding down. He was right. It had been a long one. "I am lucky you found me."

"Tamsyn and I went in search of you. We caught sight of you just as you were climbing into the cart."

"Why didn't you call out?"

"How did I know you weren't trying to escape me? You were highly upset upon seeing me in my altogether."

*She had seen him naked.* "I'd forgotten. In all that happened, I put it out of my mind."

"Glad I was memorable," he said dryly. "When I saw you take the ride, I assumed you were leaving on your own. Although Tamsyn and I did trail behind. We kept to the tree line in case you didn't want to have anything to do with us."

"Am I that ferocious?"

"Yes," came his quick reply. "You are lucky oxen don't travel fast. When the driver turned off the road, I started to have doubts about him."

"And so you followed?" She was fortunate he had.

"*We* did. Tamsyn was upset from the moment you climbed into the hay cart." Hearing her name, the dog moved even closer as if wanting to be a part of their huddle.

"The driver seemed kind. He reminded me of my father," she admitted. "Which is silly because Simon looks nothing like him. Well, his eyes reminded me of Father." Or so she had told herself. Now she realized how foolish she'd been. "I suppose I was tired and not thinking clearly."

"It has been a rough adventure."

She appreciated that there was no censure in his tone.

His stomach rumbled. She lifted her head and made as if to move. "You haven't eaten all day."

He gently pressed her back against him. "I found some berries while following you to Simon's. Besides, this isn't the first time I've had to wait for a meal."

"We should have been at the next posting house by now."

"But we aren't."

No, they weren't . . . and it was fine to be right here, stretched alongside him in the haven of the oak—

"Tell me about your father."

His request surprised her. "I don't talk about him." He was hard to explain. Instead, she changed the subject. "After removing all that scruffiness, you actually appear honest."

He winced. "Your flattery knows no bounds, Elise. I smell. You don't want to see me *naked*. I was a *dishonest* ruffian."

There was no heat in his words. Just openness. And acceptance.

Dara had harped on numerous rules about what one should say and not say around the opposite sex. But from the beginning, perhaps because of the trauma of the accident, Elise had never been anything but herself around Kit. It was a radical thought—and she realized she'd not even been her complete self around Michael, and she'd wanted to marry him. She'd always been trying to impress him with her political opinions . . . something she admitted few men valued. They would rather look at her instead of listen to her.

In the end, Michael had been pretending interest in Elise to annoy Dara.

And suddenly, for the first time, that thought failed to bother her. The feelings of humiliation or resentment that had been her constant companions of late had vanished. She seemed free of them. *Because of a good cry?*

Elise started to laugh in surprise. It was what she'd wanted, why she'd run away—

"And now you are laughing at me?" Kit noted—with *mock* hurt.

She smiled. Who was this man who could be so confident in his own person that he didn't fear ridicule or criticism? Who seemed to understand *her*? Or at least, let her be?

He'd certainly proven to be a friend. He had witnessed her lose all sense and control, and he'd acted as if everything was as it should be. He'd even apologized for his own poor behavior.

Had a man ever apologized to her before? She thought not.

"Thank you." The words flowed out of her.

He pulled a face, the black eye she'd given him darker than the other in the evening shadows. "For what?"

"For being—" She paused. What was the right word? "Trustworthy." She'd believed in Michael, and yet he'd proven she shouldn't have. He had never been completely honest with her, and that had been part of her discontent and frustration with living under his roof. He'd certainly never apologized for leading her on.

But this man . . .

Silvery eyes studied her a moment. She wished she could read his thoughts. He'd become quiet.

He shifted. That was when she realized their legs were practically intertwined. Her breasts rested on his chest. Her nipples were hard, and her hip rested on his—

Kit sat up, changing their position. It put some space between the two of them, and she wished he hadn't moved.

He cleared his throat and then said, "You *shouldn't* trust me. I behaved poorly. I was irritated when I walked off. I thought only of myself, and things *could* have gone the wrong way. A brute like Tommy should have won."

"But he didn't."

"A few moments ago, you were furious with me. Rightfully so." There was a pause. Silvery eyes met hers and then looked away. "Stay that way."

Elise frowned. A small white butterfly zigzagged along the bank as if she had lost her way home. She looked lonely and confused in the day's ending. Unmoored . . . much the way Elise felt.

She should not entertain feelings for Kit, and she was beginning to. She must remember that she was Miss Elise Lanscarr, the reigning "Flower of the London Season." The Lanscarrs were gentry. They belonged to a certain class.

That didn't mean she couldn't be appreciative of what he'd done for her.

Elise swung her attention from the hapless butterfly back to him. "Regardless, I was very lucky to have your help."

"Don't forget the stalwart Tamsyn."

Tamsyn wagged her tail at the mention of her name. Elise ran her hand over the dog's head. "You were both brave."

"You are actually a good fighter yourself, Elise."

"I am." She savored that idea a moment. "I can be quite bold."

"That you are." He smiled, revealing the dimples.

A woman could bask for hours in his smile. And then she realized she had one question. "Why do you ask about my father?"

Kit moved to sit on one of the large roots as if it was a stool.

More space between them.

"You mentioned him when you were angry. You also said he was the reason you let your guard down around Simon. I wonder at a father who lets his daughter travel alone."

She'd hoped Kit hadn't heard her reference to

her father. "He's dead." She didn't mean to sound so curt, but there it was. A world of sorrow was hidden in those two blunt words. She tried to soften her tone, her pain. "He was declared dead by the magistrate a little over a year ago."

"Declared dead?"

"Yes, we don't know where he died. He was a military man and"—she smiled sadly—"a gambler. He never could pass up a game of cards when money was involved. When he sold his colors, he didn't return to Wiltham but had to go wherever he thought there was a good play."

"Wiltham? This is a place in Ireland?"

She nodded. "It's our family home, from my mother's side. She died shortly after I was born. Papa always returned but his stays were never longer than a visit. He would appear once or sometimes twice a year with his arms loaded with presents. He'd be with us a while, almost a week, but then he'd need to leave. Gram said he *had* to go. He was a bit like you, I suppose. Wanting to wander."

"But his death was never confirmed?" Kit sounded a bit stunned by the possibility.

Elise shook her head. "When we noticed how long it had been since he'd visited, Gram sent letters to the last place he'd posted a letter to us. There were no answers. It was as if he'd vanished."

"You have no proof of death?"

"Not formally in a church ledger, no. However, he would have returned to us if he could.

He may have been absent most of my life, but he *adored* us." That was one thing she knew about her father. "Everything was very special when he was home. He taught my sisters and me all his favorite card games. I'm not a good gambler, but Gwendolyn knows every trick."

"Gwendolyn is a sister?"

"My oldest. The next one is Dara. She just recently married." More words that sounded simple and weren't.

"And you are traveling back to your Gram?"

Her heart turned heavy. "She died a little over a year ago."

"Elise, why are you traveling alone? Why wouldn't a sister be with you?"

"It is complicated."

"It's not," he countered. "You shouldn't be out in the world without an escort. Your complaints were exactly correct. We men think every woman should be ours for the taking, especially when the woman is young and attractive. We are louts. There are more Tommys lying in wait."

"I'll be more cautious in the future," she insisted. Who was he to tell her what she could and couldn't do? "I'll also be safer in Ireland."

"I wouldn't count on that."

"I'll be fine."

"There it is again. That word *fine*. You use it every time I say something you don't like."

"I'm *not* returning to London," she answered.

"I can't." Her anger at Dara was easing, but the source of it was not forgotten.

He made an impatient sound. "You can. You are just too stubborn to. Your sisters should never have ever let you go off alone."

"They don't know where I am," she shot back.

That seemed to shock him. He sat straighter. "They don't know you are traipsing around England?"

"You traipse around England," she said.

"I'm male—" he countered as if that carried the weight of the world, and then caught himself. There was a beat of silence between them. Then he said in the patient tone of someone explaining to someone who was simple, or obstinate, "Yes, you are right. Men can do as they wish. That doesn't mean women don't need protection."

"But that is unfair."

"No," he countered as if he was being reasonable. "That is just the world we live in, Elise. Right or wrong, those are facts."

"I refuse to acknowledge those facts. Why, if I listened to you, my sisters and I would never have gone to London."

"Except now you are returning to Ireland. Where is the logic in that?"

"Your arguments make my eyes cross. No one tells *you* where you can go. Or insists you have a chaperone at all times."

"No one tries to climb under my skirts or take

me captive. The other night the coachman made a suggestion that was so foul, I wanted to choke the life out of him."

The suggestion had been shocking, but Elise could not afford to admit it. "You do not need to worry about me."

"Of course I do. You are the most stubborn, willful woman I've ever met. But if Our Maker had wanted you to do as you please, He would have given you something more between your legs."

Elise didn't miss a beat. "Perhaps *She* should have."

Kit shook his head as if he hadn't heard her correctly, paused, and then he burst into laughter.

Elise was ready to take offense. Was it so difficult to consider that a higher power could be female? After all, the ancients had many goddesses. She and Lady Whitby had put forth this argument several times at her ladyship's afternoon salons.

But before Elise could expound upon her opinions, he said, "Damn, Elise. You are an Original. Perhaps *She* should have," he repeated. "And you are right. You should be able to travel where you wish without worry."

He'd said she was right. Unequivocally. No one had ever paid her a better compliment. They were usually too busy patronizing her. "Thank you—"

Her voice broke at the change in his manner. His brow had darkened as he looked down at her. "Your dress. Did Tommy do that?"

Elise glanced at her exposed shoulder. So much had happened, she forgotten he'd ripped her gowns. She'd been caught up in escape and arguing with Kit. "Apparently." She tried to pull the pieces together. The soft muslin was shredded. It might not be able to be repaired. If Tommy had pulled harder, her left breast would have been exposed.

Kit jumped to his feet, already lifting the oilskin over his head. He removed his jacket and placed it on her shoulders. The stain of her tears still marred the fabric.

Gratefully, she slipped her hands through the sleeves. They hung well past her fingertips, but at least she was covered. "I'll think of a way to repair the dresses. I'm good with a needle."

"Dresses. One on top of the other." He spoke as if solving a riddle. "You are a runaway, aren't you, Elise?"

Instead of answering, she ran a hand along the front of his jacket. "This is excellent wool, Kit. The tailoring is good as well."

"Elise?" There was a warning in his voice. He expected an answer.

He wouldn't receive one. "My sisters and I make our own clothes," she said as if he had asked.

An appraising look came to his eye. "Who are you, Elise? I thought at first you were some lady's maid and yet I've never met one with an opinion of her own. And yet you sew your own gowns?"

She turned his question on him. "Who are you, Kit? I thought you were some poacher or vagabond, but you are well-spoken. What is your story?"

He pointed a knowing finger at her. "Like I said, you are a quick one." He turned. "We'll stay here, Elise, for the night."

She nodded. It would soon be too dark to walk on. The growl in her stomach reminded her she would be going hungry, too. He started to move away from the tree. "Where are you going?"

"To check the area. You are safe with Tamsyn."

"You will be back?" The words came out in a rush. She hadn't meant to sound alarmed, but it had been a long day.

Kit turned, met her eye. "I *will* be back in a moment. Will you be *here*?"

She copied his tone. "I *will* be here."

A grudging smile pulled at the corners of his mouth. "Then we are fine. Good night, Elise. Sleep."

"I don't know that I can."

"You'd best try. After all, I'm taking you to Ireland on the morrow. You need an escort. And *no* argument. I'm thinking of your safety." With those words, he walked off, his tall figure silhouetted in the twilight.

Why would she argue with his offer? Today had been a very hard day. She realized she might not even have made it through last night without his help.

"He is not a bad sort," she confided to the dog,

and then she did a quick little jig. Tamsyn, tail wagging, tried to join her. Kit would accompany her to Ireland. Her relief was immeasurable because the trip would be easy now.

All at once, Elise found herself so tired she could barely think, and she knew it was because she was safe. She settled in to where the tree's curved roots made a comfortable space to relax. Tamsyn moved to snuggle up to her. Huddled in Kit's jacket, Elise curled her fingers in the dog's long hair. She meant to stay awake for Kit to return. She couldn't.

*HE HAD JUST promised to see her all the way to Ireland.* The offer had seemed natural, even nobly sensible . . . but as Kit circled their small camp, he wondered what he had gotten himself into.

And why?

Elise was a riddle he wasn't certain he wished to solve. Wiltham was her family home? Her father had been in the military? Those clues smacked of landed gentry, a bloody innocent alone, and a problem for him if she ever discovered *his* true identity. There wasn't a soul in London, including his mother, who wouldn't believe he hadn't compromised her. His reputation had become that bad.

Still, he really had no choice but to offer to accompany her. There were dangers out there she couldn't even imagine.

But *he* needed to be careful. Not only because Elise was a tempting bit, but also because his heart was still tender after Kate's rejection. So much so, he didn't know if he could ever trust himself or a woman again. He had clearly misunderstood Kate's opinion of him. The humiliation had set him on his present course.

That didn't mean he didn't find Elise intriguing. In spite of her beauty, she was a bluestocking. She was too opinionated not to be, and he liked a challenging woman. Admired them. A woman should be more than her looks. She should have substance, which had made Kate's rejection doubly hard. She'd found *him* lacking.

And she would probably be even less impressed now.

One problem at a time, he reminded himself. Take Elise to Ireland. Then, see what he could do to cobble together the rest of his life.

As for his motives? Well, he didn't wish to examine those either.

When he finished patrolling the area and was reasonably certain they were safe from the likes of Simon and Tommy, Kit returned to the oak. He glanced down at Elise. A child could not have slept deeper than she at this moment. Tamsyn didn't move either. Instead, the two of them presented a tableau of a moon maiden and her faithful dog.

Kit walked around to the *other side* of the tree. He wrapped his greatcoat around him, and soon was lost in sleep as well.

# CHAPTER TEN

*Don't be breaking your shin on a stool that is not in
your way.*
IRISH PROVERB

&ach and every time Beckett Steele saw Gwendolyn Lanscarr, he was struck anew by her
grace, her unhurried movements, her regal bearing. He'd immediately noticed those qualities
when their paths had first crossed. She was a
true beauty, a willowy figure with raven-black
hair and skin that always appeared as if the sun
had kissed it.

Now, with the sounds of Lord and Lady
Mersey's ball behind her, she walked through the
dark garden. She didn't know he was there, waiting in the shadows, watching. Steele prided himself on being a mystery. His business depended
upon it. He traveled through Society as easily
as he passed through London's underworld. He
would make contact with her, but on his terms.
He could have joined the soiree, even without an

invitation. But he held back. He always wanted the lay of the land before he made a move.

Meanwhile, he wondered what she was doing out here alone. Certainly, someone would notice her missing from the ball. Or perhaps she had an assignation?

The idea did not rest easy with him. He wondered who the man was. Morley? Lindell? Many were pursuing her. He knew. He paid attention to every morsel of information he heard about her.

She surprised him by stopping, right in front of where he stood hidden. She faced another direction. He caught the scent of her—

"I know you are here, Mr. Steele." Her voice was cool and well modulated with just a hint of the music of Ireland in it.

Beck didn't respond immediately. Instead, he stayed in the darkest shadows—

"You *are* here," she reiterated. She looked around. "I sense your presence."

Sensed? Well, in that case . . .

He stepped onto the path. She turned, smiled her satisfaction at being right, and every muscle inside of him tightened.

However, when he spoke, his voice was distant, controlled, the way he liked it. "I was planning to go inside." He indicated his black evening clothes.

"There are too many people in there."

"Including Brogan. He is looking for me." He referred to her brother-by-marriage.

"Actually, my sister and *I* are the ones asking for you, and we don't have time for you to be sociable."

That emphasis on *I*. He liked knowing she turned to him.

He'd once helped Gwendolyn when she was in need. That was how they'd met. He'd almost kissed her then, an unusual lapse in judgment. He was saved from making a fool of himself when one of her sisters bashed him over the head, and that neatly summed up the Lanscarr sisters for him. There was no anticipating what they would do.

"What may I do for you?" he asked.

"My sister Elise is missing. We believe she has run away."

"Run away?" That surprised him. Hunting people is what Beck did best. He made an excellent living of it. However, Elise had struck him as being very sensible, even as she was claiming the heart of every man in London. Hers was a resounding beauty, the sort that brought men to their knees. "That seems out of character for her. Are you certain it isn't something . . . worse?"

"She left a note." Gwendolyn spoke as if he was being tiresome. "She said she was going to Ireland. She's been very angry lately. Michael hired men who confirmed a young woman matching her description left from the Bull and Mouth two days ago. Michael wants to go after her, but his absence would be noticed if he left London right now. Then people might ask questions."

"Has anyone noticed her missing yet?"

"We have put it out that she is ill. To be honest, most of the debutantes and their mothers are overjoyed Elise is not present at balls and parties."

"The better the opportunity for them to shine."

"Exactly. Will you help us, Mr. Steele?"

"She could be in Ireland by the end of tomorrow or the next day."

"Then she will find herself in the hands of our vile cousin, who feels no obligation to the care and well-being of his female relations. Elise is naive in many ways. She doesn't understand all of the dangers."

"You do not trust this cousin?"

"I detest him."

"And Elise didn't know this?"

"She doesn't like him either. However, Elise is overconfident in herself. She doesn't obey all the rules that guide polite society, or feels they should be ignored, often times just on principle. She could walk right into a desperate situation for no other reason than her own boldness. It's Dara's and my fault. We have protected her. Perhaps too much." Then she said in her direct manner, "You must find her."

It seemed an easy task.

He had come to admire the Lanscarrs. They had set out to marry dukes using their looks and their intelligence. He imagined them as female pirates, swooping in to gather what booty they could. They had certainly given this Season's scheming mothers and anxious debutantes a good shake.

However, Beck already had a commission, one that was proving to be frustrating. He had been searching for a missing duke whose family was most anxious for him to be found. All Beck had to do was learn what drove the person, gambling, womanizing, other darker vices? Following their trail was easy after that.

Except, this Winderton case confounded him. He'd caught word of a sighting here and there, but by the time Beck arrived, the man purported to be the duke would be gone. He never used his title and there was no apparent pattern to the duke's actions. It was almost as if the man was roaming to roam. That meant he could be anywhere in the world since he'd been gone close to a year.

However, this was the lovely Gwendolyn asking for help.

How could Beck resist?

"Of course I will find your sister," he told her.

She was so grateful, she almost fell into his arms, but she stopped herself, stepping back. "Thank you, Mr. Steele. Please come to the house tomorrow. We will tell you all we know."

"I shall leave tonight, Miss Lanscarr. You've already told me all I need to know. She is heading toward Ireland. What is her exact destination?"

"Wiltham in County Wicklow."

"Ah, yes. If I am to reach there before your sister, I must ride now."

Gwendolyn nodded, her eyes shiny with unshed tears of relief.

And it made him feel insanely proud that he could offer this to her.

"Whatever price you want, I shall pay it," she promised. "Money, another favor. We need your help." Some paid for his services with coin, but from others he asked favors. Those favors gave him power. They were more valuable than money. Gwendolyn already owed him a favor, one he would soon ask her to act upon.

"We already have a bargain," he told her magnanimously. After all, he didn't want to see Elise Lanscarr run into the sort of people he knew preyed on the innocent out there in the world beyond the haven of her family. "I shall be in touch. You need to go in now before you are missed."

She backed out of the shadows, moonlight turning her white muslin dress to silver. He wondered how long her hair was. Right now, it was piled high on her head, but did it reach between her shoulders? To her waist?

But as she started to turn, Beck had one last question. "How did you know I was out here?"

Gwendolyn shrugged one elegant shoulder. "I don't know. I just knew." On those words, she returned to the house.

# CHAPTER ELEVEN

*It is the quiet pigs that eat the meal.*
IRISH PROVERB

*W*hat *is* your story, Kit?" Elise asked. She followed him on a narrow path through a meadow of tall grass.

They had been walking for two hours and more. Tamsyn had run ahead. The dog would charge off in a direction and then circle back to them, seemingly with endless energy. Elise even gamely moved along. She had assured him the blisters no longer bothered her. She had sacrificed her cotton stockings, using them as bindings around her feet. Apparently the extra padding helped protect the raw and tender places because she had not hobbled once.

Kit was not so graced. Granted, his ribs no longer pained him, and even the bruising around his black eye was just tender, but he was hungry. He and Elise had found some wild strawberries and a thicket of blackberries, but that was not enough sustenance. Not for him.

He now trudged on, going in the direction he thought the road lay, hoping to reach either it or a village before he perished from hunger.

Meanwhile, Elise acted as if a handful of berries had obviously sated her. A bit ago she'd been busy collecting a bouquet out of the oxeye daisies, ragged robin, and cocksfoot. He knew the names because she babbled on about them. She'd even started wandering off in her pursuit of something "pretty" to add to it.

Her wandering around truly annoyed him. It had taken all of his willpower not to roar at her. They were on serious business. They needed to reach the posting inn—and *food*. *Real* food, meat and bread and ale. *Good* food. He'd give his arm for a beefsteak.

And now she was asking for *his story*?

"I don't have a story," he answered.

"Yes, you do. You had a life before this moment." She batted at a thistle head. Kit wanted to tell her not to do that because it would spread thistle seeds, and also because he was irritable. And sweaty. The day was warm.

"Why don't you tell me *your* story?" he grumbled back.

"I did yesterday. You know I have sisters. I told you about my father and that I'm traveling from London to County Wicklow. But I know nothing about you."

"Seems a dilemma," he replied dryly. She didn't need to know anything about him. He was No Man, a person who felt honor-bound to keep her out of trouble and nothing more—

"Are you married?"

Kit almost stepped into a rabbit's burrow over her intrusive ask. He frowned his answer back at her.

Elise was undeterred. "It is a good question. I should know."

Should she? For some reason, it felt like a dangerous question.

Or was it that *she* felt dangerous?

Elise didn't appear to sweat at all. If anything, she looked like Our Lady of the Meadow. She'd undone her braid, leaving her hair to fall in large golden waves, which she'd caught up high on her head with what looked to be a swatch of the lining from his jacket she still wore. Her eyes against the field of green grasses appeared bluer than cornflowers. A sprinkling of freckles spread across her gently sun-kissed cheeks.

Her curiosity about him suggested a deeper motive. That perhaps she found him as attractive as he found her—?

What the devil was he thinking? And then he knew what was truly on his mind as his little beast stirred. That is how Kit thought of his penis. A demanding little beast that had already led him astray one time too many. However, right now, he was sober. He had control.

Kit drew a deep, steadying breath and told his impudent, strong-minded organ *no*. There had been a time, not too long ago, when he would have acted upon his desires. He wouldn't have forced himself upon her, but he would have been in hot pursuit.

"I'm not married," he said in a curt tone, answering her question. He started tromping through the grass toward the line of trees ahead. "And the other thing you should know is that I am not that good a man. You shouldn't trust me, or any of us."

There, he'd given her fair warning.

"It is too late. I already trust you," she answered, walking up behind him.

"You shouldn't." If she knew some of the things he'd done . . .

"But I do."

He ignored her. This was not an argument he could win. What was it with women that you state a fact, and they answer that you are wrong?

They had almost reached the trees. Almost to shade.

Elise said, "I'll tell you what I do know about you."

Kit could have groaned his frustration. He didn't. What would be the use?

"I know that you are well-educated," she said confidently.

He wondered how she'd gleaned that bit of truth. Probably the same way he had her pegged for a bluestocking. All one had to do was listen. He scratched his jaw with gloved fingers. He hadn't shaved this morning. He hadn't the time, and he'd used the last of his soap.

"I also know you think you are a bad sort," she went on as if they were having a conversation. "You aren't . . . but you *think* you are."

They'd reached the trees. It was a relief to be out of the sun. Earlier, he'd taken off his oilskin coat, rolled it up, and wore it over one shoulder. This coat with its deep pockets was everything to him. Better than a pack. He removed his hat and dabbed his brow with the back of a gloved hand as he whistled for Tamsyn. The taller meadow grasses shook and waved as the dog happily wormed her way to join them.

"You are ignoring me," Elise said.

Kit ignored the accusation.

He caught sight of a trail and began following it. They had to be close to the road by now.

"All right," she mused, "what else do I know about you? Oh, this is important. You are grumpy when you are hungry. You should have eaten my share of the strawberries I offered you."

He should have. He'd refused because he believed she needed the food.

His stomach rumbled at the thought of them.

Elise heard it and smiled as if it gave her great pleasure to be right.

Kit stepped over a large tree that had fallen over the path. He offered his hand to help Elise. There was no way she could climb over it gracefully in her skirts. So, he lifted her up and over. Tamsyn had found a stick she liked and was waiting on the other side for him, her tail wagging.

He set Elise on her feet, threw the stick, and continued on. Elise skipped a step to keep up.

"Thank you for your help," she said.

He grunted a response.

"You don't like talking about yourself, do you?"

"Oh miracle of miracles, you finally understand," Kit answered.

She made a little humming sound that could mean she agreed with him or disagreed. He couldn't tell.

What he did know was that having his hands around her waist had felt good. This was not the first time he'd carried Elise. But this was the first time the little beast whined for her. He felt like slapping the damn thing to make it behave. Of course, that would be hurting himself.

Why had he gallantly promised to see her to Ireland?

"Here is something else I know," she prefaced pleasantly as she drew up beside him on the path. "You snore."

Kit came to an abrupt halt. *What?*

She took a step or two more before turning to him. "You snore," she repeated as if it was simple, common knowledge.

"I do *not* snore."

He didn't . . . or believed he didn't. No one had ever told him he snored.

She winced as if she felt a bit sad for him, but did not retract her statement.

"I don't," he reiterated.

Elise pressed her lips together as if holding back words, and Kit had enough.

"I *reek*, I *snore*," Kit complained. "You delight in cataloging my bad habits."

Instead of remorse, her response was a laughter, the sound as light as dandelion fluff. It mingled with the dappled shade of the forest.

And made him feel humorless.

As if she could read his thoughts, and *agreed with them*, Elise began walking.

Kit watched her go, tempted to let her do as she wished.

Of course, that would be the humorless thing to do.

Kit moved to catch up with her. He couldn't help but notice that even in his jacket, which was oversized on her, her hips had a gentle sway as she walked. Tamsyn nudged him with his stick. He threw it, but his gaze didn't leave Elise's charming movement.

And he realized what the true problem was. Oh, yes, he was hungry, and that weighed on his mood, but there was something else amiss—she didn't act in any fashion attracted to him.

Without being vain, he knew women liked his looks. They liked that he was tall. They flattered him, even when he was plain Kit without title or fortune. If he had so wished it on this adventure, he could have had plenty of female companionship.

But he hadn't encouraged that sort of thing because women distracted him from sorting himself out. He was working on being a better man.

However, Elise had the looks that could make any male daffy headed. She was Helen of Troy and Hades's Persephone—all wrapped up in a lovely little landed gentry package.

So perhaps it was good fortune that she thought he snored—

Elise came to a sudden stop, her arm outstretched. "Do you smell it?"

"What?" He sniffed the air himself, and then caught the scent. Baking bread. "Come, this way." He took her hand without a second thought to the promises he'd made to himself to keep his distance. He would have dragged her in the direction of that blessed aroma if she hadn't been willing to come with him. Even Tamsyn dropped her stick and ran alongside them.

There was a bend in the path. They followed it and found themselves in front of a trio of cottages with well-tended gardens. A woman was coming out one of the doors. She juggled a baby in one arm and a basket in the other.

Kit moved forward swiftly, reaching her in front of her garden gate. She'd been so busy, she hadn't noticed him immediately. His presence surprised her. She almost dropped the basket.

He stretched over the gate to save it. "I'm sorry. I didn't mean to startle you."

"I wasn't expecting to see someone there." She was perhaps a few years older than Elise with apple cheeks and ginger hair beneath her mobcap.

"We are heading toward the posting inn," he explained. "I saw you leave your stoop and thought to help." He opened the gate.

"Well, thank you." She glanced at Elise and then, apparently believing they meant her no harm, relaxed. She crossed through the gate.

He sniffed the air. Bread now mingled with other smells. Earthier ones. Animals. Stables? A barn? "Could you tell us—how much farther is it to catch the Mail?"

"A stone's throw," she answered. "My husband's father owns the George Inn. Come with me."

"Before I do—" Kit paused. This was going to be a delicate ask. "We are very hungry. My nose is telling me that you have buns in that basket."

"I do, just from the oven."

"May we purchase one?"

"They are for the inn," she said.

"I will perish if I don't eat something now," Kit vowed. He lifted his oilskin pack from over his head and started digging in the pockets. He found his coin purse in a pocket. It was very light in his hand. He opened the drawstring and shook out all he had and was disappointed.

He'd known he was low on funds but he'd forgotten exactly how low. He'd have to do something to replenish the larder, as he liked to call it. But how much could a bun cost? He was at a point he would have paid her a hundred pounds if he'd had it. He offered what he had. "Please."

She looked up with doubtful eyes and then glanced again at Elise, who was doing her part by smiling at the baby, who smiled back and giggled. "Your daughter is beautiful," Elise said to the woman.

Daughter? How could Elise tell? The baby could be a boy or a girl with her bald head under a cotton cap.

The innkeeper's daughter smiled with maternal pride. "Thank you." Then, she looked down at her basket. "I suppose letting you purchase one will be all right." She took only a pence, letting him keep the rest of his meager hoard.

Proving he still had a semblance of manners, Kit offered the bread to Elise first. She tore it in two. He noted she took the smaller portion and he was so hungry, he let her.

"The inn is this way," the woman said, starting in that direction. "I'm Mrs. Sarver."

Kit followed, his mouth full of bread. Manna could not have tasted more heavenly. His whole being rejoiced in true nourishment.

Elise had only taken a nibble. If she offered him her food, he would not turn it down this time. She spoke up, "I'm Elise," she said to Mrs. Sarver.

"Elise?" She glanced at Elise curiously and then

seemed to notice that she was wearing a man's jacket. Kit had a sinking feeling. If the wholesome Mrs. Sarver jumped to conclusions, which was something wholesome people always did, then she might imagine that he and Elise were not a proper couple. Some inns, especially ones built around family, could be very particular.

So he stepped in. "Elise Cox," he said smoothly, using part of his family's hyphenated name Fitzhugh-Cox. It was an old and respected one in England. However, no one raised an eyebrow when he used just part of it. "I'm Kit Cox, her *husband*." He said the lie with a smile.

Elise started to choke on her bun. Kit rubbed between her shoulder blades as he imagined a husband would. "My wife and I were in the coach accident the other night."

Mrs. Sarver's eyes widened in alarm. "Oh, no. It was a dreadful accident. But how could you have survived? We thought everyone in the coach had been killed."

"The driver and the guard died. We are still alive."

"Why didn't you come in when they brought the bodies?"

"A very good question," Kit said, allowing a touch of his ire to show. "The coach was full and the driver told us to walk to the—what is this inn?"

"The George."

"Right, to the George. It has not been an easy journey."

"I can't imagine it would be after all that has happened." Mrs. Sarver shot Elise a commiserating look. "Now I understand why you are dressed oddly, Mrs. Cox. It must have been a frightful experience. And your eye, Mr. Cox, does it still hurt?"

"Terribly," he assured her, hoping it would earn him a free bun.

It didn't.

Elise spoke up, "My dress was torn at the shoulder. Do you think I can find needle and thread? I believe I can repair it."

"We should be able to find you something." Mrs. Sarver shifted her daughter to her other arm. The child was good-sized and as rosy-cheeked as her mother. Now Kit could see the feminine features marking her as a girl. She kept trying to reach out for Tamsyn. The dog warily hung back, apparently as ignorant of babies as Kit was.

Mrs. Sarver tsked. "Such an ordeal. The accident was terrible news for all of us. It is nice to learn there were survivors."

"Especially for us," Kit answered, and Mrs. Sarver laughed as if he was being humorous.

The inn was in sight now. The George was a very small establishment. It was actually a way station for a quick change of horses. There were paddocks and a small barn. The inn itself was a low stone building painted white with a few window boxes of bright flowers and a picture of a very ugly George on the tavern sign.

Leaving Tamsyn outside, they entered the establishment to find it was one big taproom filled with trestle tables. A group of village men sat hunched over their drinks and conversations in a corner.

Mrs. Sarver called for her father-in-law. Her husband managed the horses, she explained.

The innkeeper, Mr. Sarver, was the typical jovial sort whose face looked very much like his granddaughter's whom he had immediately gathered up in his arms, heedless of the bloody apron around his waist. Kit could picture him carving up a haunch of beef. The image caused his stomach to rumble.

He, too, was astounded to hear that Kit and Elise had been part of the crash.

"They told me there were no passengers," Sarver said officiously, bouncing his granddaughter on his arm.

So, Kit was a touch curt when he replied, "There were passengers. If you heard that information from the coachman, it is because he left us behind. You and I both know he didn't want to take us because we'd already paid the other driver. He was afraid of not receiving a fare."

Sarver made a commiserating sound. "Christian charity should be more important than coin, but it isn't."

He was so blunt, Kit had to laugh. "True." He tapped a hand lightly on the counter in front of him. "So, my lady and I would like rooms for the night."

"I only have one room and it is spoken for. Most travelers sleep on one of the benches if they are staying for the night." He nodded to the tables and benches around them. "Of course, we are the only public house for several miles. It can be noisy."

Well . . . sleeping on a bench was certainly about all Kit could afford, although he had a plan to change that. "Do you think there will be a good crowd tonight?"

"There always is on a Wednesday night. The lads like to come together in the middle of the week."

More good news. "Is there a place that we may see to ourselves?" he asked.

"The privy is out back. There is a place to wash as well."

"Thank you." Now Kit had to ask the question that might be problematic. "You wouldn't be needing some help? I mean, my wife"—he pulled Elise forward, draping a husbandly arm over her shoulder—"and I were left stranded. I will cut wood, nail boards, help with horses?" There had been a time when, beyond the care of horses, those other tasks had been a mystery. Dukes didn't do manual labor. However, since setting off on his travels, Kit had learned to become quite skilled with his hands. He would never have survived otherwise. Elise hadn't moved from under Kit's arm and seemed to lean into him so that he imagined they presented a lovely picture of a young, stranded couple.

"My Clive could use help," Mrs. Sarver jumped in, with a beseeching glance at her father-in-law. "It would be nice to have him home early one evening."

"All right then," Sarver said. "Cox, you can help with the horses. Maybe I'll gain another grandbaby out of this evening. I would happily take a hundred of these—"

"Mr. *Sarver*," his daughter-in-law exclaimed, her face a bright, but happy red.

He laughed. "Ah, lass, you are too easy to tease." He turned his attention back to Kit and Elise. "Help my son and I'll serve you a meal that will fill your belly for days. And I am sorry for your troubles. It isn't your fault Morris drove into a storm. I always said the man's driving was dangerous. I'm just glad you are alive. My wife will set plates out for you when we are ready to serve supper."

"I'll fetch needle and thread for your dress," the young Mrs. Sarver said to Elise. She took her baby from her father-in-law. The child made some sort of silly noise as if wishing to be back in her grandfather's arms.

Kit eyed that little being with a touch of surprise. He'd rarely been around babies. His family circle was very small, and he'd spent most of his youth in school. He wondered why that little scene among family made him feel . . . envious.

The Sarvers disappeared through a door that must have led to the kitchen and back rooms.

And Elise stepped out of his hold. *"Wife?"* She didn't bother to whisper.

Kit sent a warning glance at the table of villagers. She was so cross, she seemed not to care. "What else should I have said? My paramour? My mistress?"

"Your traveling companion?" she suggested.

"Elise, do you really think Mrs. Sarver would believe that we are marching around together and not a couple of some sort? We can be a couple in sin or a couple by all that is holy."

"I think it is a sin to lie about something like that."

When she was angry her Irish truly came out and brought a sparkle to her eye. He liked it—

"What are you grinning at?" she snapped.

He knew better than to answer that question. "Elise, we will never see these people again. They don't care what I claim as long as it fits their definition of what is right or wrong. I decided to be right."

"But it isn't right to lie."

"It isn't right to run away. And if you are so upset, then correct me the next time I make such a claim. Tell everyone that we are not married, that you have been in my company for days."

"Not by choice. There was the accident."

"Do you think this country society is different from London Society?"

She opened her mouth to argue, but he wasn't

about to let her. "People always assume the worst, Elise. It is as if they can't help themselves."

The worry line made its appearance between her brows, and he had the urge to smooth it away. "It will be fine," he promised.

The line didn't budge.

However, at that moment, Mrs. Sarver popped through the kitchen door. "I found thread and needle. Come, Mrs. Cox. You can repair the tear in the back room."

Elise did not correct her use of the title.

As they left, Kit heard Elise ask, "Where is your daughter?"

"In the hands of her grandmother," was the reply, and then the women were gone, the door closing behind them.

Kit went outside and over to the barn to talk to Clive.

Tamsyn was happy to see him. There were other dogs, but Kit noted she was a bit standoffish. Perhaps she considered herself above the hounds. She had found a few bones and as she trotted after him to the stables, she held two in her mouth.

Clive was as amiable as his wife. The last stage had left sometime earlier, so all that was left of chores was feeding the horses for the night. It was an easy enough task for Kit. He helped Clive shovel some manure and sweep and, once done, left Tamsyn gnawing on her bone collection.

He stopped at the back of the inn to wash in a

long horse trough. Blocks of lye soap were available for the task.

Kit removed his well-worn gloves and grabbed the soap. He missed the sandalwood soap he'd used for shaving and bathing at Smythson. Funny, but of the life he left, it was the small conveniences he mourned. He'd always believed cleanliness was a good thing. Elise's comment the day before had struck hard. However, it was hard to bathe when one didn't have servants boiling the water and carrying it to and fro.

And perhaps he had needed Elise's bluntness. He had been growing complacent and forgetting who he was. He had set out on this journey with some vague idea it would make him a better man. He'd need a respite, a different way of looking at the world—

A deep, innate honesty, cut him off.

*Whom* was he fooling? Embarrassment had driven him out of London. He'd reached a point when he couldn't meet his mother's eye, let alone anyone else's. He'd run.

Just like Elise . . . only she was going to Ireland. He'd never run *toward* anything.

Perhaps the time had come that he should. Because he was discovering there was no running from himself.

Kit shook the water from his hands. He walked into the inn through a back door, entered the taproom, and stopped, struck by the sight before him.

The room had grown more crowded. Men

and women from nearby had gathered for the evening. Sarver had been right when he'd promised the place would be busy. Kit had noticed patrons arriving while he was out helping with the horses.

But in the middle of this busy room, Elise shone like a morning star, and she was all he could see.

Yes, she was a physically attractive woman. Many eyes, especially male ones, drifted toward her and lingered.

However, what caught Kit was how composedly she sat, how there was an inner serenity about her. A *presence*.

Her body shifted. She straightened and craned her neck to search the room. She was looking for someone—

Deep blue eyes lit up when she spied him. She smiled and, for a beat, it was as if the world disappeared. Her smile told him she was glad he had returned. *Him*, the prodigal.

Many women had smiled at him. Most as an invitation.

Elise smiled because she trusted him.

And Kit's heart, which he had declared hard as stone, softened, and began to beat again.

# CHAPTER TWELVE

*There's no use boiling your cabbage twice.*
IRISH PROVERB

Elise had been anxiously waiting for Kit's return.

The taproom had been growing busier. She'd felt the curious looks from the women and caught the way the men stared, some covertly, a few openly. In London, it had been assumed she enjoyed being the center of attention. She did not. She was a country lass who had grown up knowing all the people around her. No one mentioned her looks in Wicklow. However, after her experience with Tommy, the attention made her uneasy. She shouldn't be so skittish, but she was.

And then she sensed Kit's presence. She *knew* he was close.

The men in the room averted their gazes from her. It was as if they, too, understood she wasn't for the taking.

She looked to the front door. Kit was not there.

She glanced at the crowded bar around the tap. He was not among them. She also didn't believe he would go for the ale first before letting her know he'd returned. That was not the man he was.

Then, a tingling at the back of her neck told her exactly where he was. She turned in her seat.

Kit stood by the back door. His large frame seemed to fill the space, making him seem taller and broader than he was. His neckcloth was looped around as if he couldn't be bothered to knot it. He held his wide-brimmed hat in his hand, and his hair was wet as if he'd been washing. He held his oilcloth coat rolled up under one arm.

Their eyes met. She smiled, both relieved and pleased to see him. She motioned him toward her.

Was it her imagination? Had there been a moment's hesitation, almost as if—he was uncertain? If they had been in a ballroom and this exchange had taken place, she would have thought him shy.

The idea made her laugh.

But as he made his way toward her, she felt happy he was here. She'd become accustomed to him. She liked having him near.

As he took his seat on the bench directly across the table from her, she held up his neatly folded jacket. "Thank you for its use."

"You are skilled with a needle," he commented, noticing the repair she'd done to her dress. She'd managed to piece together the sleeve of the blue walking dress. It had been the least damaged of her gowns. She now wore it on top of the others.

"When I say I am good at a task, you should believe me," she responded lightly. "Did they work you hard?"

He laughed. "Not hard at all. Most of the work had already been done. However, there is clean hay in the barn. I suggest we sleep there rather than on these hard benches."

"Is that where Tamsyn is?"

He nodded. "I left her stealing bones from her dog friends." He paused, searched her face. "Is something the matter? You appear worried."

Elise was surprised he'd noticed and then admitted in a very quiet voice, "I have no money. It was in the cloak we had to leave behind. And I don't think you have any money either?" Her voice went up at the end because she wasn't certain.

At that moment, the innkeeper, Mr. Sarver, came to their table, a serving lass behind him with two plates of hot food. "Here you are," Mr. Sarver said proudly, nodding for the lass to put the plates in front of them. He raised his voice. "These two were in the crash during the storm the other night. They survived it, they did."

"I heard there were no survivors," a man from another table piped up.

"Same here," chimed in another.

Kit stood. He clapped his hand on Mr. Sarver's shoulder. "My wife and I have quite a story to tell.

We were in that crash. And Sarver has been the best of hosts. I appreciate you, sir, for your generosity. Now, I'm going to tuck into that beefsteak and then afterwards, we shall share tales. But before I do, a huzzah for Innkeeper Sarver."

"Huzzah," many voices answered him.

The innkeeper chortled his embarrassment. "I have done nothing."

"You have been kind to strangers, sir," Kit said, "and that is far from nothing."

And Elise wondered—who was this Kit Cox who had so many obvious talents and nary a penny to his name? With his praise of the innkeeper, he had won over many in this room. Now, both Kit and Elise were accepted, which was no small feat in a village community.

Within earshot, she overheard one man repeat, "But I heard there were no survivors."

She turned on her bench, wishing to correct the man's misunderstanding, but Kit had sat down. He gave life to his promise to "tuck" into his beef with gusto. She had never witnessed a man enjoy his food more.

To be honest, the beef, peas, and parsnips tasted delicious to her as well.

The serving lass asked what they wished to drink. Kit ordered ales for both of them. The combination of good meat and drink had a restorative effect on her.

Kit's manners were good, she had to give him that. He knew how to handle a knife and fork with some dignity. Proper manners and a rough exterior—more riddles than clues to the person Kit was.

The moment their plates were clean—Kit having eaten his and half of hers—a villager invited himself to sit down to discuss the crash. He was a surly sort and asked many questions. Kit was patient in answering them. She wondered if this man was the doubting Thomas who had made the comment behind her. Instead of listening to what they discussed, she found her attention wandering to the other people in the room—

"Elise, I'm going to spend some time with the group of men in the corner. Will you be all right here?"

His questions startled her out of her woolgathering. "Well, yes, of course." And then she noticed the men Kit wanted to see were gambling over cards.

Elise stood up in alarm. "You are going to gamble?"

Kit leaned toward her. "We need money. I have no more than maybe a few pence."

"But is this wise?" Panic rose in her. "How will we go to Ireland if you lose?"

"Why are you anxious? I thought you said your father was a gambler."

"That is why I know you can lose. We could end up with no money."

"I won't lose," he assured her.

"Chance is never certain."

"Is this the same woman who has risked everything to reach her home?"

She didn't answer.

"Trust me," he murmured. "Gamblers lose because they either aren't paying attention or don't understand how to play the odds. I may not win a lot but I think I can manage our fare to Liverpool. I can find another game from there. Come, sit with me. You will be a powerful distraction to the other players at the table."

The compliment caught her by surprise. Or was it a compliment? "Distraction because . . ."

"Elise," he said, a warmth coming to his voice, "you know your power."

She did. But really until this moment, he'd seemed oblivious to her . . . and something stirred inside her with an intensity that was both provocative *and* slightly unsettling.

It threw her off balance. Because she was beginning to like him. She'd not deny that she was attracted to his looks. Even the fact that he was a bit of a rogue pleased her. It shouldn't have. A person being exactly, and boldly, who they were was a powerful draw.

However, something else was happening as well. The farther she was from London, the more she was beginning to see that Michael had never been interested in her other than as a friend. She'd imagined him the Love of Her Life, but she hadn't really known him that well. Perhaps she'd just liked the "idea" of Michael? And she'd picked him out without actually bothering to understand the first thing about him.

The realization was radical.

Over the past weeks, rarely a minute had gone by without her thinking about her anger, about the betrayal. Those were the terms in which she'd thought about Michael. They had nothing to do with the actual person. Pride and self-righteousness had twisted everything inside her toward Michael and her beloved sister Dara.

And with insight came relief. The knot of outrage and discontent that had been her companion for so long vanished. Because of Kit?

She prayed not. They were of two different classes. He was completely unsuitable to be anything other than a friend to her, and even that would be frowned upon by those who believed in the proper social order.

Still, to keep the matter in perspective, there was no doe-eyed look in Kit's gaze or lustful interest. She'd been more of a burden to him than a help.

And yet he'd stayed by her side. He'd included her, just as he was now.

"Come," he said, picking up his still full tankard with one hand and their measly belongings with the other. "Adventure awaits." He started for the table of players.

"So, are you a seasoned gambler?" she asked. It made sense. He had never spoken of work.

"Every man games. Unfortunately, I was a

terrible one for a long time. I made all of the mistakes. Then I met Old John. He took me in hand and taught me a few truths—not that I gamble that much," he added quickly.

At last, Kit was talking about himself. That must mean he trusted her. Or that his belly was full. Whichever way, she was determined to encourage him. "Where did you meet this Old John?"

"In this village called Moorcock."

"Like the bird?" The name made her laugh. He smiled as if he had anticipated it would.

"Exactly. Old John took me in hand and told me it hurt his eyes to see someone as bad at cards as I. A few days with him and I was cured of ever thinking a fortune could be won gambling."

"My sister Gwendolyn gambled and won the money for us to travel to London," she confided.

"Your *sister* gambles?"

"Women gamble," she replied, a bit stung by his incredulity. "We all had to learn Papa's tricks. When he came to visit, we played with him. He preferred playing cards over any other endeavor." What had once been a happy memory now seemed rather sad. "I'm very good at hiding a pea in a walnut shell and no one guessing where it is. Not even Gwendolyn is as good as I am."

"I can picture you, a young girl, learning how to play the simplest swindle in the world." He looked down at her. "You are a contradiction, Elise."

"I am?"

"Ah, yes, you have the grace and manners of a lady, but you aren't idle. Or afraid to take action. Your father teaches you the shell and pea game, but you preferred books, didn't you? And you probably always did what was expected, right? Even when your mind rebelled?"

Was that true? He might be correct on the first part, but—"I'm not doing what is expected now."

Kit laughed. "That is a fact." He drained his tankard. "Come, let's see if they will let us in the game."

"Do you really think you can win tonight?" The stakes were whether or not they reached Ireland. The thought made her anxious.

"If not, there will be another game."

Her father had often made the same claim. For the first time, Elise wondered why her papa couldn't just stay at Wiltham and find his games in Ireland. What drove him to insist upon traveling the world?

Neither she nor Kit were wearing gloves. He'd grabbed her hand many times during their time after the crash, but this time it was skin on skin.

And she noticed.

His hands were callused, but then, he wasn't afraid of manual labor. So different from the lords and gentlemen who had wooed her in London.

Yet, there was an uncommon grace to his hand as well. The fingers were long and well-formed. His hold confident. The grip exactly right.

Pulling out a single coin, a measly pence, from his leather purse, Kit set it on the table, a sign he wanted in the next round. He didn't act embarrassed about his offering.

The game was vingt-et-un. Her father had played it with her and her sisters for hours. They'd used twigs from the garden as money. Elise rarely won. The stakes here seemed just about as modest. No wonder the pence had been accepted.

She reminded herself that all they had to do was earn the fare to take them to Liverpool. She could be hopeful.

Another woman also watched the game. She sat at the trestle table next to the game table. She was older than Elise and had brought knitting. No one seemed to find that odd. Kit indicated that Elise should sit at the table with her and still watch everything that was going on.

When the round finished, a player in front of Kit decided to leave. He offered his place to Kit, who took it with a nod.

"You aren't coming in with much," a grizzled man remarked as Kit pushed his coin forward.

"With her by my side for luck, I don't need much," Kit answered. The men at the table openly looked over to Elise. She glanced down modestly, feeling a rush of heat to her cheeks. She was the decoy, was she not?

"Aye, you are a lucky one," the man said. The play began.

Kit won the first round and the third.

He did know when to play and when to pass. He seemed to remember what cards had been played and suspect which ones would appear. That was the way Gwendolyn played. Her memory never lost track of the cards.

Kit's little pile of coins grew and then ebbed. New players joined in, others left. They had enough for their fare, but he kept playing. Did he really need her to be a "distraction"? She didn't think so. She was also beginning to suspect that he liked gambling more than he wished to admit.

Elise had been exchanging pleasantries with the village woman when it was Kit's turn to shuffle. Her interest in the game had been beginning to drift at that point. She barely noticed what was happening at the table next to her. Instead, she was thinking she might take herself out to the barn to see if the hay was as clean as he claimed. She was tired. However, recent events had taught her she would be wise to wait for Kit. She was about to ask if he was nearly done playing when she noticed from the corner of her eye an unusual sight.

He was shuffling the cards . . . *with her father's signature style.* Her father had always bragged about the shuffle. It was unique to him. She and her sisters had all tried to master it without success.

Kit had it right.

The cards cascaded from one hand to the other. And then, he deftly flipped them, one section over the other. Her father had even been able to position cards so that he knew when they would come up. Gwendolyn had accused him of that. He'd just laughed.

Across the table from Kit, the grizzled player said, "That is a neat trick."

"Easiest way to shuffle them, I assure you," Kit answered.

That had always been her father's answer.

Elise stood. Old *John*. He'd taught Kit this method. John had.

And her father's name had been John. Captain Sir John Lanscarr.

An idea struck her so outlandish and impossible, and yet, what if it was true? *"Who is John?"*

The men at the table startled at her abruptness. Kit squared the cards. He turned his attention up to her, a quizzical look in his eye.

"You said Old John taught you to play cards," she reminded him. "Did he teach you that shuffle as well?"

"Yes, in Moorcock." He started to deal the cards.

Could it be that Kit had met her father? She grabbed Kit's arm, wanting answers. "What did he look like?"

"Elise, we are in a game."

He spoke politely, reasonably. However, she was in no mood for reason or delay. "Kit, what was his *last* name? What did he *look* like?"

"He looked like a man, Elise. He was of the age of my friend over here." He waved a hand to the grizzled man.

"And his name?"

"*John*. Happy? Elise, let us play."

But Elise was in no mood for being put off. Could Old John have been her father? It was fantastical . . . but possible?

Old John had taken Kit under his care. Her father had loved cards, he would help any player. He also must have liked Kit or else he wouldn't have shared his secret shuffle.

The play continued. Elise looked down at the cards on the table, her mind a scramble of theories and possibilities. "When did he teach you that shuffle?"

Kit didn't even look up. He kept his focus on the cards but he did answer. "A few months ago." He turned a card over for a player.

Elise almost fell back to the bench. A few months ago?

*Her father could be alive.*

She had to repeat the idea several times before it started to make sense, and then—

*He was alive.*

The moment she accepted the thought, the truth of it rang through her. Her father was alive.

In fact, what if her running away had *not* been a mistake? What if this was what had to happen for her to find her papa? Could it be there was a purpose to *all* of this? Even to Dara and Michael's marriage?

And what *had* kept her father from returning home?

She had no idea, except that he must be in danger, or ill, or suffering from a mental affliction. He would never willingly ignore the girls he called his "precious daughters."

A sense of purpose more powerful than she had ever known surged through her. Her father needed her.

"Kit, where is this Moorcock?"

He made an impatient sound. "Elise, I'm the dealer. My attention needs to be on the cards."

Elise did understand, and didn't. She had questions, and he believed cards were more important? Her temper ignited. *Why did men think games were more valuable than people?* Well, she was done with it. Done with always being of second importance. Wasn't that truly why she'd run away from London?

Certainly it had not been to be dismissed when her father's life might be at stake.

Without pausing to consider her actions, she reached out her hand and swept it across the table. Cards and money went flying. Men shouted. She ignored them. Whether Kit confirmed her suspicions or not, there was only one way to be certain if Old John was her father, and that was for her to go to this Moorcock and see for herself. She snatched up her gloves from the pile on top of the jacket, knocking his hat to the floor where it would probably be stepped on. She didn't stop to pick it up. She knew how much he liked the dratted thing. She didn't care.

Instead, she marched out of the George, the sounds of complaints and Kit making apologies behind her.

The night was quiet after the hubbub of the taproom. The only light came from the George's windows and the moon.

Elise pulled on her gloves. She meant to leave, *right* now.

The problem was, she didn't know where Moorcock was. She believed she could figure it out. The place had such an odd name, there must be people who were familiar with it—

A hand hooked her arm and whirled her around. A furious Kit confronted her. His hat was on his head but with the crown slightly bashed in as if someone had stepped on it and he had pushed it out. He had his rolled oilskin slung over one shoulder. "What are you doing? Do you know I had to leave most of my winnings to keep everyone happy after you cleared the table?"

"Tell me about Old John. I want to know everything."

He looked heavenward as if begging for patience and then shook his head and answered, "I told you what I know."

"How tall is he? What are his facial features? What is his last name?"

"His last name," Kit repeated as if she had asked the impossible. "I don't recall him saying."

"Please, Kit, this is important. *Try* to remember."

He frowned and snorted out his breath as if she had backed him into a corner. "Why is it so important to you?"

"I believe he is my father."

Kit's posture changed. He lost the defensiveness. "He can't be your father."

"Why not?"

"If you saw him, you would understand. He is a tough old codger. Rarely spoke about himself. In fact, I don't think he even lived in Moorcock proper."

"Had he been in the military?"

"I don't know." He shook his head with exasperation. "Elise, why do you think this man could be your sire?"

"The way he taught you to shuffle cards. He was very proud of that shuffle. He rarely shared it."

"And you think that because of the way I shuffled that I have a connection with a man who has been declared dead. Perhaps he taught Old John the shuffle? Or a hundred other people? You need to be reasonable, Elise. A shuffle doesn't mean your father is alive."

"But no one knew for certain he was dead. He just disappeared. Can you not understand why I need to know?" She walked three steps away, stopped, looked back to him. "I must go to Moorcock."

"No, you 'must' not," he answered. "We are going to Ireland. All of this"—he circled his hand in the air to encompass not only the two of them but the crash, the days of travel—"is to take you to Ireland."

"Ireland means nothing if my father is alive. Kit, I have to find out."

*"Fine."* He said the word like an epithet and then shook his head. "I can't believe I just said that."

"Said what?"

*"Fine.* I'm starting to sound like you."

"Is that bad?" She wasn't certain whether to be offended or not.

However, before he could answer, some villagers came out of the inn. They grumbled in their direction. One man put his hands on his hips as if warning them away from the establishment.

Kit took her arm and led her toward the barn for privacy. "Listen, Old John is a hardened gambler. He could never have sired a daughter like you."

"My father was a hardened gambler. His name was John—and Kit, if he didn't come back to my sisters and me, there must be a reason. I *must* find out."

"You can't traipse all over England alone. There are a hundred Tommys out there. You are lucky you have made it this far." He held his breath as if there was more that he wanted to say, and then understood any lecture would be wasted. He let his air out with a huff of resignation. "Here is what we will do—I'm going to take you to Ireland. I will deliver you as far as the doorstep of the family estate. I will then see what I can do about bringing Old John to you."

His was a sensible offer, but not one she could accept. "Your plan seems a waste of time. We go here, we go there. Kit, if Old John is my father, he needs me. There is something wrong. He would not just disappear from our lives without a word. He'd never do that, not in his right mind. We must go to Moorcock."

"Well, then, here is another problem. Moorcock is a thieves' den. It isn't the sort of place for a woman like you."

She rested on his words a moment, and then thought of her laughing father, the man who had taught her games, took delight in how well she read, and had boasted he had daughters who could outshine the sun. "If what you say is true, he needs me more than ever." She walked into the barn.

Outside, Kit groaned his frustration. "Elise. Come back here."

She ignored him. She didn't have time to put up with his naysaying.

The barn was dark, but there was enough moonlight for her to see a giant stack of hay. The dry, sweet scent of it filled the building. Several horses munched quietly in their stalls.

Tamsyn hopped to her feet and approached her, the white parts of her coat silvery. Her tail wagged its greeting. Elise thought to leave right now, this minute, except she was tired. She needed to sleep to make any journey.

Kit marched into the barn, his manner imperial. "That's it, Elise. I will *not* take you on some fool's chase to Moorcock."

She settled in the hay, ignoring him. She used her arm as a pillow. She was going to Moorcock. She'd leave at first light. She yawned.

Kit stood by the rick. She could feel him studying her. She kept her back to him.

Then, "And how do you think you are going to get there? You just threw any money I made around the taproom. It's gone, Elise, except for a bit. We'll use that to reach Liverpool—"

She rolled over to glare up at him. "You go to Ireland if you so wish. However, I have my own plan." With that, she gave him her back.

"You're stubborn, Elise."

She didn't answer. There was nothing left to say.

And to her surprise, she fell into a deep sleep where her dreams battled with doubts. But there were no spiders.

The next morning, as she'd wished, she woke at first light.

Tamsyn was snuggled in the hay beside her. The dog snored.

Kit was on his side, one arm outstretched toward where she'd lain, his head resting on it. He slept soundly.

Elise eased out of the hay. She was covered with the stuff and shook out her skirts, and then she remembered her purpose for this day. She rubbed the sleep from her eyes. Her braid was a mess. She undid the binding and quickly rebraided it. Was she a bit intimidated by the journey ahead of her? Absolutely.

It was also difficult to leave Kit's protection behind. He'd called Moorcock a thieves' den. Would her father be in such a place?

There was only one way to find out. She must go.

Still quietly brushing the hay from her bodice and pulling it out of her hair, she tiptoed past Tamsyn and then past Kit, where she paused, giving them one last look.

The dog was on her back, sleeping as if she had not a care in the world. She would be better off with Kit. He'd take care of her.

Kit shifted, and she had an impulse to kiss his cheek. To thank him in some way for what he had done for her. If Old John was truly her father, then that would be the greatest gift of all.

She pictured how surprised her sisters would be at her return to London with their father. Then they could throw Cousin Richard out and reclaim Wiltham. It was a good thought.

Elise also discovered it was going to be hard to leave Kit. She'd miss the snap of humor in his gray eyes and his bluntness. He talked to her as an equal, as a companion. No one had ever done that . . . and for the briefest second, she wavered in her determination.

But then she thought of her father, of all his

homecoming would mean, of how her sisters would be impressed—and she knew she must leave.

Except, just as she started to move away, to set out on the task of finding her way to Moorcock, a hand shot out and grabbed her skirt. Kit looked up at her with a grim glare. "Give me a moment. I'm going with you to Moorcock."

Not only was she relieved, but her heart gave a happy skip.

They were together again.

# CHAPTER THIRTEEN

*A beck is as good as a wink to a blind man.*
IRISH PROVERB

$\mathcal{I}$t was early afternoon when Beck rode into the George's small innyard. He was tired and discouraged. The news about Elise Lanscarr was not reassuring.

At the last posting inn down the road, he'd heard of Monday's crash. They claimed there had been no survivors. The Mail had been running behind, the coachman had pushed it, and he had wrecked his vehicle in a nasty storm.

No one from the inn had remembered seeing Elise on the coach, which was unusual. He'd had no trouble tracing her path out of London. She was alone and beautiful. People noticed. Men noticed. Gwendolyn had also drawn a fairly good likeness in a pencil sketch for him to share. It had been a great help.

But this news of a crash? Of no survivors—?

He had no wish to tell Gwendolyn that her sister was dead. Then again, Beck had learned over the years to never assume the whereabouts of anyone. People started off in one direction, changed their minds, and took off in another.

He didn't think this of Elise. What he remembered about Miss Lanscarr, beyond her singular beauty, was her willful determination. The young woman had a firm belief in what she wanted and what she didn't want. If she said she was on her way to Ireland, then he had no doubt she was.

But there was always the chance that someone he spoke to had just not recognized her.

There was even the possibility that rumors and gossip about the accident could be incorrect. And considering the stakes—Gwendolyn—he was determined to ferret out the truth.

The stable master took the reins of Beck's horse. Beck pressed a coin into his hand. "Rub him down and give him grain."

"Aye, sir."

"By the way, my name is Steele. I'm searching for someone." He'd learned long ago to never play with subterfuge when a direct inquiry was faster and more effective. He took the picture from his coat. "This young woman. She is missing. Her family is very concerned. Have you seen her?"

The stable master shook his head. "Not that I recognize. My father is the innkeeper. You might ask him. It's just me and a lad here most times.

You know what that means. I'm too busy working to see who is coming and going much."

"I understand. Thank you." Beck walked into the building. It was a pleasant place with flowers in the boxes and a fresh coat of paint on the stone structure. There were a few patrons in the inn's one main taproom.

The innkeeper's name was Sarver. He was happy to serve Beck a tankard and a mutton chop. Once Beck felt settled, he looked around and threw out a statement in a general way to the patrons around him. "I hear there was a coaching accident the other night."

A man who had the arms of a smithy said, "Aye, no survivors."

"There were survivors," said a man who sat beside his wife, who was knitting. "A young couple. Ask Sarver."

"I didn't hear tell of any," the smithy argued.

At that moment, the innkeeper came out with his chop. Beck drew out the picture. "We were talking about the coach accident the other night. Some say there were no survivors and say some there were."

"There were survivors," Sarver assured him.

"Do tell? Was this young woman one of them? She's hard to forget. Her family is most anxious for her return."

Sarver barely looked at the picture. "She could be a number of women." The smithy and the couple came over to look as well.

"You can't tell anything with a pencil drawing," the woman agreed. "What color are her eyes?"

"Blue. The color is so bright they can rob a man of speech."

She nodded. "If you are looking for blue eyes, you might mean that lass that was in here last night."

A look crossed the innkeeper's face as if he wished she hadn't mentioned the woman. Interesting.

"The one who ruined the game?" the smithy asked. "I heard Rawley was furious about that."

"Rawley made out better with the game being disrupted than if we'd kept playing," the man with the knitting woman answered. His dark hair was streaked with gray. The others laughed their agreement.

Beck felt hope. "Do you know where the woman is now?"

Sarver answered, "She and her husband were heading to Liverpool."

"Her husband?"

"Aye, Mr. Cox. Good man he is," Sarver said.

"Especially since his wife has a temper," the man with graying hair added.

Cox? Beck had never heard that name. "A temper?"

"She lost it. Destroyed our game."

Beck sat forward. Could Elise be traveling with a man? Was she in danger? "Did she act fearful?"

Everyone laughed. "They were a *couple*," Sarver

said, "if you understand my meaning. Didn't take their eyes off of each other." Heads nodded agreement.

Beck asked, "Did they take the Mail in the direction of Liverpool?"

"Cox asked about it. However, it hasn't come in yet," Sarver answered. "It should be here in about two hours."

"So, the couple is here?" Beck could not believe his luck. "Where are they now?" *If* this was Elise, then who was the man? And why was she with him? But also, if this Cox did anything to Elise, Beck would happily peel the skin off of him.

"I don't know where they are. I haven't seen them," Sarver answered. "But then, many people take a walk while waiting for their coach. They should be here by and by. Then again, I haven't seen their dog either. My son told me Cox said he didn't know what he'd do if the Mail driver didn't let him bring his dog. Attached to the animal, he was."

*A dog?* Beck sat back on the bench. "Did his wife like the dog, too?" He was trying to make sense of it all.

"I assume so," Sarver said. "Another tankard?"

"Thank you," Beck responded. He picked up his fork and knife, his mind busy. He needed time to consider all of this.

There was nothing to do but wait for the Mail to arrive.

A few hours later, he watched the coach drive

off. No couple had taken a seat. He'd also talked to the stable master, who hadn't seen the couple or their dog all day. "They slept in the barn," the man had said. "We don't have more than one room in the inn, and it had already been claimed. The husband helped me with chores and asked if they could sleep in the stables for the night. I said he could. Never saw her. I know they slept in the hay, but they were gone when I came to feed the horses."

"Where do you think they went?"

"For a walk."

Was that the answer to everything in the country? Beck swore under his breath. A hundred wicked things could happen to a young, beautiful woman traveling alone.

He prayed none of them had happened to Elise. Gwendolyn had put great trust in him and he had no desire to disappoint her.

In the end, Beck decided to ride on to Liverpool. It was his safest gamble. He believed he would find Elise, or some word of her, between here and the port city.

He mounted his horse.

# CHAPTER FOURTEEN

*Two people shorten the road.*
IRISH SAYING

$\mathcal{K}$it had come of his own volition with Elise, but she knew he was not happy with her decision to travel to Moorcock—mainly because he let his feelings be known.

Granted, he was obviously *not* at his best in the morning. In the short time she'd known him, he'd never been particularly communicative before the sun was well up in the sky.

This was different. While yesterday he'd been fine, even gallant about seeing her safely to Ireland, today the hard set of his jaw and his conversations of grunts let her know he believed she was wasting their time.

She was just as certain they weren't.

Tamsyn tried to cheer him up. She found a good stick and brought it to him to throw, something he always did for her. Not today. He ignored her prodding. He gave her a pet, but little else.

Eventually, she dropped the stick and settled for walking right at his side, staring up adoringly at him. Kit didn't notice. He was too wrapped up in putting one angry foot in front of the other, stopping only to roll up his oilskin and drape it over one shoulder as the day grew warmer.

Elise had no trouble disregarding his attitude. She had sisters. She understood sullenness. She was very good at practicing it herself. In time he would grow tired of feeling put upon.

Still, someone had to counteract his nonsense. She hadn't insisted he take her to Moorcock. *He* had made the decision to come along. Consequently, his surliness only served to make her more *pleasant*. In fact, she delighted in being sunny and bright.

Her stockings padded and protected her healing blisters to the point that she had no trouble on the path. She didn't hold back her joy at the sight of the primroses and other wildflowers that patterned the side of the lane they traveled.

And she hummed. Elise didn't have a good singing voice, but she could hum a tune. The one she chose for today was a jig the Wiltham stable lads had whistled. It was a bit of a one-note melody. She liked it. The humming helped her pass the time since Kit hadn't answered when she'd asked how long it would take to reach their destination. It kept her annoyance over his pouting at bay—

*"Would you stop?"* Kit practically spit the words toward her.

Elise pretended to not understand that he meant the humming. Instead, almost gleefully, she froze in place—still humming.

Tamsyn looked confused but Kit kept walking. He didn't notice Elise was not trailing behind him. Tamsyn barked. Kit frowned and looked around, and that is when he realized Elise was some forty feet behind him, a "frozen" foot raised, a "frozen" arm outstretched.

He skidded to a halt. *"What* are you doing?" he barked.

"You told me to stop."

His scowl deepened. He saw no humor in the matter. Instead, he shook his head without comment and continued on the way. Elise lifted her skirts and ran to catch up.

She fell into step beside him.

"I know you didn't wish to accompany me to Moorcock," she said. "But you *chose* to."

Kit did not reply.

Elise said, "You think this is a fool's errand."

He didn't answer.

Undeterred, she went on. "I mean, it's fair that you are not invested in this trip. But"—she continued as if he was interested—"my sisters and I never believed Papa was dead. Not truly. There was no proof of it. Our cousin Richard and the magistrate were the ones who pushed the matter. Richard wanted Wiltham. He refused to give more time for Papa to return."

"How long had he been gone?"

He spoke!

Elise had been tempted to say those words aloud. She caught herself in time.

Kit even unbent enough to pick up a stick from the side of the path and throw it for Tamsyn into the surrounding woods. The dog joyfully flew after it, and Elise smiled.

Kit might occasionally be considered moody— who wasn't?—but he was a good companion. She was glad he was with her. She trusted him. He was also pleasing to her eye, something she was appreciating more and more—

"Do you not know?" His voice interrupted the drift of her thoughts.

She blinked. "Know?"

He lifted a quizzical brow as if he was surprised by her woolgathering. "I asked how long your father has been gone? When did you see him last?"

"My father, yes," she responded, trying to catch the thread of the discussion.

How long had it been? They were in mid-July now. Gram had passed over a year before they went to London. That had been when Richard had swooped in with his claim to Wiltham. Her father had not returned for close to two years before her death. "Over three years." Perhaps even four.

"Three years," he repeated. The words seemed weighted in the favor of an untimely death.

"I understand how that sounds, except you didn't know my father. He wasn't one to sit in front of a hearth. He couldn't be in one place too long, even for a visit with us. But he did love us. He *did*."

She wanted him to understand her father. "People always asked questions about Papa. About why he didn't stay with his girls and why he left the running of Wiltham to Gram, even when he was with his regiment, as if a soldier had a choice about military service. However, Papa wasn't the doting type and . . . that was fine. I had Gram, Tweedie, and my sisters. Gram always said that we must accept people as they are. She claimed the world would be a better place if we did. That doesn't mean there weren't times it was hard to not know where he was. We missed him. But Kit, when he'd return, we were all so happy. He'd bring presents and call us his girls and, well, it was just the best time. He was a good man. He was knighted for his service. Captain Sir John Lanscarr."

"Elise, it is not that I am unsympathetic to your plight. He was your father and, of course, you saw the best in him."

"I saw the worst, too. I'm not blind, Kit."

"I'm certain you weren't. However"—he drew the word out—"this information you share convinces me more than ever that Old John is not your father. I've never known a man with a title

who didn't use it. Even a knighthood. The fellow
in Moorcock is a dodgy sort. Moorcock draws
disreputable characters from all over. It is almost
the middle of the country, and thieves come from
all over to change what they stole into money.
Old John makes his livelihood separating the
lowest of the low from their ill-gotten gains. He
is quite good. Then again, those who steal are not
the brightest of fellows. Old John can easily out-
play them. He certainly taught me a thing or two.
Perhaps, at some point, Old John met your father,
who taught him his unique shuffle?"

"So you have suggested before. And that is all
the more reason I must go to Moorcock. I need to
know the truth."

He shook his head. "And if the truth is disap-
pointing, Elise?"

"If he isn't my father, then I've lost nothing,
have I?" But this Old John *was* her papa. Deep in
her soul, she knew it.

KIT HAD DONE his best to warn Elise.

He knew Old John. The man played at being
a genial gentleman but beneath his exterior, Kit
sensed he was a lying, thieving fox. Old John
could not have sired anything close to the intelligent woman Elise was. But she wouldn't listen,

and perhaps he didn't blame her. At one time, he'd wanted to believe his father had given a care for him, too.

Except men weren't afraid to take off the blinders.

Women, on the other hand, believed they could fix anyone. Elise had looked up at him with eyes as clear and bright as stained glass and babbled the things that women always say. It was the way they were. Eternally optimistic.

Of course, a new trouble had begun niggling away at Kit. What if she was right and Old John *was* her sire?

He couldn't leave her with him. It was one thing to learn Old John's card tricks and laugh with him over an ale; it was another to hand Elise over. A loving father didn't abandon his family, and that is what he'd done, all of Elise's excuses to the side. If Old John was that man, what other sly acts could he be capable of against his daughter?

And she would be his unwitting victim. She had unshakable faith in him. Old John could make up excuses to explain away his bad behavior, and she would believe every one of them. He knew. His mother had been that way.

She'd held his father up as a paragon. She'd claimed his father was a great statesman and had admonished Kit that he must work very hard to measure up to his sire. A sire who rarely came home from London. Oh, yes, he understood what

Elise meant about eagerly waiting for a father to make an appearance.

On the rare occasions when the former duke had come home to Smythson, his mother had acted like a giddy girl in love. There wasn't anything she wouldn't do for him. She'd held dinner parties where Kit remembered his father would wax on about the important generals he knew and how he'd been in discussions over the French. Whitehall needed his advice, he'd claimed. That was why he couldn't come home often. After all, he held the king's counsel.

What were a wife and a son when compared to Affairs of State?

All of those stories had been lies.

Kit had learned the harsh truth at school. When he had bragged of this father's connections, he'd been set straight. His father had rarely made an appearance in the Lords, let alone offered time to his king. He'd been too busy spending his money on women and gambling. *Whoring Winderton*, they had called him. The name was one they'd overheard their fathers use to describe the Duke of Winderton.

He'd never shared this information with his mother. She'd loved her husband. Her faith in him had been rock solid, even when it was discovered upon his death that he had gambled away most of the Winderton fortune. There had even been a fear they would lose most of Smythson's lands as well, but did she criticize him? No, she'd held on to her theory that he had been a good man led astray.

Fortunately, the estate was saved by her brother, Kit's guardian, his uncle Balfour . . . the one who had won the lovely Kate's heart, even after knowing Kit loved her.

Was it any wonder he didn't trust families?

Of course, he'd not handled Kate's rejection well. And so had started his downward spiral into self-pity. He'd been so angry, he'd acted out as if he'd had this need to prove himself to be—a what?

A man? A duke? A lover?

And when he'd failed at all of those roles, when he'd botched everything, he'd run . . . which actually hadn't been a terrible idea. He had been given a title, an education, and wealth. And he had taken them for granted.

He could have turned to his uncle. Balfour was highly respected and had tried his best to give Kit guidance. And Kit might have listened—until the lovely Kate. After that, Kit had been too proud and stubborn to ask for help.

Consequently, his ruin had been quick.

Except his mother had not been so understanding with her son as she'd been with her husband. He remembered his mother confronting him. The words she'd used over his appalling behavior still rankled. *You are Winderton. That must stand for something.* Then she'd told him he needed to go out into the world.

He needed to make something of himself. His father, she had assured him, would never have behaved as he did.

It had been on the tip of Kit's still slightly drunk tongue to set her straight, to tell her that her husband had been no saint.

He hadn't. He'd kept his mouth shut. Her husband's behavior had not been her fault.

Instead of arguing with her, he'd just left. He'd walked away from Smythson and had been walking ever since. He didn't even understand what he searched for. Or how to find his way back.

And now, here was Elise hoping against common sense to find her father. A father she expected to love her. Perhaps his own difficult history with his sire explained why, in spite of Moorcock being the last place he should revisit, he felt an obligation to stay by her side.

Or was it obligation? Did he feel something else?

Yes, part of his purpose was to protect Elise, but there was more. He felt a connection to her and not just because she was strikingly beautiful. He understood her. Not only was she proud but she had an intelligence that made it hard for her to suffer fools. What must that be like for a woman of her social standing? She would be expected to grace a table and breed babies and nothing more.

One thing that Kit had learned on his journey was that many women liked having control over their lives. Certainly Kate had. She'd run her own theater company, something he'd admired.

And now here was Elise, younger than Kate but no less fiercely determined.

How could a man not admire such women?

But was it worth his life? Moorcock was not a safe place for any woman alone, but especially one with Elise's uncommon beauty. She needed protection. However, he was well aware that he might have powerful enemies lurking there, the sort who would happily string him up.

Holbert and his men had been chasing him ever since he'd spoiled the plans they'd had for a very naive country lass. They hadn't appreciated his interference. Kit had been running from them the evening he'd met Elise in that ill-fated coach.

He hoped Holbert was still roaming the countryside searching for him. It was possible. The man was not that quick.

His other wish was that Elise would meet Old John, realize he couldn't be her father, and agree to Kit's escort to Ireland. Then they would be done with one another.

Or did he wish for them to be done?

He knew it was for the best. Sooner or later, he must return to his rightful role in life. Just as Prince Hal had become king, he must be the duke. He'd marry a woman of suitable rank and a very grand fortune to secure his estates and his heritage. Meanwhile, Elise would be snapped up by some man far wealthier than himself.

In the future, perhaps their paths would cross. Would they recognize each other? Or pretend this adventure had never happened? That they were mere strangers?

And from deep within him came an awareness that he didn't want to lose this bond between them. He liked her company. He liked her trust. One of them bumped into the other, almost as if they were drawn together.

He caught her hand. She did not draw away. Their fingers laced together and it seemed the most natural thing in the world for them to walk hand in hand.

Her mind was always active and she chattered away. He found himself laughing and making his own comments. Anyone coming across them would think they were more than just a couple out for a morning stroll.

More important, Elise acted as if he mattered to her. *Him*, disguised as—what had she called him? A ruffian. A common fellow . . . walking beside a golden goddess—

"Do you know women *want* to have a say in government?"

"Why?" Her statement truly astounded him, bringing him back to the moment. He rarely took his seat in the Lords and had been avoiding government service or any position of authority, reasoning that he was too young, even as a duke, for such dreariness.

"Because there are changes we desire, and we are being ignored."

A stream blocked their path. Tamsyn had already leaped across it. Kit could straddle it and, waiting a moment for her permission, lifted Elise up and over so she wouldn't get wet.

"Thank you," she said, straightening her skirts. She had released his hand.

"I see no reason for women to vote," Kit said. The moment he spoke the words, he realized his mistake. He'd been ready to take her hand again.

It was not offered.

Instead, she tilted her head. "Ah, because men take care of us?"

He'd walked into a trap, one of his own making. However, Kit was nothing if not stubborn. "We do," he asserted.

She made a scoffing sound.

"We do," he reiterated. "On the important matters." He was sure of that. He'd not heard his mother complain . . . he didn't think?

Come to think of it, they had never once talked about issues before the Lords. She was more involved in Maidenshop village affairs than matters of state.

Elise was different. She arched a brow. "It seems to me that all the rules favor the men. Then again, as you said so eloquently the other day, you have an extra body part. Isn't that how you put it? Endowed by Our Maker and all that. Perhaps what Our Maker wants is for men to share some of the spoils in life with their better halves."

At first, Kit was taken aback, and then he burst out laughing because she was so very right. "I can't argue with you. We have made the rules in our favor."

"I know," she assured him. "I would like to have a say. I have a list of changes."

"And what is on your list?"

"So many things," she answered promptly. "Starting with the laws of inheritance. But also, I believe women should have the right to attend schools like men do."

He thought of Eton, where he'd gained what education he had, and gave a shiver. "You need to desire something better."

"Own property?"

"Some women own property."

"Not enough."

"True."

"See? I knew you were an intelligent man," she said.

"All I have to do is agree with you."

"Not always," she responded lightly, "but it makes conversation easier." She punctuated her words with a smile that made him almost trip over his feet. There was a sparkle in her eyes. Sunlight spun her hair into gold.

And suddenly, just like that, Kit was hooked.

He could make all the excuses he wished about why he should keep his distance from her. She didn't know his true identity. If she did, she might have a different opinion of him. Knowing Elise as he did now, she would be angry at his deception . . .

It didn't matter.

Standing in this country path in the July sun, he found himself falling in love.

Real love. Not infatuation but something earthier and stronger.

A love that—without his realizing it—had been building from the moment she'd been willing to strike out on her own back in the woods after the Mail crash. He laughed to remember her darting around the coach, ready to give him a club over the head. Or informing him that he "reeked."

Then there were those moments he could almost divine her thoughts . . . when their eyes met and he experienced a sense of connection. Why, he could have no more have let her go off to Moorcock alone than he could have flown to the moon, even if it meant facing a hundred Holberts—"What are you thinking?" she asked, interrupting his thoughts. "You have the strangest expression on your face."

He wasn't about to tell her. This awareness of what she meant to him was too new, and made him surprisingly vulnerable.

"I'm hungry," he said in answer to her question.

Elise laughed, the sound happy as if his statement explained everything. "Of course you are," she said. She held out her hand. "Let's keep going. We'll find food soon."

He wrapped his fingers around hers, his palm in hers.

And he knew he was in trouble.

## CHAPTER FIFTEEN

*Beauty never boiled the kettle.*
IRISH PROVERB

Around midday, they came upon a village. Several stone-and-board cottages lined a road leading to an old Norman church. The graves around the building appeared neatly tended while two hemlocks and a rangy crab apple tree with twisting roots provided shade.

There was a small public house at the other end of the road, and Kit caught the whiff of meat and pastry in the air. "I could use an ale. What of you?" he asked her.

Elise hung back. "And how will we pay?"

"After you swept the table clean last night?" he reminded her.

For the first moment since he'd met her, she appeared somewhat contrite. "That wasn't my wisest move, was it?"

"Not the best," he agreed easily.

"I lost my temper."

"Isn't there a limerick about a lass and a temper?" he wondered.

"Not one that should be repeated, I'm sure."

"Fortunately," he confessed, "I learned long ago to not keep one's winnings on the table. Not unless you wish to start bad feelings. I'd been slipping some into my pocket from the first hand I won."

Her face lit up. "You are the most clever, wise, remarkable person I have ever met, Kit Cox," Elise announced, her praise raining on him like the most blessed of benedictions. "I am famished."

And he liked the feeling of not only pleasing her but surprising her. "Come, let's see if we can find a good meal."

From the public house, they purchased three cold pork pies and tankards of foamy ale. They ate them outside on a stretch of grass in the afternoon sun. Tamsyn sat between them, and they broke half a pie into pieces that she thoroughly enjoyed.

Two neighbor women wearing aprons over their dresses and the wide-brimmed hats of the gardener were gossiping across the stone fence between their cottages. One held an arm full of roses, which the other admired. While Elise had a moment to herself, Kit approached them, a coin in hand.

By the time she rejoined him, he was holding

one of those wide-brimmed straw hats with a low crown. It was a shabby thing that had probably seen many hours in its former owner's garden, but Elise acted as if the hat had come from a London milliner. She smoothed her hair back and put it on her head, giving it a rakish tilt.

"What do you think?" she asked, looking up at him from under the brim.

What did he think? That she was beautiful. Perfect, actually. Her smile alone could hold him spellbound. He'd also never known a woman who could be so pleased with a secondhand hat.

That was her gift, wasn't it? Her obvious enjoyment of life.

"It suits you," he said.

She took off the hat, picked at a piece of the weaving that was coming undone, and then said, "My sisters and I searched for hats like this. We'd buy them for a pence and then we'd spend hours refashioning them with whatever we could find." Her gaze swung up to his. "Thank you, Kit. I feel a proper gentlewoman. Everyone needs a hat." She set it on her head.

As a duke, back in London where he enjoyed servants and all the best of life, he could afford to buy her a thousand hats. But this hat was special because she took so much pleasure in it—and it had been purchased with money *he'd* earned.

As they left the village, they waved at the village women who'd been watching him give Elise the gift. They waved back. Then Kit offered Elise his hand and they were back on their way to Moorcock.

✦✦✦✦✦

KIT HAD SURPRISED her with the gift.

Elise didn't know why this made her so happy, but it did.

She wasn't a fool. She knew when a man was attracted to her. Kit was showing all the signs—the touching, the thoughtfulness, the hat.

He had to know they were of two very different classes. She was landed gentry. She was expected to marry well.

And what of him? She knew little of his story, but she saw how worn the heels of his boots were.

Still . . . he was like no other man she'd ever met. Quick-witted, protective, and not only open to her opinions, but he also understood her sense of humor. She'd never considered that an important quality before. However, now, listening to him laugh when she said something outrageous or clever made her feel appreciated. After all, looks would fade—but a man who acted as a counterbalance to her?

That man was to be valued.

The single country lane was a well-traveled one and soon ran into a better, wider road. Kit claimed he now had his bearings. He explained that Moorcock was close to Stoke-on-Trent. He asked questions of fellow travelers and learned there was a posting inn several miles up the road. "The stage will take us the better part of the way," he told her.

Tamsyn had stopped bothering them with a stick. Instead, she trudged alongside them.

"We must take Tamsyn," Elise insisted.

"Of course. We'll sit on the roof. I'll hold her."

She smiled, pleased with his answer. But then a new concern followed. "Do we have enough money?" she asked.

"If we don't, we'll sell your hat," he said.

"Why not sell yours?" she returned gamely, interested to hear his response.

Kit acted offended. "I can't part with this hat. I like it too much. We've been through adventures together."

Here was an opening she had been waiting for. "What sort of adventures?" She tried to sound nonchalant.

He made a hushing sound. "They are secrets. The hat won't talk."

"It won't, hmm? Have you and your hat not heard of the law of traveling companions?"

"The law of traveling companions?" His eyes crinkled with amusement.

"Yes, it states that to while away the time, I can ask you questions and you must answer. I know very little about you."

"I like it that way."

"But I don't," she replied as if that should settle the matter. "My sisters and I play a game called three questions. I ask you three questions and you answer them."

"I thought a game was something that went back and forth."

She considered that a moment and then said, "You already know everything about me."

"Do I?"

"Almost everything," she amended. "By the way, I truly adore this hat." She pulled on the brim of her new bonnet. "Thank you. I didn't realize how much I needed it."

"You are welcome."

Elise smiled and took his arm, leaning into him. He didn't complain. "My first question—"

"I don't know that I agreed to play?"

"You *are* playing," she informed him. "What do you do for work? Are you a gambler like my father?" This was important to know.

"That was two questions."

She made a frustrated noise. "You quibble like Dara."

"I hope that is a compliment."

Elise thought of her sister, the one who always needed to control everything. "Yes, it is a compliment."

"Well, thank you."

When he didn't say anything beyond that, she nudged him in the side. The man's body was as hard as a rock. "I asked you a question."

"Two questions."

"Kit, answer *one* of them."

He grinned as if he enjoyed playing her game. The smile was a bit crooked, which was good. It gave his face character. Then he countered, "I'm more curious about what you imagine I do for work? I mean, since I'm not a gambler, other than for survival."

A clue, and one that pleased her. She did not want him to be a gambler. "Truly? You did well last night."

"It was vingt-et-un, and you brought me luck. So tell me, what do you think I am?"

He asked his question in a tone that warned her he didn't expect her to guess correctly. However, she thought his challenge fair. "You don't strike me as an ostler or some sort of driver. You can't be a yeoman because with fields to till, you wouldn't have time to march around the countryside. You could possibly be a horse trainer. However, I suspect you are some sort of salesman because you seem to like traveling."

Kit came to a halt. "A salesman?" He frowned down at her. "I'm no damn *peddler.*"

"You are right," she agreed. "You are not pleasant enough."

"Elise . . ." he said, a warning—if she was wise enough to heed it.

Her response was to laugh as she held up her hands, asking for quarter. "Fine," she answered. "You could be a tutor. You are well-spoken."

"Thank you . . . I think." They continued walking.

"Or a squire."

"A squire," he repeated, acting as if she was elevating him.

She looked up at his amused expression, knowing full well he could be cool and disdainful, if he wished. Under that scruff of beard was a handsome man. Patrician handsome, save for the crooked smile. So, she said, "You might even pass for a prince or a *duke*."

For some reason, her statement seemed to give him a start. "Why would you say that?"

She laughed. "I'm jesting. You can't be a duke. You are too young and you haven't a paunch over the buttons of your breeches."

He pondered a moment. "That sounds distasteful."

"It is," she assured him. "All dukes are old. That is one thing I learned in London. And they can't dance. None of them, at least not in my experience."

Kit gave her a strange look. "You danced with dukes in London?"

His tone confused her. Many people believed titled lords were to be revered. She hadn't pegged Kit as one of them, but one never knew.

*Or*, and this was important, his learning her station might set her apart from him—and she didn't wish that to happen. "It isn't your turn to ask questions."

"You only have one more question to ask."

She made a face. "That second question was part of the first."

Kit looked regretful. "A question is a question."

"Very well. Here is my question. Why do you wander homeless?" She was determined to learn something of substance about him.

"You make it sound as if there is no purpose to my wandering."

"Is there? Please explain, dear sir."

"I don't know that I could." He shot her a look as if he was slightly embarrassed, which made her want the answer all the more.

"It is the rules of the game," she softly reminded him.

He took that under consideration and then said under his breath, "Very well." He looked to Elise. "But don't lose sight of the fact *you* asked."

"I'm remarkably curious."

"That is an understatement."

She gave him another nudge. This time because she liked moving closer to him.

Freedom to be herself was a heady thing. There were no "rules" or eyes watching her on this road. The other travelers weren't paying attention. They had no expectations of her, unlike her sisters and Society.

"I wanted to have an adventure," he said. "My chance to pretend to be Prince Hal."

"Prince Hal? From Shakespeare?"

"And other stories."

"But why him? Wasn't he a wastrel?"

"Wastrel? What quaint language you use."

She laughed at the "scholarly" tone he had adopted. "It is the description Vicar Perry used. He was our tutor. 'From wastrel to ruler,' he said."

Kit shrugged. "Perhaps I was a wastrel as well."

"I can't imagine you as one. You have too much talent, too many gifts. You could be whatever you wished." She meant those words. She'd noticed how people reacted to Kit. He made them feel at ease and they were always eager to accommodate him.

Her compliment seemed to make everything about him tighten. "You don't know me, Elise."

She refused to be deterred. "Then tell me, Kit. Wanting to pretend you are Prince Hal—?"

"It was my favorite boyhood story."

"Yes, but it sounds more as if you ran away. And that means something set you off."

"Same as yourself?"

She didn't balk at the description. "Is it what we have in common? What are you running from?"

Kit shook off her arm. She let him. He walked several steps before he said, "I needed to be away. The gambit of playing Prince Hal seemed as good of a ploy as any. It was a fancy. Go out into the country. Meet the people. See how they live."

"Because?" she prodded.

"Because, who knows? It might make me a better man." His expression said he didn't believe that possible . . . that just like herself, he had doubts, and possible betrayals of his own. And her heart hurt for him.

"Have you gained any insight or wisdom as Prince Hal?"

He held up a hand. "You've had your three questions."

"I've always been one to push the boundaries."

"Except it is *my* turn."

To her mind, their conversation had just taken a serious and important turn. She realized that she'd be wise to back off and give him a bit of room. "Very well. What questions do you have for me?"

"What do you value most?"

"Honesty," she replied without missing a beat. "I don't care what people say, as long as they are telling me the truth. No one is honest with each other in London. *No one.* And the truth becomes a waffly thing. Perhaps if I'd known the truth of Michael's feelings earlier, I could have prepared myself."

"Michael?"

Embarrassed heat rushed to her cheeks. She'd given away too much, and then decided it didn't matter. Out of all the people in her life, she'd already been the most honest with Kit. And Michael was the past. "I'd wanted to be his wife." She gave a little shrug before confessing, "Instead, he chose my sister."

"Which one?"

"Dara."

Kit made a face. "The one you compared me to? You claimed it was a compliment."

She shook her head. "It is. Well, it is *now*. I mean, I was angry when they expected me to live with them. That is what happens with unmarried sisters. They are expected to live with relatives." She didn't hide her bitterness. "I couldn't watch them be so happy every day. And they are, Kit—very happy. Happy enough for me to be jealous." There, she'd admitted it aloud. She'd been consumed with jealousy. "That was the reason I bolted. My pride was very hurt."

"But your heart?" His voice was gentle.

"Untouched," she admitted—and it was true. "Although I didn't realize it until I was away from them." She considered a moment. "I understand what you mean when you say you needed to leave to become a better person. Apparently I needed to do the same." A thought struck her. "It is as if I am playing the role of Falstaff to your Hal." She held out her arms, pretending to be a big man as she imagined Prince Hal's companion had been.

Kit laughed. The sound filled the road. "You are a far more attractive Falstaff than Shakespeare could have envisioned."

"What of yourself?" she asked, liking this easiness between them. "What do you value?"

He shook his head. "I don't know. I'm not as clear about myself as you are." There was a moment of silence, and then he said, "Looking back, rethinking, I'm beginning to believe I may not be running *from* something. I might be running *toward* it."

And that is when Elise realized she'd fallen in love. She wanted to be what he was running toward. She wished to be included in his life.

The intensity of the emotion caught her off guard. It was three things at once—unexpected, unbidden, and a complete revelation.

She loved Kit Cox. She may have unknowingly been in love with him for some time, including last night when she'd been so furiously angry with him.

And he was absolutely the *worst* choice for her to love. He wasn't anyone important. He may be uncommonly handsome in spite of his roughness, but he was a ne'er-do-well by any of Society's standards. Her sisters would be horrified. Even Tweedie might disapprove.

Except, walking by his side, she couldn't imagine loving anyone else. He allowed her to be exactly who she was.

Those feelings she'd claimed for Michael Brogan meant nothing when compared to this mixture of loyalty, trust, and, yes, desire that she experienced right now. She was safe with him.

Suddenly, he grabbed her hand. "Come, the posting inn is ahead at the crossroads, and it appears as if the coach is there." His simple action of drawing her with him to catch the coach only served to make her love him more because he included her. He thought of her as being with him.

They reached the inn just as the driver was

getting ready to climb into the box. Kit called out to him. "Is this the coach to Stoke-on-Trent?"

"Aye."

"We'll ride on top," Kit said. He was already helping Elise up. There were no other passengers there. "And we are taking the dog."

"The dog can run alongside the coach. You don't need him up there," the driver said.

"Yes, we do," Kit answered. "What are the fares?"

"You pay for the dog if you insist on letting it ride."

"Done."

Elise was settled on a seat behind the driver by the time Kit climbed up to join her. He carried a squirming Tamsyn under his arm and sat her across their laps. She calmed down, although she was still not certain of this idea of riding. Kit and Elise both removed their hats. Otherwise the wind would blow them off—and they both liked their hats.

"How long is the drive?" Kit asked the driver.

"We'll be there in three hours," the coachman said. He picked up his whip. The guard sitting in the back of the coach blew his horn.

Kit's arm came around her, and Elise moved to be as close to him as she could be, completely taking advantage of the situation. She rested her hand on Tamsyn's shoulder.

Then, with a flick of the whip and a call to the horses, they were off.

# CHAPTER SIXTEEN

*You've got to do your own growing, no matter how tall your father was.*
IRISH PROVERB

𝒯he time to Stoke-on-Trent flew by.

Kit purchased buns for them at the next posting inn. Other passengers joined them on the roof. One woman sniffed at seeing poor Tamsyn up there. And even though the dog would have preferred to run alongside the coach, Kit made Tamsyn stay with them. He vowed he was not going to let anything happen to her.

They had become friendly with the driver and guard. Kit had decided to play the three questions game with them. Elise wasn't sure about the idea, but to her surprise, the two men had joined in with good humor.

It had helped the time pass. Kit incorporated each new passenger into the game, even the lady who had disapproved of Tamsyn. By the time they reached Stoke-on-Trent, the woman was hand-feeding Tamsyn pieces of the cold sausages she'd prepared for her own meal.

"What now?" Elise asked after they'd climbed down from the coach. She kept her eye on Tamsyn, who made three quick circles, happy to be on solid ground, and then ran off a short way to see to herself.

"We need more money," Kit said. "I suggest we find lodging and go from there."

A few inquiries directed them to the house of an elderly couple named Forkner who had a room to offer. Again, Kit introduced them as Mr. and Mrs. Cox. He was wise to do so. The husband was a deacon at his church. He declared them a lovely couple.

Their room had one bed. Elise stared at it as if she'd never seen a bedstead before. In truth, she was exhausted. It had been a long day. However, the sight of that single mattress with tall, confident Kit standing right at her shoulder . . .

She glanced up at him, wondering if she should say something . . . or allow things to happen.

That would be the easy way, wouldn't it?

To let circumstances carry her toward what she was beginning to desire? As a young woman of lineage and class, she shouldn't even be thinking about wrapping herself around him, holding him, disappearing into him. At least, not intentionally.

However, if Fate intervened—?

"I'll take the floor," Kit informed her briskly. He moved away from her to hang his hat on one wall peg and the oilskin on another, removing a flat leather kit from its pocket. He then walked to the washstand and took off his jacket. He rolled up the sleeves of his shirt.

Elise watched, slightly disoriented. It was as if she'd been leaning against him and now that he'd marched off, she had to catch her balance. And with that little bit of breathing room, all the rules she'd been taught raised their ugly little heads. He was right about the bed. They should not share it—because she did plan to return to her life . . .

So, why was she so disappointed?

"Although," he continued, "I shall not be here a good portion of the night. I'll try not to wake you when I return." He began shaving, using the cake of soap by the pitcher and bowl.

She watched as the whiskers disappeared. "You are going to gamble?"

"It is the quickest way to scratch together some money." He wiped his face with a cotton towel. "Don't wait up. Sleep while you can. Enjoy the mattress for me." With those words, he picked up his jacket, grabbed his hat, and was gone.

Gone to do what he must to take care of them.

The elderly couple would not let Tamsyn in the house, so Elise, feeling at loose ends, went out and sat with the dog. Tamsyn seemed to understand Elise's mood.

Finally, the soft twilight gave way to evening's darkness, and the midges were annoying enough to chase Elise inside. However, she had reached a decision.

The depth of her feelings for Kit was true. She didn't believe she felt mere infatuation or plain lust. She was not a milkmaid. She understood expectations.

But it was easier to obey expectations when she'd believed love was a series of checklists built on hopes and good values. A heart and mind endeavor.

She'd been wrong. What she felt for Kit was all heart, and there were no boundaries or musts. Not since he'd entered her life.

One moment, she'd been alone and lost. In the next, her world had opened to include *him*.

And it was a *wonderous* thing, and so she would tell him when he returned. She'd declare herself.

The decision released all the prickliness inside of her. He'd want her declaration.

He'd tell her he felt the same.

She knew he must. He had to feel the heat of awareness between them. And then, there was the way he had begun reaching for her hand. Also, the small touches. A brush of his arm, his hand going to her waist to steady her, a touch of his fingers when he gave her the bun—it was all there.

Elise had misjudged Michael. Could she be

wrong about Kit as well? She didn't know but she discovered she was willing to risk her pride to find out.

Now came the waiting. Elise did lie on the mattress, surprised at how good it felt after so many nights on the ground. That didn't mean she fell asleep. No, she had other plans, because as she waited, she discovered she couldn't hide her feelings. Not anymore.

There was a sound outside the house. Kit was at the front door. He said something Elise couldn't hear to Tamsyn.

The bedroom door squeaked as he opened it. She caught her breath. The moment had come. She'd been rehearsing in her mind what she should say. However, what had seemed logical and simple even a few moments ago was suddenly now, in his presence, terrifying.

He was being very quiet and Elise watched as he crossed in the moonlight, treading carefully so he didn't make a noise.

"Did you win?" She spoke in a hushed tone, not wanting to wake their elderly hosts.

Kit gave a start and then laughed quietly. "Why are you awake?"

"I couldn't sleep, not until I knew you were home. Did you see Tamsyn outside?"

"I did. She is very comfortable in a bed of pine needles."

Elise sat up. She wore the white muslin. Her other two dresses were on the peg beside his oilskin. The material was thin without a chemise beneath it, the left shoulder still torn. "Did you win?" she repeated.

He had crossed to the bowl and basin. Elise had emptied the water when she'd used it earlier. He now poured in fresh and splashed it over his face. He took the cake of soap and washed his hands before answering, "Enough. I earned enough."

Kit walked toward the bed. Elise straightened. There was room in the bed for him . . .

She should speak. She couldn't. Her tongue couldn't move because he'd stopped and removed his jacket, the neckcloth, the shirt. The moonlight from the room's two windows bathed him in silver. She caught a moonlit glimpse of a flat abdomen, hard muscles, and strong arms before he moved back into the shadows.

He lowered himself to the floor, but he didn't lie down. Instead, he leaned against the bed frame, his back to her. "It was a long night," he said quietly.

She slid off the bed to sit alongside him. Not touching—she couldn't be that forward. She wanted him to come to her. "It was a long day," she whispered.

"It was." He smiled at her.

She looked down at his long legs. He'd removed his boots and she'd been so nervous, she hadn't registered the action. Now she noticed the hole in his stocking. "Why didn't you tell me?" she said, pointing to it. "I could have repaired that. I'll do it in the morning. I'm certain Mrs. Forkner has needle and thread."

"I've become accustomed to it." He wiggled his toe. "I rather like it. Well, unless I have water soak through my boots."

And then he did something truly amazing. He removed his socks.

Elise watched with a feeling akin to amazement. She still wore her socks wrapped around her feet. She'd always thought feet ugly. They were just necessary appendages, but his were different. He had beautiful feet. They were long with well-formed toes, and the sight of them in the moonlight was remarkably intimate.

"You didn't braid your hair." He spoke as if he'd just noticed.

Elise didn't say anything.

"And what are you wearing?" he asked. His gaze ran over her. The simple gown with its graceful lines was what she and her sisters were known for in London. While others went to parties wearing lace and satins, the Lanscarr sisters made their entrance in white muslin, and no one forgot them.

His gaze lingered on her bare shoulder where she'd tucked the frayed edges under. And then dropped lower.

Under his scrutiny, her breasts seemed to grow fuller, rounder. The nipples hardened.

Did he notice? He must.

She wanted him.

And he knew it.

He reached out and ran the back of his fingers against her cheek. "Elise?"

His touch set off a steady, impatient thrumming deep inside of her, and she braced herself. Of course, she'd been kissed, but there had never been this heady anticipation.

But he didn't move. Instead, his brows gathered as if he weighed the consequences, and she knew that if she didn't act now, she'd lose her courage. And so, when he didn't move beyond a touch, she threw her arms around him and kissed him fully on the lips with all the power of her fervent being.

✦✧✦✧✦

KIT WAS SHOCKED when she slammed her lips on his. She pressed hard against them with an enthusiasm that would have been appreciated . . . if her mouth wasn't closed tighter than a clam's shell.

For a long moment, they sat, Elise's arms holding him trapped because he dared *not* move. Or laugh.

It wasn't as if he hadn't wanted to kiss her. A man couldn't be with her day in and day out and be oblivious to the feminine perfection that was

Elise Lanscarr. After all, men fell in love with their eyes.

But he knew what lay beneath the surface. She was quick-witted, spirited, kind, bold, and generous—and it pleased him to no end to learn that she was such a terrible kisser.

He could remedy that. This was an opportunity he could not pass up.

Would she thank him? Kit wasn't certain.

And he also knew he'd best be wise. Her hard kiss only reinforced her innocence. He was a gentleman. He needed to see her returned to her family that way. In fact, if he was truly wise, he would tuck her into bed and then go outside and sleep with Tamsyn.

But before he did that, the truly noble thing would be to teach her to kiss.

Kit lifted her into his lap. Comically, her lips didn't budge from his. When Elise took action, she carried through. Few could deter her.

However, he liked the weight of her. She felt good in his arms.

And something stirred within him . . . not the little beast, although that part of Kit had been excited from the moment he'd realized they would be sharing a room.

No, what moved was Kit's heart. Another crack formed in the hard shell he'd worn around himself. He could feel himself growing whole.

A voice whispered inside of him that the last thing he should be doing was offering kissing lessons. But her nipples pressed against the soft white material of her gown as if begging to be touched. Her hips rested across his thighs, making him all the more aware of his erection. And Kit knew he couldn't let this beautiful, willful woman believe the hard press of lips was a kiss.

He gently pressed her shoulders. The kiss broke. Elise opened her eyes as if startled. He leaned toward her. "Elise, do you trust me?"

The small worry line appeared between her brows. She nodded.

That was all the consent he needed. He took her hands still on his shoulders and brought them down. Lacing their fingers, he whispered, "Close your eyes."

Elise obeyed, her body tense.

Kit savored the moment. He breathed in the scent of her skin. She reminded him of the deep green forests they walked through, of the sparkling water they waded across, and of the rising of the moon that gilded them now. Her scent spoke of all they had experienced together.

He bypassed her lips. Instead, he lowered his head so that he lightly followed the line of sensitive skin right below her jaw with the very tip of his tongue.

Elise gasped at his lightest touch. That was how responsive she was.

A primal beat began in Kit's veins. He had to remind himself that this was about a kiss. He *owed* her a kiss. *One*, he reminded himself, but he could take his time with it.

With the tip of his tongue, he traced the line between her closed lips. They naturally parted—and that is when he kissed her.

He held his passion in check. He wanted this to be good for her. His purpose was to show her how a kiss should start—

A cynical voice inside him, the honest one, pushed back on selfish excuses. He'd wanted to kiss her since that day she'd rounded on him for his rude comments about Tommy and his father, the day she'd forced him to see her as a person and not an unwelcome obligation.

She had challenged him. Often thwarted him. Always fascinated him.

There was a hesitance, a sweetness about her trust in him . . . but then Elise's natural curiosity took hold. Her tongue experimentally stroked his, copying his own actions. From deep within him, lust roared and their kiss took on a deeper dimension.

It was no longer a lesson for her.

*He* was the one being schooled.

He buried his hands in the thickness of her glorious hair, and he kissed her the way he wanted to kiss. No reservations; no pretense; no holding back.

The heat of her was pressed down upon him. He held her close and rained a line of kisses to her ear. The moment he touched a sensitive spot,

Elise reacted, her hold tightening. His hands cupped the curves of her buttocks—

*God, what was he doing?* What were *they* doing? Because Elise was as much of a participant as he was. She pressed her breasts against his chest and he wished there was no thin material between their bodies. This was dangerous. She might not completely understand what was happening, but she was learning fast.

Kit took hold of her arms and brought them down to her sides. Their lips met again, like flint to steel. Sparks flew, and he couldn't let it go on.

He broke the kiss. Parts of his body howled in protest. In response, Kit stood, carrying Elise in his arms up with him. She snuggled into him. Her hands reached to go around his neck. But before she could, he dumped her on the bed, and then he moved himself across the room.

His heart was pounding and his breathing was ragged as if he had run a long race. He braced against the washstand, willing himself back into control.

"Kit?" Her voice was soft, confused . . . a bit dazed.

He gathered himself. "Elise, we can't." He turned to her and then realized that was a mistake.

She sat on her knees in the middle of the bed, her hair curling down her shoulders. Her gown was hiked up above her thighs.

Her lips were swollen from his kisses.

It would be nothing—a mere two joyous steps—to cross the room to her.

But it wouldn't be right.

"We can't, Elise," he repeated.

"Because?" She gave him a small smile. "Everyone believes we are man and wife."

"Elise—"

"And if you are worried about what people will think, Kit, I don't care. Do you understand me? *I don't care.* I don't want to spend my life with a duke or marry for money. I don't want a man for his title. I want him because I respect him. Because I trust him. Because he *values me.*"

There was something wrong with what she was saying. He heard it but didn't understand it . . . until he did. She was declaring herself to him, and she couldn't. She mustn't.

He'd known she was gentry. Certainly, she wasn't a woman to trifle with. She came from a good family.

*He* came from a good family.

There were expectations for both of them, and a little sojourn with a person she thought was a ruffian playing Prince Hal could destroy her. It could cost both everything, which was fine for him. He understood what was a play. She was the one clueless to his identity.

"Elise, will you pull the skirt of your gown down? It is quite distracting." Gawd, he sounded like a governess.

Instead of taking his chiding to heart, her

response was the opposite. Her smile turned wicked and intriguing. She leaned forward, and for a second it appeared as if her breasts were in danger of popping out of her bodice.

"Elise." The word was a plea and a warning. Meanwhile, his hips seemed intent on crossing the room to her. He gripped the edge of the washstand and stood his ground.

Her teasing stopped. She sobered and slid to the edge of the bedstead, pulling her skirts down.

Kit didn't know if that helped. Elise could have been wrapped up in thick blankets with a hood over her head and he'd want her. That kiss had opened a door that should have remained closed.

"Better, Kit?" she asked. Her voice was tight.

"Hardly," he admitted.

"Then can you explain why you are—" Her voice broke off. She looked away and then finished, "Are you rejecting me?"

"You were in London for the Season?"

Her brow furrowed. "Yes. My sisters and myself."

"I imagine you did well."

"Are you asking if I had suitors? Of course. However, none of them compared to you."

He let his breath out slowly. He didn't doubt her sincerity, but what would her feelings be if she knew exactly who he was? He didn't trust that she would be pleased to realize he'd been gulling her for the past several days.

At last, he found himself with a bit more control over his lust, but he didn't move close to her. He didn't have that much of a hold on himself. Her story. He needed to know her story. "Elise, you ran away over a man, no?"

"No." She swung her gaze back to him. "I left because I believed my sister had betrayed me. Yes, Michael was involved . . . but he doesn't matter. I thought having him would mean I would be out of the fray. Actually, to be candid, I wasn't comfortable with all the attention. I would dance with a gentleman once, and the next day he would appear on our doorstep with an ode pledging undying love. It was nonsense. The trip to London, the scheme to marry dukes, that was all Dara's dream. Because my cousin had taken over Wiltham, Gwendolyn and I went along. What else were we to do? We couldn't stay behind. We are sisters."

Clarity was a strange thing. It appeared at the least expected moments, as it did now. He was ready to stop running. "Elise, you are going to return to your life." As he would his. "We both will."

She reacted as if he'd struck her. "You are not hearing what I'm saying. Kit, I wish to be with you. My life in London means nothing to me."

"You deserve better than what a fellow like me offers."

"You are wrong. From the moment we met, you have been the noblest man of my acquaintance."

He frowned. "I am no hero."

"You are to me. No matter what has happened or how much we have disagreed or what I've done, you've guided and protected me. You were even the one to stop that kiss. I would have gone further, Kit. I—" She paused, met his eye. Even in the moonlight he could see her question herself and then she rose to her feet.

"I'm Elise Lanscarr, a homeless Irish lass, possibly an orphan. See? There is nothing special about me. However, the one lesson I learned from my father that matters is that when you have found something good, hold on to it. You are *my* choice, Kit." She paused. "I pray you return my feelings?"

God help him, he did. And he needed to tell her the truth. To be honest with her. Wasn't that what she said she valued?

Before he could speak, Elise reached behind her and pulled the laces of her dress loose. The gown dropped from her shoulders. The tips of her breasts stopped it from falling to her feet. Thin white material clung precariously. One shrug of her shoulder and she would be naked in front of him.

And he wanted what she was offering. He wanted to know if her nipples were pink and rosy or dark brown. To admire the indentation of her waist and the golden triangle he knew was there. He wanted to hold her, make love to her, watch her laugh, and ease that little worry line that appeared between her brows. In short, he wanted all of her.

But if he took her, if he despoiled her, she'd be ruined. There were those who would already label her damaged goods because she'd been in his company unchaperoned for so long.

Aye, he could protect her with his name, but she would be losing the freedom to make her own choices. If Elise knew everything about him, she might not be so anxious to declare herself to him. She could end up being trapped by Society's standards.

He walked across the room to her. Her eyes grew rounder the closer he came. She lifted her chin as if determined to see this thing through.

Kit reached out, took hold of the shoulder of her gown, and pulled it up. It was the hardest thing he'd ever done in his life.

Then he admitted very quietly, "I care for you too much to let you do this, Elise." He turned and left the room.

ELISE SANK TO the bed, her legs shaking.

What had just happened? She didn't understand.

She had offered him everything . . . and he had turned her down?

He'd said he cared for her, but there had been heaviness in his voice. This did not make sense.

She had taken a huge risk. And then, just as she'd believed he returned her feelings, she'd lost it all. It was because she'd been too bold, she told herself. That was why he'd left. She shouldn't have been so honest with her emotions.

Elise lay back on the bed. She looked up at the ceiling. She turned the memory of their kiss and his words over and over in her mind. He was not like those oafish lords who made declarations that had no meaning.

No, Kit had thought out his words.

She rolled to her side, curling into a fetal position. The bed felt very empty. How did one miss something they had never had?

It was her last thought before she fell asleep, full of regret and exhausted by loss.

The next morning, she woke shortly after dawn. Kit had not returned to the room.

Elise was careful with her toilette. She wanted to be at her best, even if her hair was just worn in a braid. She went to the door, not certain what to expect when she left the room.

The cottage was a small one. She heard sounds around the hearth. Kit was there along with the Forkners. They seemed all in good spirits. They were eating porridge. A bowl was prepared for her.

"I hear your man was lucky last night," the elderly man said.

"Lucky?" Elise inquired, looking to Kit.

His expression was calm, but there was a distance. "I won," he admitted. "Enough to lease a carriage to see us to Moorcock."

"Then we shall arrive in style," she answered, equally distant.

And that is how they treated each other, as if they were strangers.

Kit hired a vehicle from the small posting house and brought it back for her. They set off for Moorcock. Kit drove and Elise sat inside the open-air vehicle. Tamsyn ran alongside until she was tired and then begged to ride with them. She happily curled up on the seat beside Elise.

They were continuing their journey, but the search for her father was no longer uppermost in Elise's mind.

No, she was dreading the moment she and Kit parted.

She feared it would come too soon.

# CHAPTER SEVENTEEN

*When the apple is ripe, it will fall.*
IRISH PROVERB

They had stopped to stretch their legs.

The leased carriage had seen better days. The springs were loose and it might have been an easier ride if they had sat on hardwood boards. No wonder the owner had been willing to let Kit drive off with it.

Elise didn't complain. Her mind was elsewhere. She was glad for the presence of Tamsyn. The dog allowed them to pretend to act normal with each other.

However, after an hour or so of travel, her thoughts began eating away at her. She had attempted to discuss the night before. There was so much that didn't make sense.

But Kit had not responded to her questions. He'd changed the subject, talking about the weather, asking her questions about the roadside flowers, and teasing her about always wanting to know too much.

Finally, she'd given up.

She'd decided she would just not talk to him at all, and that is how they had traveled for the last two hours.

Elise had needed this stop. She walked a bit of a ways and then returned. That small amount of exercise did her good.

Kit was throwing a stick for Tamsyn. The dog never tired of the game. "Are you ready?" he asked upon her return.

"Do we have much farther?"

"Actually, no. A half hour, a little less."

Elise nodded. She reached for the handle of the carriage to help herself in. Kit was by her side in a blink.

"Here, let me." He offered to take her hand.

"I'm fine," she said, ignoring his help.

He made a face. Then, instead of speaking to her, he spoke to the dog. "There is that word again, Tamsyn. She is *fine*."

Elise pretended she didn't hear him. She rearranged her skirts. Actually, she was heartily tired of traveling. She didn't know how Kit could make a life of "wandering."

A new thought struck her. Perhaps Kit believed she would expect him to change. That she would expect him to give up his aimless travels. Would she?

*That* was a humbling thought. Elise hadn't

considered it before. She did now and acknowledged that she had no desire to lumber around from village to village. Or to live off of whatever he could win.

When she was younger, she'd wondered why they couldn't travel with their father. Now she knew. It would be too much for her father to follow wherever luck took him with three daughters in tow. Nor would she wish to raise children that way.

In truth, she'd never thought about a future beyond what was expected of her. She'd assumed she would have children, but she hadn't considered the matter very deeply. Could she trundle her babies around like a peddler's wife—?

The carriage leaned as Kit climbed in. "This is for you," he said. "Tamsyn and I found it." He offered the feather from a jay's wing. He twirled the black-and-white feather with its cap of vivid blue between two fingers. "For your hat."

When she didn't move toward it, he added, "You adorn your hats with feathers, no? Isn't that what you and your sisters do?"

For a moment, Elise feared she would break down into tears. This was a perfect gift. A feather, a simple, humble, beautiful feather from a man who would soon fly away. "I think you are a fool, Kit Cox."

He looked down at the feather. "I might agree with you."

"But that doesn't change anything, does it?"

"It can't." He held up the feather, offering it again. This time she took it. He picked up the reins.

While he snapped the reins to send the horses forward, she removed her hat. The feather was five inches long. She wove the quill into the straw until she believed it was attached securely. What was needed was a hat band. Then she could sew the ribbon and always keep the feather secure. Just as she wished to hold Kit forever.

She ran a finger along the feather's edge, admiring its complex pattern. She would probably wear this feather on every hat she owned from now on.

Elise put on the straw bonnet. Last night, Kit had said they would each have to return to their lives. She pondered his words a moment before saying, "Three questions?"

"The game again." He didn't sound happy.

She didn't care. "We have to pass the time."

"You can do that humming thing you do. You know, where you don't have any melody."

Elise tilted her head in mock offense. "I'll have you know I've been humming an extremely popular Irish jig."

"Now I know why they kept it in Ireland," he quipped, and in spite of herself, she laughed.

The reserve between them broke. First the feather, then the teasing . . .

"Three questions," she pressed, holding up three fingers like a promise.

"Nothing about last night." It was a statement, not a question.

She nodded her assent.

"Go on then." He sounded like a man facing the gallows.

"I asked this question yesterday. You never answered so, I'll ask again—have you learned any lessons while pretending to be Prince Hal?"

"I wasn't pretending to be a prince," he said. "I was following his example."

"I understand. But wasn't it Prince Hal's experiences that made him a good king? So, I'm asking if you gained any insight into your own life."

He was quiet for so long, she began to believe he was going to ignore her, and then he said, "I learned there are good people in all walks of life. I've met yeomen who were more noble-minded than their lords. I've also come to realize that for every good person, there is a cheat, a trickster, or an unscrupulous lawyer lying in wait."

Kit fell silent and she thought he was done when he said, "I learned I don't want to be one of the latter."

"Was there a danger in that?"

"Your second question, Miss Lanscarr," he pointed out. "*Was* there a danger? Yes. I'd become selfish. A selfish man is an unpleasant soul."

Such honesty. How could she not love such a man?

"One more question," she said, her voice quiet. "Last night, you said we would both have to return to our lives. Where will you return, Kit? Who will you be?"

❈❈❈❈❈

WHO WOULD HE be?

That was the heart of the matter, wasn't it? The reason he had not returned to Smythson by now.

He could have told Elise other lessons that he had learned—that women and children were not protected under the law. He had not needed Elise's experience or her complaints to be convinced that was wrong. He'd always believed that men should inherit, until he'd witnessed cases such as her own where families were turned out because they received nothing. Just as her cousin had treated her and her sisters.

He'd seen children as young as four doing repetitive dangerous work under stern masters because their families needed money. In every vale was a widow who could barely feed her children now that the husband was dead.

During his travels, he'd met freethinkers and clergymen who declared it was time for a change in this country. They hadn't known they were talking to a man who had rarely taken his seat in the Lords as was not only his right but his responsibility. Kit had been too immature to rise to the task. He had not realized how much it mattered.

Elise had played a part in changing that. She didn't know the meaning of the word *indifference*. And he was grasping how his apathy about his responsibilities had hurt the very people whose plight touched his heart.

He was also aware that there were always men like Holbert willing to take advantage.

Of course, he had never had a full grasp of what it meant to work hard for one's bread. Smythson had treated their tenants and workers fairly, or so Kit had believed. He and his mother had left daily matters up to Smythson's factors and agents. Everyone had seemed well-fed and happy.

However, supporting himself through his work, hiring on here and there with the harvest or planting, had brought home the harsh realities of life. He'd come to remember incidences and reports he'd received as Winderton—reports that had never really interested him, to be honest. And Kit suspected that his estate had been like any of the others that he'd hired onto during his rambles. As owner of Smythson, all Kit had wanted to know was that he had money, and he hadn't been particularly interested in the details.

Over the past year, he'd come across estates where the owner was very interested in farming methods. Those estates had been the envy of their neighbors. He'd also realized there was a new class of landowner rising across the country comprised of merchants, nabobs, and builders.

They were often better stewards of their property than landed lords.

Elise watched him expectantly. She was waiting for an answer, and he smiled. If her sisters were like her, then the Lanscarr sisters were probably setting the wagging tongues of the *ton* on fire. He was sorry he had missed it.

"When I return," he answered her, ignoring the first part of her question, "I'm not certain whom I will be."

Her lips twitched as if disappointed. She spoke. "You are hard on yourself."

"And you think that because—?"

She touched his arm. "I think you had reason for why you left. You already have said you wished to be a better man. That is more than what I have wanted. I left because my feelings were hurt."

He nodded, and could have confessed that he had run with exactly the same excuse, except Tamsyn barked, pulling their attention from each other. She had been following her nose and disappearing into the surrounding country a time or two. She now trotted happily back to them.

"We are reaching Moorcock," Kit said, nodding to the stone roofs in the distance.

Elise sat up in anticipation, and they fell silent as they concentrated on reaching their destination.

The day had grown cloudy. Moorcock was much like any other village they had passed through. There were stone cottages with moss-covered roofs, gardens, and children playing.

The ruins of a small church stood tall and quiet as a sentinel at the far end of the village.

But there was also a difference. Several taverns lined the streets. More than one would expect for a village of this size.

Closer now, one could see that the stone walls between gardens were crumbling. And there were no flowers, no climbing roses or tall larkspur. Pigs and chickens ran loose while mangy dogs watched them without making a move toward them.

"Tamsyn, up here," Kit ordered.

The dog jumped into the carriage. Elise put her arm around her. "This is . . . different," Elise said.

"Moorcock is its own place. It draws gamblers, petty thieves, and, strangely, religious fanatics of all sorts."

"Why were you here?"

He grinned. "Do you mean, which category did I fit in? I came here because someone told me we all end up in Moorcock or a place like it from time to time. They say the village was taken over by Cromwell's deserters and it hasn't changed much. It is a good place to sell a stolen silver plate or my lady's jewelry. Rumor is Gentleman Bristow made his home here until they caught him. No one in Moorcock gave him up." Gentleman Bristow had been an infamous highwayman.

"Why would my father be here?"

"I don't know about your father. However, Old John is here because the play is always good."

Kit stopped at a posting inn called the Thorn and Thistle. The placard was of a hand with a nail-shaped thorn through the palm. The inn was a dilapidated-looking place, with no flowers surrounding it and a shutter hanging from one hinge.

A stable lad ambled over to them. Kit started giving him instructions on the horse and carriage, but the boy completely ignored him. Instead, he was rudely ogling Elise. Kit clapped him on the shoulder with such force that the lad jumped, and *then* he listened.

Once finished, Kit tapped his leg. He'd taught Tamsyn that this was a command to follow him. The dog learned quickly. Kit then offered Elise his arm and escorted her into the inn.

"I want to meet my father as soon as possible," she said.

Her statement didn't surprise him. Instead, he turned his attention to the lean man coming out of a back room to greet them. He had a bald pate with tufts of hair going every which way over his ears. He reacted in surprise. "Cox! I didn't think we'd see you again for some time. If ever."

"I didn't imagine myself returning," Kit said, taking the man's hand. "How are you, Runyon?"

"Well enough. Did you shake Holbert? I've never seen a man so angry."

"He's not here, is he?"

"He hasn't been since he and his friends took out after you." Runyon's eye had drifted toward Elise.

"She's my *wife*, Runyon," Kit said. He immediately fell into the ruse. She was going to need protection in Moorcock.

The man snapped his wandering gaze back to Kit. "Wife? You?"

"Me," Kit said, holding out his hands as if to prove he had no tricks. "We need rooms."

"I have them. One."

Kit mulled that over quickly. Two would be safer for his peace of mind around Elise. However, this was Moorcock. He needed to watch over her. Which meant another night on the floor. Or pretending they'd been in a fight and sleeping on the floor in front of the door.

Either way would be on the floor.

"Come this way," Runyon said. He took them up the stairs at the back of the inn, Tamsyn with them. The Thorn and Thistle was not the sort of place to quibble about a dog, or clean linens, or sweeping the floor.

However, Elise seemed too preoccupied to notice.

Nor was their room anything special. Unlike last night's stay, Runyon didn't fetch water. There wasn't even a basin to hold it, and the hay-stuffed mattress slumped in the middle.

Elise surveyed the sparse furnishings, although Kit didn't think she was truly seeing the room for what it was. She proved him correct when she faced Runyon. "Where may I find Old John?"

The funniest expression crossed Runyon's face. "Is she serious?" he asked Kit.

"She is."

"Well, today is what—Thursday? He'll be at the Devil's Door. It is one of our choicest establishments. Although, Cox, I don't think she should go there. You know why."

Kit did indeed.

Elise made no comment. She was focused on her mission. Other than the name of the gaming hell, Kit doubted if she'd registered anything else.

He pressed a coin into Runyon's hand. "Thank you. And if by some chance Holbert does make an appearance, don't tell him I'm here."

Runyon touched his finger to his nose and left. Kit shut the door while Tamsyn jumped up on the bed. She sniffed it as if she wasn't certain of it either.

"Why is this Holbert angry with you?" Elise asked.

So she had been paying attention. "I turned loose a young woman he had plans to sell in Manchester."

Elise startled. "*Sell?* As if she was a slave?"

With a sigh, Kit recounted the story. "Holbert owes money to a group of men whom one shouldn't cross. To pay off the debt, he kidnapped this lass with the idea to sell her."

"*Kidnapped?* He'd kidnapped her?"

Kit agreed this did sound bad. "Yes, and she

didn't want to be kidnapped. She was just some country lass who believed Holbert's promises, and when she realized what he was about, he had her tied up. I helped her escape. Quite naturally, Holbert is upset with me because the man he owes money to is not very understanding. That's why I left Moorcock. Holbert had some idea about killing me. He said I hurt his reputation."

"Well, that isn't good," Elise said, sounding slightly shocked.

"I didn't think so," Kit agreed.

"But good for you for freeing that girl," she continued stoutly, apparently ignoring the part about killing. "Did she make it home safely?"

"If she did as I instructed, she did." Then he'd purposely drawn Holbert out so that the man would chase Kit instead of chasing after her.

Elise looked around as if finally noticing the shabbiness of their surroundings. "I don't think I like this place."

"I'm not fond of it either. But it is the best in the area."

"Oh dear," she said under her breath.

"We could leave—" Kit offered, but she cut him off.

"Where is this Devil's Door?"

"Down the road."

The worry line appeared between her brows. "Will you come with me?"

"Of course." He'd had every intention of

following her every step of the way since the moment she'd insisted on this ill-advised trip.

She walked over to the door. "Tamsyn will stay here?"

"I wouldn't want her out there."

Elise nodded her agreement. "Let me change. I can't see my father wearing everything I own."

Kit bowed out. A moment later, she came out into the hall. She wore the blue day dress and the straw hat. She had rebraided her hair.

Outside, he led her to the Devil's Door. The place was as dingy as the Thorn. But then, men didn't need much to gamble. Many could go without drink or food once they started playing.

Several tables of men were already seriously at it when Kit and Elise arrived. There was also a faro table but no one sat there.

The owner was a brute of a man named Davis. Kit put a protective arm around Elise and a smattering of coins on the table next to where Davis stood. "Where is Old John?" he asked for Elise.

"Not here yet." Davis shot him a side-eye. "And I don't think you should be here either. Holbert was very angry."

Kit ignored the comment. "Where does Old John live?" He'd never known.

"Down the road. He has a place there. It has goats."

"Down the road *where*?" Kit pressed. "Can you give a hint to the direction?"

"Past the church." Davis shook his head. "That

is all I know. And why are you asking so many questions?"

"I owe him money," Kit lied.

Davis snorted. "Are you daft? You returned to pay Old John with Holbert on your tail?"

Kit sighed. This was becoming tiresome. "I hear that Holbert hasn't been seen around Moorcock."

"I saw him yesterday sometime."

Now this was news Kit needed. He had assumed Holbert was still chasing around England for him. "Around here?"

"Where else? I never leave this place."

Kit took Elise's arm. "Thank you, mate."

Davis slid the coins into his pocket. "You should have left Holbert's girl alone. He liked her."

Elise came alive then. "Leave her alone to be sold—?" she started in outrage.

Kit swung her toward him. "I'll remember your advice for next time, Davis. Can you forget you saw me?"

Davis grunted his response.

The second he and Elise were out the door, she whirled on him. "I think *you* need to return to the inn. We don't wish this Holbert to find you."

"If Holbert is around, it is too early in the day for him to be up."

"It is the middle of the afternoon."

"Way too early," Kit agreed. "Come, the sooner we find Old John, the sooner we will be done." He took her hand and started for the old church.

"You never knew where my father lived?" she asked as they walked.

"I never cared."

Elise was quiet for a moment. "This is a strange village."

"I did warn you. And it is full of unsavory people. I'm not trying to upset you, Elise, but I fear you will be disappointed."

"And that my father is truly dead."

"Yes."

Her mouth formed a grim line. She walked for a few minutes in silence, then said, "I was so certain when I saw you use that shuffle." She shook her head. "Now, being here in this place." She shivered. "It's uncomfortable."

"That is one of the nicer things I could say about Moorcock."

"If we do find my father, we must take him away from here."

Elise was nothing if not persistent. And loyal. Kit bit back a heavy sigh.

They walked past the church ruins. As they left the village proper, there were several cottages, but no goats.

Some twenty minutes later, they came upon the drive for a small country house. It was not more than fifteen feet off the road with high, overgrown hedges guarding it from view. It was a respectable, albeit somewhat shabby establishment. There was not a bit of grass around it.

Both he and Elise might have walked on by

but Kit heard the bleat of goats. "Elise," he said, surprised, "we may have found the house."

She turned, her focus still on the road ahead, and then she heard the goats. She moved to the drive's entrance and started down it. Kit trailed behind her.

The house was not large, perhaps six rooms at the most, and it had two floors. Kit caught a glimpse of a makeshift barn fashioned out of twigs and saplings off to the side of the home. The bleating was constant and the air smelled of goat, something Kit had never been close to before. However, this was far better quarters than he had imagined Old John living in.

Elise walked right up to the weathered wood door. Kit stayed back a few feet, wanting to be prepared for whatever happened. Elise didn't seem to notice he was not right behind her. Or perhaps she felt she didn't need him.

Well, she did—and he was there.

However, before she could lift the darkened brass knocker, the door opened and Old John started out.

He was a tall fellow with broad shoulders stooped with age or from spending time bending over cards and dice. His face was craggy and worn. He had a long, hooked nose and the sharp blue eyes of a seasoned gamester. There was absolutely no resemblance between the man and Elise.

Old John reacted surprised to see someone on

his step. He made an awkward sound and moved back, just as Elise stiffened and then gladly cried, *"Papa."* She followed him into the house.

Kit stood a moment, stunned by what had just transpired. *Old John truly was her father?* It didn't make sense, but before he could act, the door shut and he was on the outside.

## CHAPTER EIGHTEEN

*An empty sack does not stand.*
IRISH PROVERB

*He was alive.* Elise couldn't believe her eyes. Her father, the one she had grieved as dead, *stood* in front of her.

And what a good house he had. Granted, it was not as fine and large as Wiltham; however, the floors were wood, the walls plaster, and there was a sense of hominess in the furnishings. Stairs led from the front hall to another floor. The scent of cooking food drifted toward where they stood. Over his shoulder, she saw into a dining room with pewter plates set around the table as if ready for a family meal.

When her father had been missing for longer than a year, Elise and her sisters had imagined all sorts of terrible things happening to him. He'd always talked of returning to the Indies, where he'd once served the king and been married to

Gwendolyn's late mother. The tropics were a haven for the worst sort of diseases. Could he have been struck ill? Or even lost at sea?

Dara believed he might be on the Continent. He'd once told them of traveling through Holland and Belgium. The sisters had feared that, out of patriotic duty to his country, he had jumped into the battle of Waterloo. He might be one of the many buried where they lay.

Then Gram had died and their grief had seemed never-ending.

In spite of their father being declared dead, it hadn't seemed true, not to Elise. When things at Wiltham were upsetting, she would lie awake at night imagining him in the Americas. Far away, where it was hard for him to reach them. He didn't know about Gram's death or cousin Richard claiming the estate. He couldn't send money. The Americas were too far away. And there were wars and native uprisings and all sorts of danger that would make traveling home to Wicklow impossible.

However, none of the sisters had pictured their father in England.

And yet, here he was.

He'd aged quite a bit. Elise reached up as she had done as a child. Her hands easily landed on his shoulders. He stooped now as if the world was heavy. He'd also missed several spots shaving, and the wrinkles on his face had multiplied.

But he was still her beloved Papa. The one who

had swept in and out of her life with presents
and stories before leaving just as quickly.

Tears, happy ones, filled her eyes. "I told everyone you weren't dead. I knew it in my heart."

"Elise?" He spoke as if he hadn't recognized
her until this moment.

Well, that was to be expected. She was twenty,
grown up. She began chattering. There was so
much she needed to tell him.

"You are not going to believe all that has
happened. Dara's married to a very good man.
He's an MP, an Irish one. Can you imagine? We
traveled to London to take part in the Season
because your cousin Richard claimed Wiltham.
You remember him? You never liked him. I don't
think you knew his wife, Caroline, but she is *odi-
ous*. We couldn't stay at Wiltham. They kept trying to marry Gwendolyn off to sluggish men. I
think her suitors were paying Richard to marry
her. You should see Gwendolyn now, Papa. She
is beautiful and lords queue up to dance with
her. They dote on me as well, but I—hmm . . .
we don't have to talk about that. Suffice it to say,
I found you. *I found you.*"

She ended by hugging him. Her papa was safe.

And then a door opened and closed in the
back of the house. A male voice called, "Father? Are you still here? If so, come and look at
this pony . . ."

The voice trailed off even as her papa grabbed
her arms and removed them. He placed them at

her sides before turning. Elise looked in the direction of the booted steps coming their way.

"I was just leaving, Charles," her father said.

Charles came into the hall. He was about Elise's age, perhaps a year older or maybe more. He had dark curls, very much like Dara's. His face was lean with a strong nose. Her father's face. But his eyes were green.

His brows came together. "We have a visitor?" he asked.

"Someone from my past," her father answered.

The words confused Elise. Someone? Just *someone*?

"Does Mother know we have a guest?"

Before her papa could answer, there was the clatter of feet running across the floor above. A door in the hallway not far from where Charles stood opened. A dark-haired woman of some forty years of age in a mobcap enter the hall. "Oh, Charles, supper will be served within the hour. I had so wanted it ready before your father left—"

Her voice broke off as she looked toward the front door where Elise and her papa stood. She was a handsome woman with hips that had borne children and an expression that didn't suffer fools.

Elise took a step aside from her father.

The footsteps from the floor above came charging down the stairs, accompanied by laughing. Two boys of perhaps eight or ten years of age, one trying to hold a hat away from another, came to a tumbling halt almost at Elise's feet.

And from the room across the hall, a sitting room, a lad who was a few years younger than Elise entered through another door, a book in his hand.

They all looked like her father, although there were some subtle differences. But Elise realized that if they were queued up beside her, save for her light coloring, she would fit in.

The woman spoke. "John, you didn't say we had company." She came forward. "Who is here? Please, make introductions."

The younger boys had scrambled back, the hat forgotten. The one with the book now stood in the doorway between the hall and sitting room, gaping at Elise. Charles had moved to the dining room door, his gaze sharp and distrusting.

Her father acted confused. "I—ah . . ." He blew air out from his cheeks.

Elise faced him, waiting for what he would reply, uncertain as to what this all meant.

There was an awkward silence.

Her father opened his mouth to speak, his brows coming together. "I don't—" he started.

The woman cut him off. "Never mind," she said briskly. And then to Elise, she added, "John was never one for manners. He was in the military but you wouldn't know it. He spends too much time in Moorcock. He makes a good living, but there are those in that village who are not good influences." There was a coldness in her eyes, as if she suspected Elise was from Moorcock. "I'm Sally Lanscarr. You know my husband. Did you meet my son Charles?"

*Lanscarr?* Husband? Uncertain, hoping she wasn't mistaking the matter, Elise looked to her father, whose gaze had dropped to his boots.

"We weren't introduced, Mother," Charles answered. He was well-spoken, and there was the air of a country prig about him.

Deep inside Elise could hear her heart drumming, the sound growing louder and louder in her ears.

Meanwhile, *Mrs.* Lanscarr made introductions. "My son Charles is here with us for the moment. He's purchased his colors. He is going to be a military man like his father. He leaves in a few days." She walked over to the younger boys. "This is William and this is Michael. And, in the doorway, is our John." She spoke with a mother's pride.

Her attention shifted to Elise. "And you are?"

She was *shocked* was what she was. *Astounded. Hurt.* Those words and more roiled through her.

Elise swung her gaze to *Mrs.* Lanscarr. Yes, introductions *should* be made. She lifted her chin. "I'm Miss—"

"*Faircloth,*" her father cut in, finding his voice. "Sally, my dear, this young woman came to me with the hope that I could help her."

"Help her? In what way?"

"Well," her father said, "she is collecting for the Vale Society."

"Oh, the parish box," Mrs. Lanscarr said. She sounded as if she didn't trust her husband.

She shouldn't.

"We can talk about it as I go to Moorcock," Old John said, his hand moving to shepherd Elise out the door.

Mrs. Lanscarr stepped forward. "Must you go, John? You did well last night. Can you not be with us this evening? The table has been set." She nodded to the dining room.

"Ah, love," he said, sounding as if he hated to disappoint her, even if he must.

Mrs. Lanscarr's eyes dropped to his hand on the door handle. "Charles will be gone soon. Please *stay*."

Elise felt as if she was an intruder. The boys all eyed her with suspicion.

And she thought about how triumphant this moment should have been for her. She had envisioned returning to London and sharing with her sisters that she'd found their father. It would help remove the sting and embarrassment over her impulsive actions in running away. They would be happy with her then and she'd not be forced to explain herself.

But what she'd discovered was worse than if he'd been dead. He had another family.

A family he had apparently abandoned her and her sisters for.

All that time she, Gwendolyn, and Dara had thought he was traveling the world going from one game of cards to another, he'd actually been in Moorcock—with his *sons.*

Her father was again studying the toe of his boot. He hadn't answered his wife. He wasn't making a move to appease her either.

What had he called Elise? Miss Faircloth?

She'd be damned if she accepted that deception.

Elise found her voice. "I am Miss Elise Lanscarr. Sir John's youngest daughter." Each word was strong and steady.

Did they understand what that meant? That he had a family they hadn't known about?

Or did it even matter to them?

Suddenly, Elise felt hollowed out. There was no time to fully grasp the import of what she suspected. Some of it was too volatile for her to consider—especially at this moment with all eyes on her.

Her courage spent, but her pride still intact, Elise pushed her father's hand away from the handle, opened the door, and left the house.

For the briefest second, she stood on the step. Kit had been right. She shouldn't have come. She should have left things as they were.

She walked down the step and moved toward the road—

"*Elise.*"

Kit's voice surprised her. She'd forgotten about him.

She turned. He had been waiting by the corner of the house. He walked toward her.

"Is everything well?" he asked, concerned eyes searching her face.

A simple question. She didn't know how to answer, especially standing where they could both be seen by anyone looking out the window. There were emotions bubbling inside of her that defied words.

So, she took the only action she could. She lifted her skirts and began running. She raced to the road and into the tree line. She ran through the woods, almost slipping on pine needles before reaching the hardwoods. She couldn't draw a full breath because her chest was tight with *betrayal*. But she did not stop. She kept going because she *wanted* her lungs to explode. Wanted something to take away the shame. Once more she had *believed* and she'd been deceived.

That seemed to be the story of her life.

People lauded her looks and yet no one saw her heart. No one cared for her. Least of all her father, whom she'd idolized. He'd been the center of her world. Even when he wasn't there, he'd been a presence.

But now she understood his absences. Why had he needed to return to Wiltham and his daughters? Why, when he had *sons*?

And one of them he'd obviously had while still married to her mother. How convenient of her to die soon after Elise was born. She'd saved him from bigamy—unless there were more wives and children out there?

Her thoughts were dark—her world careening out of control. She fell into a walk, pushing herself so that she wouldn't think, wouldn't *feel*. What would she say to her sisters? They had trusted him as much as she had.

They'd all been proud to be his daughters.

Elise came to a halt. She could go no farther. She leaned against the rough bark of a tree, a stitch in her side, and forced herself to do nothing but breathe.

Her heartbeat returned to normal. A bead of sweat rolled down her spine . . .

Her father was a liar. A deceiver. She was certain *Sally* hadn't known of his other family.

Other questions crowded her mind—could she be a bastard child? Her? The Belle of London? Or Dara, MP Brogan's wife?

Hopefully Gwendolyn, whose mother had been their father's first wife when he was stationed in the Indies, escaped this taint of scandal.

Elise pushed away from the tree and realized she was in a small clearing. It was green and lush and there was a woodland pond with a mossy bank, water reeds, and dragonflies.

She walked to the edge of the pond. The sky was turning the rosy shade of twilight and the colors were reflected in the water. The calming water.

Elise bent and touched the surface with her fingers, watching the ring of light ripple, and suddenly she began laughing. She couldn't control herself. She doubled over she laughed so hard, her hands pressing into the soft bank.

Kit's voice asked from behind her, "Elise, are you all right?"

She rose, her palms muddy. "Of course you followed me," she said through her laughter, but there was no mirth in the sound now. "Kit and Tamsyn—I can trust you. But no one else. Oh, no. Those closest to us always betray us."

And then the laughter changed. It became a howling, angry, vicious cry against the world.

Kit was in front of her in a beat. He took her by the arms. "What is it?" he asked, his voice gentle. She closed her eyes against him. Oh, he was going to pity her. She *should* be pitied.

She steadied herself, his touch helping her regain control over her crazed emotions. "*Was* he your father?" he asked her.

Elise nodded and pulled away from him. She marched the length of the pond and back, trying to settle herself. She found her voice. "It was him."

"Then what is wrong?" Kit asked.

In response, Elise sank to the grassy ground. A sob rose from deep within her. The sound was almost inhuman.

Kit was on his knees in front of her in a blink. He took her in his arms and she dove into his chest, holding him as if she would collapse without him.

And she gave in to those deep heaving sobs.

A Lanscarr never cried—or so her "father" had told them. But the truth was, she'd cried over him many times. She had cried every time he'd left. She wept when he'd been declared dead. He'd been important to her. Now, he was *nothing*.

Kit pulled her closer. He repeated softly, "Go on. Let it out."

She did. Years of disappointment and confusion poured out of her. She wished she didn't know what she knew now. She wished she could deny it. But wishing didn't change what was true.

That was the lesson she was learning, wasn't it? Life never met expectations.

And the best thing she could do was accept the reality—whether it was losing Wiltham to a male cousin or that her father was not the man she'd imagined him.

She took hold of herself. They sat on the ground. She was in his lap, tucked into the shelter of his arms and chest. She sat up, faced Kit. "He has another family."

If she had blackened Kit's other eye, he could not have reacted with more surprise. "Another family?"

"Yes." She took a deep steadying breath. "All these years Gram and my aunt Tweedie took care of us because father was serving his country and then later—" She lifted her shoulders, dropped them. "We were told to accept him the way he was. That was what Gram said. He was the man Mother married." Another bubble of hysteria threatened her. "She probably didn't know he was married to another woman as well."

"What?"

His kindness, his willingness to listen were what she needed right now. She curled her hands resting against his chest into fists. "He has children. The oldest is my and Dara's age. They are all *sons*, Kit. He chose them over being with his daughters. Apparently, he tried to split himself between two families and then finally, he chose one. It wasn't mine."

"But what of this Wiltham? Doesn't he own the estate?"

She shrugged. "Gram, the overseer, and the factors ran it. There was not much money in it. Wiltham paid its bills and little else. I don't know why he chose to just stop visiting . . . he could have abandoned them and come to us. He didn't. Instead, he let us believe he was dead. That is hard to accept. He let us grieve. We lost our home. *And*," she stressed, "we were being sold off to suitors and had to make our own way to London and try to create lives for ourselves. *And* all this time, he was here with *his* sons." Shock was giving way to anger. "That is the way of the world, isn't it? Women don't matter."

"Not everyone is like him—"

"I thought my sisters and I mattered to him," she cut in, the tears in danger of flowing again. "I thought *I* mattered."

"You do matter, Elise." He wrapped his arms

around her and gave her a fierce, tight hug. "You matter very much."

"But not to him." She bowed her head but he cupped her face with his hands forcing her to look at him.

"*To the devil with him.* He is of no account." Gray eyes searched hers. "Do you understand? You are worth a million of your father. And his sons? They will be like him. Entitled and lazy."

"He has a nice house." She felt she must point that out, although Kit was saying all the right things.

"The house was probably in his wife's family. Isn't that how he had Wiltham?"

"Yes, it came through his marriage to my mother."

"I wonder what the courts would say if we showed that your father was a bigamist."

Elise winced. "That is an ugly word," she whispered.

"Deceiving women is an ugly action. However, you might be able to reclaim Wiltham. Isn't this Richard related to your father?"

Elise nodded.

"Well, he had no right to Wiltham then. If the marriage is invalid because of bigamy, then he married your mother under false pretenses."

It became easier for her to breathe. "I don't know which one he married first. My mother or this Sally."

"That can be discovered."

"Except, it won't change anything. Some male on my mother's side will claim the estate. And it still won't make my father care for me or my sisters." Once more she felt as if her heart was being torn asunder. "You should have seen him. He pretended in front of his wife as if we were strangers. He tried to introduce me by another name."

"He'd been caught in his lies. He's probably incapable of honesty."

She frowned. "How could that be?"

"How could he be so selfish?" Kit clarified. "Because that is what he is. And I understand having a father who only thinks of himself. My father married a gentle, loving woman and every day he was alive, she had to pretend that his disregard didn't wound her deeply. *You* are not one to pretend, Elise. You are vibrant, bold, and unafraid to fight. Of course this hurts. You would never treat someone the way your sire has you and your sisters. You have too much integrity. I'm glad you were raised by your Gram. I'd hate to think of how little character you would have if your father had been around more."

Some of the tightness in her chest eased. He was right. Her Gram had encouraged her spirit, her love of books and ideas.

Then again, her half brothers had not appeared as if they had lacked guidance. "Charles, the one who is around my age, has purchased his colors."

"So?" Kit boldly challenged her.

She glanced up under wet lashes at him. "So . . . I don't know how much it costs to buy one's way into the ranks of officers, however, my father did not provide a dowry for any of us."

Her face felt hot. She pressed the backs of her hands against her cheeks. "His neglect stings."

"But you paid your way to London, didn't you? You managed?"

She nodded. "We've had a Season. Can you imagine? Three lasses from County Wicklow. We were going to marry dukes."

It all sounded a touch implausible—and yet, they'd made their way.

Kit's brows came together. "Dukes," he said with a sniff of disdain. She sniffed back at him, mimicking the sound—and he laughed.

The pain, the hurt began to drift away. She looked up at him. "I'm sorry, Kit."

"For what?"

"For not listening to you when you said we shouldn't go to Moorcock. For being more than a bit of a burden to you and quite exasperating—"

He kissed her fully on the lips, exactly as he had last night. Only this kiss was better . . . because she knew how to kiss him back now.

The kiss broke. His arms were around her, her breasts against this chest. He looked down and said, "Elise, never apologize for being who you are. Ever."

And on those words, he kissed her again.

# CHAPTER NINETEEN

*The cowardly man did not go to the lady.*
IRISH PROVERB

*D*amn all selfish fathers.

Kit's father had twisted his mother's heart for years. And *this*—having a second family? It was either kiss Elise or shake Old John until the bones fell out of his body.

Kissing Elise was far more pleasurable. It was also a way to show her how valued she was. He'd let harm come to her, but he would never let it happen again—because she meant that much to him. She knew him in a way no one else did. She'd accepted the wanderer Kit for exactly who he was. How could any man resist such a woman?

He understood her. He could empathize with her feelings and follow her emotions. Her disappointment was his; her pain hit him sharper than his own.

And now he felt more alive than he could ever have imagined—because she was in his arms.

Whether he wished to or not, whether it was even wise, his fingers caught the laces at the back of her dress and pulled. Elise didn't protest because her hands clasped the material of his shirt. The hem escaped his breeches, giving her access to his abdomen and chest.

Kit adored her boldness. He would have expected nothing less of her, and he wasn't about to hold back.

He carefully rolled so that she was on her back in the dry, sweet green grass, and he kissed her neck and that place right below her ear that had pleased her so much. A sharp inhale of breath and a soft sigh told him she liked it, and that was all the permission Kit needed.

Her father was of no importance. He didn't matter. *This* mattered—what was happening between them: the spark, the flame, the trust.

Running his lips up and down her neck, he drank her scent. She was fresh air, clear skies, and sun. She was the wildflowers she admired so much. She was potent, heady, and when their lips met again, it was Elise who rolled him onto his back.

She followed him, her breasts on his chest, her hips against his. Did she notice how hard he was? He was raging with need.

If she wished to stop, if she told him no?

He *would* halt. He would bring his careening

lust in line because he wouldn't do *anything* that could cause her harm. This woman meant more to him than his own life.

She'd braced herself on her hands. Her glorious hair had come loose from its braid and created a curtain around them.

She smiled down at him.

He smiled up, wanting to capture this moment to treasure in his mind.

Elise bent down. Her kiss held no reservations.

And when her tongue tentatively experimented the way it had the other day, Kit didn't hesitate to answer in kind, breathing her in, celebrating her with his desire.

He pulled her legs to straddle him. Her skirts were up to her thighs. Her heat was right over his. The only thing separating the two of them was the material of his breeches.

She placed her hands on his chest.

He placed *his* hands on her *thighs*. Her *bare* thighs. Kit wanted to kiss the insides of them. His hands moved up her legs. She didn't stop them.

Kit reached to fling an arm around her to bring her closer, the thumb of his other hand tracing small circles on her tender skin. His kisses were becoming greedier. She met him, her hunger seeming to match his own. His hands slid behind her and he cupped her buttocks. He wanted to wrap his body around her.

She shifted. "Kit, I don't know what to do next. How does this go?"

He thought she was doing everything exactly right. However, the question in her voice caught him. He sat up, bending his knees to hold her because he liked her heat.

Their faces were on the same plane. "We need to stop, Elise."

Those words were hard to say.

Her hands cupped his face. "I don't want to stop, Kit." She eased her dress down over her breasts—

Rose-hued, that was the color of her nipples. They were rosy and hard and boldly begging for his attention.

Almost reverently, he placed his palm over one. It tightened against him. Her hips shifted to sit on the length of him.

He took one nipple in his mouth and gently sucked. She whispered his name, bucking slightly and wrapping her arms around him as if to hold him there. He lifted her off of him, his mouth never leaving her breast.

Reverently, he laid her on the ground beside him. He sought out her other breast. She arched, offering herself to him. Her knees bent and her legs parted and Kit had to touch her. He needed it.

He stroked the length of her thigh to that very sweet place. She startled at the contact. He whispered, "It will be fine. I promise." He cupped his hand over her.

She turned toward him and as their lips met, he traced a small circle on that one delicate spot.

Elise moved closer. Her kiss became bolder.

He didn't want to pressure her or cause her to experience any regret. He wanted her to enjoy what they were doing. To want it as much as he did.

Kit was also aware that Elise was a virgin. He needed to think of her pleasure above all else.

He slid his fingers along those delicate folds, and to where he wanted her to open up to him.

Her arms came around his shoulders.

He broke the kiss. Their gazes met. That small worry line had appeared between her brows. He kissed it. She seemed to relax and his fingers slid inside her.

Deep muscles tightened around him. He didn't know who was more excited. "Is this all right?" he asked.

Elise nodded. She released her breath as if she'd just realized she'd held it. He touched her intimately, teaching her what she needed to know. Her gaze never wavered from his. Her trust was a gift.

Her hips began moving. She stopped as if she should be still. He kissed her shoulder and brushed his lips across her breasts. "It is all right. Let yourself feel."

Her expression turned dreamy. She nuzzled his hair. He brought his attention back to her lips and this time, he let his tongue mimic the movement of his fingers.

Her skin grew flushed. Her arms tightened their hold. "Kit?"

He found her ear, nipped the curve of it. "I'm right here. It is all good, so very, very good."

And it was.

He'd never given to a woman this way before. He'd always taken. But this was better. Her enjoyment created his.

Her knees bent. Her whole body quivered. The tension of her, the way it broke, he could feel the depth of her release, and see the beauty of it in the dazed expression of her eyes.

For a long time, they stayed in each other's arms.

"Thank you." Her voice was so hushed, he could have imagined the words.

She pushed up. She looked enticingly wanton. Her skirts were almost to her waist. The bodice of her dress was pushed down below her breasts.

It was the early evening, right as the moon was beginning its rise. A full moon.

"I hadn't imagined it would be so—" She broke off as if words failed her. Her nakedness didn't bother her. She had no self-consciousness.

Kit smiled and traced the smooth skin of her cheek. "You are a miracle."

She smiled as if both pleased and embarrassed. "Why do you say that?"

"Because," he said, half sitting up, "you make me happy."

Her eyes lit up. "That is how I feel with you." She came up on her knees and pushed her hair back. She pressed a hand against her lower abdomen. "This is so strange. My body is still humming." And then she said, "But that is not all there is?"

"Elise, we'd best not go that far." That was the hardest statement he'd ever had to make.

"Kit, I'm a country girl." She leaned toward him. Her hand brushed the length of his erection pushing against his breeches. "I know what should happen between a man and woman."

At her words, his whole body went on alert. God help him, he had unleashed a siren.

"Elise, I would not hurt you. You have a reputation to protect."

"For what? Some old duke?" She looked into his eyes. "Can't you tell that I love you? I love you in a way I've never imagined a person could feel for another—"

*Love.* She'd said it. She loved *him.* And he should be dancing for joy except, in this moment, he thought of her, of what could happen. "Elise—"

She placed her fingers on his lips. "Don't argue, Kit. Don't tell me I'm wrong or that we shouldn't or any of the 'or's' you have in mind. Here is what I know to be true—if I don't have all of you, I will die from the loss—"

"Elise—" She wouldn't die. He might, but she wouldn't, because—

"Kit, I can feel your brain coming up with so much common sense, and it doesn't matter. Nothing matters but this night. We are here together. You care for me as much as I care for you. I know that is true."

*More*, he wanted to say. He cared for her more than she could ever feel for him. His world now revolved around her. But when he started to speak, she cut him off, kissing him hard and in a way that made all of his good sense vanish.

Her lips traveled to his ear. "We shall work it out on the morrow. But for tonight, let us be completely true to ourselves."

His response was to shrug off his jacket. He tugged at the shirt she had loosened from his breeches. Almost joyfully, Elise stood. She let her dress fall to her feet. She was naked in the evening air with only her stockings and sensible walking shoes.

She looked down at herself and started to laugh.

"I see nothing amusing," he assured her, reaching to help her remove shoes and stockings. I only see your beauty. And your boldness. I admire bold woman."

"Even opinionated ones?" she asked, ending on a small gasp as he slid the last stocking off and his fingers brushed her skin.

"Especially those," he assured her.

And then, at last, they were naked—then, in the open air. Elise held out her arms. *She loved him.*

Could any man be more fortunate?

The grass beneath them was lusher, softer, and finer than any bed. He rose up over her. He never wanted to forget how beautiful she looked with her golden hair loose and spread around her.

Kit bent to kiss her temple, her ear, her shoulder. Her hands caressed his ribs and smoothed over his buttocks. He liked the way she touched him. She wasn't afraid of passion.

She wasn't afraid of life.

In fact, in the short time they'd been together, she had taught him about courage, about honesty, about openness. About being vulnerable.

He held her in his arms as he settled between her legs. He kissed her, deeply, the way they both liked. The tip of his head pressed against her sweetest spot. She gasped and, being Elise, she laughed softly as if in joy.

Kit moved the tip lower, steadying himself and then slowly entering her. She was tight and it took all his willpower to not push forward. To give her time.

Her muscles loosened as she became accustomed to him. He had reached that fragile barrier that marked her virginity.

"Ah, Elise, I'm sorry." He drove himself into her.

He felt the tear. She gave a start, a cry. He went still, held himself.

And then her lips curved into a smile, part relief and part bravery. "That wasn't so bad."

"No?"

"I was prepared for far worse."

"And how did you know?"

Her eyes sparkled in the moonlight. "Maids talk."

The response made him laugh. Her brow

lifted. "I felt your laughter. There, deep inside me. Oh, Kit, there is more, isn't there?"

Indeed, there was. He began moving slowly, his gaze meeting hers, his concentration on pleasing her.

The heat between them built. Her hips began to meet his thrusts. Her eyes darkened. She lifted herself against him.

She was going to be the undoing of him—in all ways. Elise was tearing apart his doubts, his regrets, even the arrogance that had forced him to run from all that he had once loved.

And now, she was rebuilding him. Molding him into a man he respected.

He wanted to give her everything. All of him.

Kit felt her tighten. She seemed lost, so he guided her. Paced her. And when the time was right, when he knew she was close to the pinnacle, he thrust deep and let her go.

She did. Her cry reaching fulfillment vibrated around him. Her body held him tight, tighter, and then he too was flying into his own release—and the two of them . . . the two of *them* . . . became one.

One. The thought brought the sting of tears to his eyes. He'd never grasped until this moment what it meant. But she was his; he belonged to her. Never again would he be alone. Ever. Their bodies had been joined with a force that was mystical. Wonderous. Shattering.

They lay very still. Kit's heartbeat raced

through his veins. Where their bodies were still connected, he could feel the pounding of her blood. It mirrored his own.

Elise moved first. He slid off her, suddenly aware of how heavy he might be to her. He rolled, taking her with him so she lay on top of him as languid as a cat. She looked down, her eyes slightly bemused, her lips well kissed.

"Is it always like that?"

Gently, he slipped her hair back from her lovely face. "Elise, it has never been that way before. Not since the beginning of time."

Her laugh was soft. "It was perfect, Kit." And then she added, "My ruffian." She laid her head down on his chest and he enfolded her in his arms.

Above them were the stars in a cloudless night sky. He stroked the point where her spine met her hips. He didn't know what the future held, but he did know he would never give up Elise. Never.

❈❈❈❈❈

ELISE FELT AT peace. At last the world made sense.

Fate had not set her on this trip to reach Ireland or find her father. No, she was here to fall in love with Kit.

He had not said he loved her.

Resting her head against his chest, her hips on

his, she decided it didn't matter. She wasn't reserved like Gwendolyn. She didn't measure everything like Dara.

No, she was the Lanscarr sister who plunged into life. And she had to be true to herself, no matter what the outcome. She loved him enough for both of them. She also knew the truth—he loved her as well. She'd just have to wait for him to say it.

There was stickiness between her legs. Probably blood and the life force that meant she was now a part of Kit.

He appeared to be studying the stars. She eased herself to his side and focused on them as well. "There are a million of them up there," she said.

"If the moon wasn't so bright, we could see more. This is unlike London. No one can see as many stars as possible in the sky there."

"So, you've been to London?" She drew a line back and forth on his chest, admiring the hard planes in the moonlight.

"I have."

"Another clue to the mystery of Kit Cox," she said. When he didn't offer more, she continued, "This sky is very much like Wiltham, except we have more stars."

"Of course you would believe there were more stars in your precious Ireland."

"Because it is true," she assured him. Her lover was a well-formed man. She ran her hand down his abdomen and going to parts lower—

Kit caught her hand. "What are you doing?"

"Investigating."

He laughed. She liked when he laughed. His teeth were strong and straight.

She was also mesmerized by the freedom to explore his body. There had been times when she had marveled at the way he'd moved, at his strength, and quickness. His muscles were long and lean, his arms and legs perfectly formed. Any woman would admire him, but he was hers. She'd marked him this night, just for her.

Her fingers discovered his navel. He gave them a playful slap.

She walked them lower, and he stirred. She watched, fascinated.

"You are certain you are ready for more?" His brows lifted.

"We can do that?" she asked, delighted with the possibility.

"We can," he assured her. "I could make love to you all night. Although it would be best to wait. We were strenuous and I don't want you hurt."

She understood some of his caution. She was feeling places in her body where she'd never experienced even a twinge before.

However, she wasn't ready for this night to end. What had happened between them was more than just the act of joining. It magically bound the two of them together forever.

Even the setting was enchanted. The pond was a silvery disk with the darkness of the forest all around. Their own little heaven, and Elise had a sudden inspiration. "Come," she said.

Without waiting, she stood and walked toward the water.

"What are you doing?" Kit called.

"I want a swim. The night is warm."

Kit came to his feet. "You swim?"

Elise swung around to face him. "Our father taught us. He said children in the Indies swam all the time and so his daughters would as well."

Her father. The betrayal no longer rankled. Kit's kisses had given her the sense of belonging she'd always longed for.

She waded into the water. It was cool against her skin. She took a few experimental strokes. The pond was not that deep—

A huge splash washed water over her. She turned. "Kit?" She didn't see him and then she felt a tap on her shoulder.

Elise flipped around to see him right behind her. She reached up and pushed his head down. He let her. There wasn't any possibility that she could have matched his strength.

Then she felt him come up between her legs. Elise screamed and tried to get away. He grabbed her ankle, almost upending her, but he caught her in time.

He would always catch her in time.

Kit set his feet on the bottom. For a long moment, they held each other in the pond. Kit swayed with her and she put her legs around his waist. Her heels pressed against his buttocks.

That is when she felt him stir against her.

Elise combed her fingers through his thick hair. She tucked a lock behind his ear and moved against him.

"You are incorrigible," he said, his tone low and warm.

"How else am I to get what I want?" she asked.

"No complaints in the morning," he warned her.

"Oh, I'll complain," she said. "Happily."

Kit kissed her. They made love in the water with the moon and the stars shining down on them.

When they were done, they fell upon the grassy bank, entwined in each other's arms. Elise had thought she would fall asleep. Instead, they talked. They laughed over their journeys and she dared to tell him, "I want my sisters to meet you."

His answer was a kiss, and then he said, "I will do whatever you wish, Elise."

She sat up. "I will hold you to that promise."

His laughter was deep and free. It seemed to echo around the clearing in the woods. "I'm in for it now, right?"

Her answer was a kiss.

✦✦✦

AT LAST, THEY needed to return. They dressed each other. She even managed to tie a respectable knot in his neckcloth, something she'd been wanting to do since they had first met that stormy evening.

Before the faint light of the sun could be seen on the horizon, they began walking back to Moorcock. Elise wore her hair loose. They held hands. She did not know what the future held, but she knew it included Kit.

Elise didn't look past the hedges of her father's house as they passed. She did grip Kit's hand tightly.

All was quiet in the village at this wee hour in the morning. Not even the pigs were wandering around.

"I imagine Tamsyn will be anxious for us to return," Elise said.

"We shall make it up to her," Kit agreed.

"Now I feel very selfish."

"Don't," Kit replied. He lifted her hand to his lips and kissed the back of it.

The door to the Thorn and Thistle was open. They walked past the taproom. No one was sleeping there. They started up the stairs. At the top of them, Elise heard Tamsyn whine.

She moved ahead of Kit, anxious to let the dog out. It might have been safer for Tamsyn to be shut in the room but it was not her nature.

"I feel so guilty," she said quietly to Kit and opened the door.

But Tamsyn was not impatiently waiting by the door ready to greet her.

As dawn's light streamed through the window, Elise walked in, her attention on the bed where they'd left Tamsyn, but then she came to a halt.

A large, thick-set man with a whiskered face beneath a battered top hat sat in a chair, and he wasn't alone. Two others who looked equally disreputable in their manner flanked him. One leaned against the wall. The other stood by the bed.

The man in the chair raised his brutish arm. He had Tamsyn by the scruff of her neck as if she weighed nothing. He dangled her in the air. "Are you looking for her?"

# CHAPTER TWENTY

*Never bolt the door with a boiled carrot.*
IRISH PROVERB

*P*ut her down," Elise demanded, her heart in her throat. She feared the man had done something to Tamsyn by the way she seemed to just hang in his grip.

But at the sound of her voice, Tamsyn snarled and snapped. The man laughed. He stood and gave her a hard, mean shake and Elise lunged forward—

Kit's arm came around her waist. He swung her to stand behind him.

"Damn it all, Holbert, can't you leave well enough alone?" Kit's voice was deadly quiet.

"I'm afraid I can't, Cox. You and I have unfinished business and I hate loose ends." He emphasized his words by standing and throwing Tamsyn to the wall. The dog landed with a yelp of pain.

Elise pushed her way past Kit before he could stop her and knelt by the dog. "Tamsyn?"

A golden-brown eye opened and looked at her. Tamsyn was hurt, but she moved. She tried to rise on her front feet.

Then Elise heard Holbert say, "What have we here?"

Before she knew what anyone was about, the man by the bed grabbed Elise and jerked her up. She tried to release his hold, but then he caught her hair and held her secure.

Kit was still in the doorway, his body tense. "She has nothing to do with this. I'm the one you want."

"I do want to see you dead," Holbert assured him. "And I will. You don't cross me and walk away. Do you understand?"

Elise looked to Kit, half expecting him to make some quip, but he didn't. He had never looked so serious.

"Understood." Kit raised his hands as if requesting calm. "Now release her and we shall settle this as gentlemen."

"Gentlemen of swords, right?" Holbert said with a laugh. "I don't trust you any more than you trust me. But I will say, this one is lovely. Been hearing you had a woman with you that turned heads. They said she was a nice filly, and they weren't lying. I'm partial to yellow hair."

"Actually, I didn't know your partialities," Kit

replied. "However, now that I do, let her leave the room."

Holbert walked to stand in front of Kit. "No, Cox. Since you helped my gel escape, I'm taking *yours*. This one is prettier. Brothels pay double for yellow hair."

"Trust me, you don't want this woman. She is a handful," Kit said, and as he talked, his own hand came down and touched his leg—

Suddenly, the man holding Elise screamed. Tamsyn had seen Kit's silent command for action and had sunk her teeth into the man's calf. His hold loosened. Elise didn't hesitate to shake herself free.

The man reached down to hit the dog but Elise gave him a push, costing him his balance. At the same time, Kit took advantage of the distraction and swung his fist at Holbert, punching him sharply in the center of his face.

And then he turned his attention to Elise. Kit pushed her out the door. *"Run."*

Elise didn't question the command. She started down the hall. Tamsyn charged out of the room, racing right on her heels. Elise reached the stairs and started down them when she realized Kit was not behind her. He'd stayed up in that room with those terrible men.

The door to the room slammed shut and what sounded like a body bounced off it.

However, before she could act, a tall man dressed in black from head to toe started up the stairs toward her. She looked down at him. "Please, you must help me. They are going to kill him—"

Sudden recognition in the dawn's thin light stopped her. "Mr. Steele? What are you doing here?"

"Your sisters sent me."

Elise's heart gladdened. The fabled Mr. Steele was here to help. She didn't care what his presence meant. People whispered that he could solve all problems. She hoped so. She and Kit needed support now.

Tamsyn growled at him. "Stop," she said to the dog. "Mr. Steele, there are some men who will kill my friend. Please, come help—"

Before she realized what he was about, Mr. Steele picked her up and slung her over his shoulder. "Miss Lanscarr, the time has come to return home."

He began carrying her back down the stairs and Elise went wild. *He must help.* Those men would kill Kit.

She curled her fingers into talons and ripped into him. His step faltered but he kept going. Downstairs, she rose up on his shoulder and tried to buck herself off. Meanwhile, Tamsyn attempted to bite him.

Mr. Steele kicked at the dog. *"Down,"* he ordered, but he could have been speaking to either one of them. It didn't matter. Elise wasn't going to listen, and neither was Tamsyn.

Kit needed them.

❦

IT HAD BEEN a long, frustrating journey.

Beck Steele had gone to Liverpool. He'd stopped at every village, every posting house along the way asking for Elise Lanscarr. No one recognized the name or her description.

Finally, he'd discovered the driver who had come across the wrecked coach. The man told him that the only two bodies were the driver and guard, and that there'd been a couple who had survived the wreck, but he'd had no room to take them on their way. So, he'd left them to make their way to the George.

Beck chose to ride back to the last place where a woman matching Elise's description had been seen. It was assumed the couple were man and wife, but what if they weren't?

What if some bastard was taking advantage of her?

He owed it to Gwendolyn to discover the truth. He'd returned to the George and asked more questions. This time, about the man and wife. The innkeeper Sarver told him that they'd said their family name was Cox, but he knew nothing more. He'd thought they had planned to take the next stage. Instead, they had chosen to continue along on foot.

Beck had been frustrated. They could have gone anywhere. Apparently no one saw them leave. He'd gone to fetch his horse from the stables when he decided to question the stable-master. A boy who helped around the stables overheard them. He had not been around when Beck had come through here earlier.

"Moorcock," the boy told him. "I overheard them arguing over Moorcock. It was very early in the morning. I was trying to be quiet with my chores so I didn't wake them."

Beck had pressed several coins in his hand and set off for Moorcock with all haste. Yes, he did know the place. No one could traffic in the underbelly of London and not have heard of Moorcock. It was a safe haven for those who wished to fence goods or sell a stolen horse or lose oneself in a week of gaming and not have any questions asked.

If a man from Moorcock had Elise, she was in danger—although no one he had talked to claimed that the woman acted afraid of her companion. More like, anytime someone mentioned the couple, they were arguing. Perhaps that was why everyone thought they were married. Someone even mentioned that the "husband" was not faring well in their arguments.

And Beck knew, at last, he was on the right trail. A Lanscarr woman could talk circles around any man.

Beck had hoped to reach Moorcock ahead of the walking couple. Instead, he had learned they were already there. It didn't matter. He was prepared. He had a loaded pistol in his pocket. This "husband" would let her go.

He'd also hired a driver and landau in Stoke-on-Trent and the services of a reputable woman to act as a chaperone. He had sent a messenger to the Lanscarr sisters to be ready. He had found their sister.

Except, she wasn't where he'd been told she would be.

A few coins to the owner of the Thorn and Thistle had confirmed that Cox was there. Apparently, Cox had a reputation in the village as someone who was well-liked but whom one shouldn't mess with.

Beck had gone to their room, pistol ready.

It was empty save for a shepherd's dog who barked ferociously at his intrusion. Having a healthy respect for angry dogs, he'd shut the door quickly. Instead, he'd visited the taverns and gaming dens clustered in the village. No one had seen Cox or a woman matching Elise's description, or if they had, they weren't about to tell him, not for any amount of money. Beck was a stranger here. Places like Moorcock were tight-lipped.

That was why he'd found himself hiding in the landau and watching the Thorn and Thistle. They waited down the street from the inn, not wanting to appear out of place and warn this Cox that help for Elise was nearby.

He and the landau driver had taken turns on

watch. The driver had woken him no more than five minutes ago to report that a couple had entered the inn.

Beck had thought it great luck that as he was climbing the stairs to the room, Elise had come running down them, chased by that crazed dog. But she had wanted him to help Cox?

He wasn't about to do that. He was tired. He'd chased this woman across England. She needed to go home to her sisters. When it had quickly become clear to him that she wanted to return to the room in the inn, Beck grabbed her by force.

That turned out to be a mistake.

Elise had turned into a she-devil. She tried to claw his ears off his head. She twisted and bucked, kicking at him the best she could. She almost cost him his balance several times.

And the dog was nipping at his heels. The only thing that saved him was that he wore good leather riding boots.

He kicked open the inn's front door. The landau was waiting right there. The driver, Evers, had the vehicle door open. Mrs. Banner waited inside. Beck's horse was tied to the rear of the vehicle. The hour was still too early for there to be a great deal of activity on the street.

It took almost a herculean effort; however, Beck stuffed Elise into the landau.

And she attempted to come right back out.

He grabbed her hands. "Miss Lanscarr, your sisters sent me."

*"They are going to kill him,"* she shouted right into his face.

There was a crash of glass, as if one of the inn's windows had been smashed.

*"Please, Mr. Steele, you must help him."*

"No, I must see you to London."

She whipped around, reaching for the opposite door of the vehicle. Mrs. Banner tried to stop her, except Elise gave her a hard punch in a manner very unbecoming of a debutante—and Beck realized when he was beat.

Elise would fight them all the way to London. She was that frenzied.

He reached into the vehicle, caught her arm, and yanked her around. *"Listen to me,"* he ordered in a voice that brooked no disobedience. "Your sisters are beside themselves with worry—"

"He's in danger," she responded. "Please, Mr. Steele, you must help him."

At that moment, the dog bit the driver. The man shouted in pain.

Beck swore colorfully. He faced Elise. "If I help, will you go with Mrs. Banner to London?"

"I will do anything you ask. Please, Mr. Steele, *please.*"

He stepped back. "Very well. I will help this man Cox. But you leave now. Understood?"

"Yes, sir, I do understand. Please help him."

"And this damn dog." Beck kicked back at it.

"She's mine," Elise hurried to say. "Tamsyn, come to me. Come." The dog slipped by Beck and up into Elise's arms. "She is trying to help. Kit told her to protect me."

Once in her arms, the dog watched all of them warily.

Mrs. Brunner didn't appear happy to have the dog, but she didn't say anything.

"Go now," Elise pleaded.

And that is when Beck had a suspicion about why Elise was so attached to this man. He was also surprised at his own attitude because he was incensed that some fellow had taken advantage of her. Ever since the Lanscarr sisters had knocked him over the head in a Dublin street, he'd actually felt a bit responsible for them.

Nor did he have a desire to go up the stairs to enter a fight.

Unfortunately, this is what Elise required in order for her cooperation. "Very well. I'll go save him. However, you are on your way to London, and don't give Mrs. Banner and Evers *one* spot of trouble."

"I won't, I won't. Please, Mr. Steele, help him."

He shut the door. "Are you all right, Evers?"

"The dog just nicked me. No harm."

"Good. Drive like hell to London. I shall catch up as quickly as I am able." He untied his horse from the landau and looped the reins around a post.

Elise leaned out the window. "Mr. Steele, you are wasting time."

Every man should have a woman as dedicated as Elise was to this Kit Cox. Beck didn't even like the sound of his name. Kit Cox. What a silly name.

He nodded to Evers and the landau took off.

Beck turned back to the inn. He was a man true to his word. He would rescue Cox. He'd also give him a beating afterwards. He didn't want the man close to Elise ever again.

He marched up the stairs.

The room had gone quiet except for what sounded like the steady use of fists. Beck might be too late to rescue him, but a promise was a promise.

Beck pulled the pistol from his pocket, cocked it, and kicked open the door.

It was as he feared. A heavy man used his fists on Cox's torso while another man held him. Cox didn't appear to be conscious, but he also didn't seem dead. He still stood on his feet.

Beck could say one thing—Cox could take a beating.

"You've had enough, gentlemen," he said, aiming his pistol at the man doing the pounding.

The brute rounded on Beck. "The hell I have. I'm just starting."

However, his companion was wiser. He let go, and Cox proved he was not done yet either.

Before Beck could respond, Cox came alive. Using his body as a battering ram, he tackled the heavy man, driving him all the way back to a broken window.

And then he tossed the man out it.

The man gave a shout a beat before he landed. Beck ran to the window. There was already another man on the ground. He was groaning as if bones were broken. The heavy one had landed on his back. He rolled over. "My legs," he shouted. "You broke my legs."

Cox took a wobbly step back from the window.

Beck looked at the last of the three assailants. He stood as if turned to stone. "You'd best join him," Beck advised with a wave of his pistol.

The man tore off out the door and could be heard almost falling down the stairs in his haste to escape.

Cox leaned against the wall, the morning light falling on him. He pressed the back of his hand against a split lip. Beck knew from experience that he had to be in pain.

"What did you do to them?" he asked Cox.

"It is what I wouldn't do." He pressed a thumb and forefinger against his mouth. "Thank God I still have my teeth."

"What wouldn't you do?" Beck asked, curious.

"Holbert procures for London brothels. He's angry because I helped a lass he'd kidnapped escape."

"Not Miss Lanscarr?" Beck said with a start. Did he have the story all wrong? Could Holbert have been the one they described traveling with Elise?

No. Cox's name had come up consistently and he'd seen them enter the inn together.

"No, not Elise," Cox said. "This one was younger than her. I couldn't let him have her. She was too scared. Holbert preys on country girls who yearn for something more in life."

He spoke well in spite of his bleeding lip. His face had not started swelling yet, but it would soon—and that is when Beck experienced a flash of recognition. *It couldn't be.*

And yet, this man was of the same age, the height, brown hair, gray eyes. Beck stared at the man's features. However, the missing Duke of Winderton had been described as solidly built and soft. This man was as lean and hard as shoe leather. He had taken a beating that would have destroyed someone like the duke and he was still standing. Could it be the same man?

"I must go." Cox pushed off from the wall and straightened. "I must tell Elise that she is safe—"

Those were the last words he spoke before his legs buckled and he crashed to the floor at Beck's feet.

# CHAPTER TWENTY-ONE

*God's mill may grind slowly, but it grinds finely.*
IRISH PROVERB

Kit had trouble regaining consciousness. He sensed he was swimming upward toward it, but it was a struggle. It was as if he was in a silver pool of light and Elise was waiting for him. He attempted to reach for her—

"You are awake. Good. Don't try to move right now. You experienced a vicious beating."

The haze vanished at the man's sharp words. Kit winced at them and slowly found consciousness. He squinted his eyes open. There was a candle burning on a night table. It hurt to look at it until his vision adjusted to the light.

Memory returned. He recalled tossing Holbert out the window, and he laughed.

The sound was hoarse and it hurt his ribs. Again with the ribs. He could have cursed. Only this time, he was fairly certain something was broken. Holbert had been very diligent in his attention to them. But before that happened, Kit had been giving all three of them a sound drubbing.

However, one question burned in his mind, and he called out her name as best as he could. "Elise?"

The room was dark save for the one candle. She could be here. He strained to see. *"Elise?"*

"Please, don't struggle. You are not in good shape."

That male voice again. Kit saw a shadow by the window. "Who are you?" Kit managed.

"Steele."

Kit frowned. Steele? He knew no Steele.

And exactly where was he? In Moorcock? He didn't know. He tried to think. He couldn't. His head began to pound as if he'd overexerted himself.

Booted footsteps crossed the room. A door opened. "Doctor?"

More heavy steps. Kit closed his eyes.

"He's awake?"

Steele answered, "He was."

"He won't have an easy time of it. But he will heal. He's young. Here, let us give him some more of my headache tisane."

Someone lifted Kit's head. They tried to pour liquid down his throat. It smelled of wine and something unappetizing. He turned away. He didn't need drugs. He needed to find Elise. He tried to sit up.

"He's a difficult one," the doctor said.

Strong hands grabbed Kit and held his head, tilting it back. The liquid was poured down his throat. He attempted to spit it out. The taste was bitter. "Elise—"

It hurt to speak. "I must . . ." he started, but then fatigue overtook him. He fell back on the pillow.

"I mixed a sleeping draught in with the medicine. He should be fine after some rest," the doctor whispered to Steele, and that was the last Kit remembered.

KIT OPENED HIS eyes. He expected to be in his bed at Smythson. He stared at the wall. It was plain plaster without adornment.

He was not at Smythson, and then he remembered what was important.

"Elise?" His throat felt raw. He remembered candlelight . . . and Steele.

Could he still be in the same place? Light flooded in through an open window. A bird called in the distance. How much time had passed—?

"You are awake again," a male voice said.

Kit struggled to sit up.

"Careful. You are still healing." The man sat

in a chair across the room from the bed. His jacket was off and his waistcoat unbuttoned. He was dark-haired and had almost a wolfish countenance. He was stretched out as if he had been napping in the chair. He did not appear comfortable.

"Steele."

The man acknowledged the name with a nod, and, moving stiffly, rose to his feet. "So, you do recall?"

"Elise—"

"She is fine. She should be back with her family in London by now."

Elise was in London? She was not here?

Kit had to search his mind to recall where "here" was. He remembered the silver pond, Elise telling him she loved him—what had he answered?

His mind went blank for a moment and then he remembered. He hadn't said anything. He'd been too caught up in the moment. They'd made love and once again he'd been taking when he should have been giving. What must Elise think?

"I need to find her." Kit sat up, ready to throw aside the bedclothes. Every muscle in his body contracted in pain. His head swam. He forced himself to breathe, to relax into it. "I must talk to her."

"Fortunately, that won't happen anytime soon."

"I'm sure she'll *want* to see me."

"Possibly," Steele answered. "However, you and I have unfinished business."

Kit frowned. "I've never met you before—" He paused. Or had he? "How long have I been asleep?"

"The good part of a week."

*A week? And Elise could be in London?* "Who the hell are you?"

"I told you—Steele."

"The name means nothing to me."

"It should. I was tasked with finding Miss Lanscarr. I am also the man who was hired by your family to find you, Christopher Fitzhugh-Cox, Duke of Winderton, and a merry chase you have led me on."

He revealed Kit's identity with the flair of an amateur actor proclaiming some great secret, and Kit almost laughed. After all, he'd always known who he was—

The door to the room flew open. "I heard voices. Is he better—?" Kit's mother, Lucy, the Dowager Duchess of Winderton, rushed in and then skidded to a halt when she saw him. She was dressed for traveling and hadn't bothered to take off her stylish bonnet or her gloves.

Her gaze took him in, and for a moment, Kit feared she was going to swoon. Steele must have thought so as well because he stepped to her side. "Please, sit, Your Grace."

She didn't. She held up a hand to stave him off. Huge tears filled her eyes. She'd aged since Kit had last seen her. She'd worried for him . . . and he realized the impact of his actions on her.

"Mother, I'm sorry."

She waved the words away and sank down on the edge of the bed beside him. "I'm just happy to see you safe. But, Christopher, you look horrid."

Her candidness made him laugh, something his ribs did not appreciate.

Seeing his distress, she said, "I'm so sorry. You are in pain still, aren't you? Here, drink this." She reached for the cup on the bedside table.

Kit shook his head. "I've had that. It is full of sleeping draught. I'm tired of this bed."

She set the cup down and looked across the room. "Mr. Steele, thank you for finding my son."

"It was my pleasure, Your Grace. And now, let me give the two of you a moment alone. I know you will wish to speak to Mr. Sutton, the doctor, when you are finished."

"Thank you," she answered.

At that moment, heavy steps sounded outside the door. They stopped as if they had run into Mr. Steele.

His mother smiled down at him. "That is your uncle. He came with me. We have been anxious for you."

Kit shifted in the bed. This time, he didn't wince at the pain. He was too ashamed.

And now Brandon, the uncle he had treated in a disdainful manner, had accompanied her because Kit had been so wrapped up in himself, he

had not been present to take care of his mother—
for any reason.

Or, had Brandon, too, worried?

His uncle came to the door. He was twelve
years younger than his sister Lucy. They had the
same dark hair, although hers had more gray . . .
so much gray.

Brandon paused in the doorway. His gaze
fell on Kit. His expression was stern. "We've
missed you."

Kit thought about the conversations he'd had
with Elise about family and its challenges. About
being angry with those he loved.

"I'd stand to greet you," Kit said, "but Mother
has me pinned down."

His mother gave a start and began to move,
but Kit caught her hand. "I'm teasing. I want you
here, and I couldn't stand if I wished." He looked
to his uncle. "Bran, please pull the chair over."

His uncle and mother exchanged a look. Kit
understood. It had been some time since he'd
spoken to his uncle with *any* respect.

He didn't want anger in his life anymore. He
was tired of blaming others for his own faults.
Tired of sopping grudges in a bucket of ale. The
time had come to ask forgiveness.

And then he was going to find Elise.

# Chapter Twenty-Two

*There are no unmixed blessings in life.*
IRISH PROVERB

*London*

Elise had slept most of the way to London, holding Tamsyn in her arms the entire time. She had believed the two of them worried together over Kit's fate. She'd quietly assured Tamsyn that Mr. Steele's ability to fix all problems was legendary, so he'd be able to help Kit as well.

Of course, she didn't say this so Mrs. Banner could overhear. The lady thought Tamsyn was only a dog. She was wrong.

They changed drivers three times on their trip to London and the horses more often. Consequently, they had made excellent time.

Her sisters and Tweedie had been at the door the afternoon the landau reached the house Dara and Michael had rented. The redbrick home was in a highly respectable neighborhood.

Gwendolyn ran out to greet Elise. She held one of her shawls open in her hands as if she had anticipated Elise to be an invalid. She tossed it around Elise as she hugged her. She whispered in Elise's ear, "Be watchful. Word has gone round that you are missing. We said you were merely visiting friends in the country."

Elise bubbled with laughter. She'd forgotten the silly London games. And it was true. She had been out in the country. But still?

Gwendolyn answered in her hushed tone to Elise's unspoken question. "We weren't as wise as we should have been when we first realized you had left."

Of course.

Elise hadn't been thinking of returning . . . or of the ramifications to her sisters. "I'm sorry—"

Gwendolyn hushed her. "We are just relieved to have you home. Come."

Elise called Tamsyn to follow and they hurried to the house.

Dara waited on the front step. Elise stopped and faced her sister.

Gwendolyn chided, "We need to go inside. There are eyes everywhere, even when we don't believe we are being watched."

But Elise didn't move. Instead, she reached for Dara's hand. They were the closest sisters. They were a year apart in age and shared the same mother. They'd always lived in the same room until Dara married. As the oldest, Gwendolyn may have watched over them, but the bond between the two younger sisters had always been the strongest, until Michael came along.

And Elise had been brutally unfair to Dara.

She looked her sister in the eye. "I'm sorry. I had no right to be angry over you and Michael."

Only then did she realize how Dara had braced herself, expecting the worst. Her shoulders relaxed. "You loved him."

"No," Elise admitted, "I loved *the idea* of him. I didn't really know him. I didn't even try to. I was wrapped up in myself. He chose you and, yes, I was jealous because—oh, dear, this is going to sound terrible."

"Yes?" Dara prodded.

"Well—" Elise paused and then confessed, "I was the one who you believed would marry first. Your words, not mine."

"I honestly thought that would be what happened," Dara protested.

"I'm glad you were wrong. You and Michael are a good match. If I hadn't been so self-absorbed, I would have seen that."

Dara shook her head as if to deny it, but Elise wouldn't allow her to. "Please, accept my apology. I shall say the same to Michael when I see him."

Gwendolyn spoke, interrupting them. "Is this our little sister speaking?"

Elise rolled her eyes. "I know . . . I can be a bit headstrong."

"A bit?" Gwendolyn questioned, and then smiled

while lightly pushing them both through the doorway. "We need to be away from prying eyes."

This time Elise obeyed, moving inside the house. "Granted, I appear a fright."

"Your dress—" Dara paused. "The shoulder is torn, and patched."

"That is a long story. It also doesn't help that I've been wearing it for days." To distract them, Elise smiled at the butler, who had shut the door behind them. "Hello, Herald."

"Hello, Miss Elise."

She handed him the shabby wide-brimmed hat Kit had purchased for her. "Please treat this with good care."

"I shall, Miss Elise."

"And Tweedie," Elise called out. Her great-aunt sat on a settee in the receiving room. She was petting Tamsyn, who had made herself at home by walking right into the house as the sisters had talked and jumping up next to the older woman. Not even Herald had noticed. Now Tamsyn sat as regal as a duchess as Tweedie scratched behind her ears.

"Where did this dog come from?" Dara asked.

"She's mine," Elise told them. "Her name is Tamsyn and she saved my life." She would eventually tell them about Kit, but not right now. She needed to carefully choose her words as she shared the news that she was in love with a man who did whatever he pleased, had only a few shillings to his name, and answered to no one. A man she prayed had survived Holbert's assault. She wanted to believe she would hear word soon, even if it came from Mr. Steele.

Instead, Elise went to her great-aunt and gave her a huge hug. The maid Molly brought in a tray of sandwiches, hot tea, and sherry. Elise and Tweedie took sherry. No one asked Tamsyn to move off the settee.

"So," Elise said, "what has happened since I left?"

"Other than every debutante and their mother trying to discover if there is any truth to the rumor you have disappeared?" Gwendolyn said.

"I had no desire to bring scandal down on the family," Elise said.

"Then you should have stayed where you were," Tweedie observed. She gave Tamsyn a sandwich.

And there it was—the truth.

Elise drew a fortifying breath. "I wasn't thinking clearly. I was so angry. I'd been angry for a long time."

"With us?" Dara asked.

"No," Elise answered. "I realize now that my anger may have started with Gram's death and the changes that happened with Richard and all. I kept wanting to find a safe place, one where there weren't any changes."

"Such a place does not exist," Tweedie declared, "because life is always changing."

Elise looked at her small family gathered around. She loved them so much.

She also loved Kit—and that is when she understood.

"There is something that doesn't change," she told her family. "Love. When I am here with you, I know I'm safe." Just as she'd been safe with Kit.

"Please, don't ever run away again," Dara said. "I admit I can be somewhat high-handed—but, Elise, you took terrible risks. Something horrible could have happened to you."

She was right. Then again, Elise had no regrets. She'd met Kit.

Gwendolyn poured more tea in her cup. Of all of them, she was the tea drinker. "Elise, you had callers. We made excuses, but men are competitive and that makes them suspicious. Then the other debutantes and their mothers began asking. It was as if they saw a chance to spread rumors. When they have seen us without you, they have been very inquisitive."

Dara nodded. "An upstairs maid we'd hired had been in the employ of Lady Byrne. Her ladyship was paying for information."

Lady Byrne and her two daughters were the Lanscarr sisters' chief rivals. Both families were from County Wicklow and on the hunt for husbands. If any spurious stories were spread about the Lanscarrs, Lady Byrne was usually behind them.

"I am sorry," Elise said. She meant those words. "I was thinking about myself. It was selfish of me."

Dara dusted breadcrumbs from her hands after sampling one of the sandwiches. "We'll be fine. We will have you make an appearance here and there. Those rumors will disappear."

"Besides," Gwendolyn said, "the Season is all but over what with the closing of Parliament this week. The last important ball of the Season is Lord and Lady Woolfolk's and then everyone will be off to the country."

"The Woolfolk ball is being called 'the last chance' for those young women who didn't make a match this Season," Tweedie added. "Surprisingly, you and Gwendolyn are of that number."

Elise glanced at her sister. Elise had been focused on Michael, her anger, and Lady Whitby's salon. Her lack of interest had turned away many suitors. However, Gwendolyn had received several offers, and she'd turned them down. Elise didn't know if Tweedie or Dara knew that. Gwendolyn could be quite secretive when she wished. Elise knew because she'd overheard the rejected complain. They had all been men of good standing. She wondered what Gwendolyn wanted?

"It will be your time to shine," Dara predicted. "Although a certain viscount has been very attentive to Gwendolyn."

Gwendolyn blushed a response and shook her head. "Not Morley."

"Why not?" Dara asked. "He is very respectable."

Elise met Gwendolyn's eye. They both knew that when Dara was busy managing, she often forgot details such as whether a sister was attracted to the gentleman.

But there was no sense arguing. Especially since Dara had turned her attention back to Elise.

"You have some sun on your skin. We shall have to do what we can to lighten it."

Elise didn't wish to worry about the paleness of her complexion. And she wasn't interested in the last ball of the Season. She was waiting for Kit. He would come. She knew it.

A new thought struck her, something that in the excitement of Kit being attacked and the mad race to London she had pushed out of her mind. But something that was very important to all of them. She set her sherry on the side table. "I have important news—Papa is alive."

They stared at her as if they hadn't heard her correctly. Elise reiterated, "He is not dead. I spoke to him. He lives in a village called Moorcock."

"Father?" Dara questioned. Gwendolyn was shaking her head.

"If he was alive," Tweedie said, "why didn't he come and toss Richard and his nagging wife, Caroline, out on their ears?"

Elise picked up her sherry before giving the answer. "Apparently, Wiltham wasn't that important to him." She paused a moment and then said, "He has another family."

There was a moment of stunned silence.

Gwendolyn broke it. "He's alive? And he's remarried?"

"In a way."

"*What* does that mean?" Dara asked. "And I'm still trying to understand that he is alive . . . and we didn't know? He didn't want us to know?"

"Something like that," Elise confessed and then shared meeting the houseful of boys, one close in age to her and Dara.

"I still don't understand," Gwendolyn said.

"He might have been married to *two* women at the same time," Tweedie answered, going right to the heart of the matter. "More than once I told my sister—your grandmother—I thought him a tomcat, so this doesn't truly surprise me. Although when they handed Wiltham to Richard, I did think John was dead."

"What was Gram's reply when you told her my father might have other interests?" Gwendolyn asked.

Elise sniffed her thoughts. "Gwendolyn, you are so kind. 'Other interests'? He had a whole separate family and a good house. It wasn't as grand as Wiltham; however, it was close to Moorcock, and you know gambling has always been his first love."

"So Moorcock is a place for gamblers?" Dara asked.

"And other unsavory activities," Elise answered.

"What were you doing there?"

Elise sidestepped that question by looking at Tweedie and asking, "What would Gram say?"

"She'd shrug and say, what can you do? And

she was right. Anything we did would have up-set you girls. You adored him."

"Because we didn't know who he was?" Dara suggested pointedly.

Tweedie's eyes narrowed thoughtfully. "Think about the truth, and where we all were several months ago. Wiltham was your home . . . but it was falling apart because of neglect."

"*His* neglect," Elise couldn't hold back from saying bitterly. "And now Richard's."

"And yet you were going there, weren't you?" Gwendolyn observed quietly.

Elise shot her a guilty glance. "I was . . . I was confused. I thought it was home."

"And now?" Tweedie asked.

Elise had been thinking on this during the long ride back to London. She answered quietly, "I now believe, home is where people you love are."

Dara took her hand. "We are glad you are returned to us. That is all that matters. As for Father and whatever subterfuge he has played . . . well, I am sorry for him."

Gwendolyn chimed in, "Although I think he wished to be there for us. He did return."

"To take what cash he could find out of Wiltham," Tweedie grumbled.

"Then he missed what was valuable," Gwendolyn answered. "*Us.*"

Michael returned home just then, interrupting them. He acted as delighted as her sisters to have Elise home. She was going to be spending the rest of her life apologizing to Michael and Dara for her behavior. She had reacted selfishly and here they were, treating her like a valued member of the family.

He was quickly included in the information about their father being alive.

"Was he happy to see you?" Dara asked.

"That is the part that is uncomfortable," Elise warned. "No, he wasn't happy. He did recognize me, but then he acted almost angry that I had come to his doorstep. He seemed to have his life there and he really didn't care about Wiltham or what had happened to us."

There was a moment of silence as those dark words sank in.

"I'm going to find him," Dara said, rising to her feet as if she would walk out the door that minute.

Michael rose and blocked his wife's passage. "And do what?" He shook his head. "I would be happy to call him out for you. I think it would be a waste of a bullet, but I would do it."

Dara placed her hand on his arm. "He's not worth it, is he?"

"He's your father. Only you can answer that question."

Elise chimed in, "He's not worth it. I prefer my memories of him to the man I met."

Gwendolyn leaned forward. "We have half brothers?"

"Several of them," Elise confirmed. "You are

no longer the only dark-haired person in the family."

Tweedie made a disgusted sound and looked at Tamsyn, her hand on the dog's back. "What do you think? Is he worth a bullet?"

Tamsyn yawned, stretching her jaws wide. The poor dear was probably exhausted after her travels, but the action fit the question so well that the sisters found themselves laughing.

Elise grew pensive. "It is sad that Wiltham is gone to us."

Gwendolyn answered, "Wiltham will always be home . . . but some things we let go of because we grow away from them. They cease to be important to us. Our life is here, Elise. With the new."

Like Kit. The time had come to reveal all the truth.

Elise spoke of the accident, of Kit's saving her life, and Tamsyn helping them find shelter. She didn't tell of Tommy and Simon. But she shared about the long walk to reach the next posting inn.

"How did you realize Father was alive?" Gwendolyn asked.

"The man who accompanied me—" That was how she referred to Kit. "He was playing cards and he used Papa's shuffle."

"His shuffle?" Michael asked.

Gwendolyn started to explain but then decided it was too difficult, and a deck of cards was found. She expertly executed the shuffle.

Michael looked to Dara. "Can you do that?"

"Only Gwendolyn," his wife answered. "And apparently this, ah, man." She looked to Elise. "Does this man have a name?"

*Kit.* "Mr. Cox."

Her sisters exchanged glances. Elise remained still. Had they heard what she hadn't said? Her sisters could be remarkably perceptive.

"What happened next?" Tweedie prodded in the sudden silence.

"He took me to Moorcock. I found Father. Mr. Steele found me." They didn't need to know anything else.

"Took you?" Dara prodded.

Elise didn't answer. But she wanted to add that soon Kit would come for her. She knew he would.

"You've changed."

Elise gave a sharp glance to Gwendolyn. "In what way?"

Her oldest sister didn't answer. Dara did. "You've matured . . . but there is something else." She had a knowing look in her eye.

"She's had quite an ordeal." Tweedie spoke as if there would be nothing more said. She rose. She was using her walking cane. "Come, I am ready for my supper. It is past time."

And that was it. They all walked into the dining room.

Elise begged a moment to wash and change.

"Let me show you the room," Gwendolyn said.

Tamsyn followed Elise up the stairs. Where once Elise had shared a room with Dara, she now shared with Gwendolyn. The room they had been given was the first door on the right side of the stairs.

Molly had poured water into the pitcher. Elise filled the basin. The soap was violet-scented, one of Gwendolyn's favorite fragrances. Elise washed, took out her serviceable green day dress from the wardrobe, and changed. She then used Gwendolyn's brush for her hair. She started to braid it, but then realized she was too tired. It had been a long, hard journey . . . and she was right back where she'd begun.

She looked around the room. "If we aren't careful, it will be as if you and I never knew Kit," she warned Tamsyn. "But he will come for us. He will."

Elise just wished she knew when.

She went down the stairs to join her family for supper.

⁕⁕⁕⁕⁕

EVERY DAY, ELISE waited for Kit to come for her.

Tamsyn kept watch beside her.

Time passed slowly with one day flowing into another. A week. Then two weeks.

Her sisters encouraged Elise to accompany them around town. They wanted her to be seen and quell any gossip.

"Lady Byrne has been spreading the vilest innuendoes," Dara warned.

"I overheard Helen Byrne tell Lady Alice Pinwood that you had some dreaded disease," Gwendolyn said with exasperation. "I practically boxed the girl's ears. It will be some time before Helen makes such a false claim about you again."

Elise didn't care about rumors. She also had no desire to leave the house. Her focus was on Kit.

One afternoon Tweedie joined Elise as she sat by the window overlooking the street, Tamsyn by her side. "He's more than just an acquaintance, isn't he, lamb?" she asked Elise, using a pet name from years ago.

"I don't understand," Elise answered, not taking her gaze off the paved road.

Her great-aunt had a piece of hard cheese for Tamsyn. Tweedie often snuck treats to the dog, who was becoming a great favorite of everyone in the family, including Herald.

"Elise, one of the hard lessons of life is that sometimes things aren't meant to be. Your struggles with that truth have been one of your downfalls."

She looked to her aunt. "He isn't just anyone, Tweedie," she admitted. "And if it is in his power, he will come."

Tweedie sat a moment, and then she said, "Do you remember the story of the three Fates?"

"The Greek or Roman?" Elise asked.

Tweedie waved a hand. "You are too clever, girl. However, you know that they weave the thread of one's life. I've had three husbands. Three men who had loved me well." She smiled. "Three Fates."

She had Elise's attention now.

"What I learned, what the Fates taught me, is that if it is meant to be, it will happen. Your sitting and waiting will not bring him to you any quicker. But I would like to meet this man who has so captured your imagination."

"He is remarkable."

"As I would expect. However, you must trust that the golden thread the Fates weave has encircled both of you. He'll either find you or not."

"It is the 'not' I fear."

"You have no power over the 'not,' Elise." Tweedie stood, bent, and kissed the top of her head as if in benediction, and without another word left Elise to her watch.

"YOU MUST GO to the Woolfolk ball," Dara insisted.

"And why is that?" Elise challenged her.

They stood in what Dara called the Garden Room because it overlooked the back of the house. It was where Dara liked to do her sewing. The sisters still made their own gowns. Even though Michael was relatively well-to-do, he was supporting a household of four women. Every economy was appreciated.

Besides, the sisters liked designing their own dresses. It made them feel useful. To this end, several measures of fabrics had been spread out over the furniture because Dara believed Elise should have a new dress.

Elise was just as certain that a new gown was not necessary because she had no intention of attending the Woolfolk ball.

"Everyone will be there. You can't miss it," Dara responded.

"This is the last ball before everyone goes off to wherever they go," Gwendolyn added. "We need you. *I* need you. I'm tired of seeing those other debutantes gloat over the demise of the Lanscarr sisters."

"They don't," Elise countered.

"They do," Dara assured her. "You can't imagine how petty they are. They say we set out to marry dukes and, well, we have missed our mark. Of course, I'll take an MP over a duke any day." Dara shook out a light blue diaphanous muslin. "Touch this. Isn't it soft? And the weight is perfect. The skirt will move in time with the music."

Elise did touch the material. The color was lovely and it was as finely woven and soft as she'd ever seen.

"The gossip is that the Duke of Winderton will be at the Woolfolk ball," Gwendolyn said.

"Who is the Duke of Winderton?" Elise asked.

"He's the one everyone claimed we should meet. Remember when we first arrived? They called him the 'young' duke," Gwendolyn answered.

Elise laughed. "I didn't know such a creature existed."

"I'd given up hope, too." Gwendolyn held the material up to herself. "However, everyone is whispering that he will be there."

Elise sat on a nearby chair. The blue was a gorgeous fabric, but, "I am not interested in a duke. Young or old," she assured her sisters.

Dara tilted her head speculatively. "It doesn't hurt to look."

"And you will be with us," Gwendolyn pointed out, holding the blue up to the light. "In a lovely new dress for the last ball of the Season. And if you don't want to dance with what must be the only young duke in London, then you can have the task of keeping Tweedie out of the punch."

"It might be easier to dance with the duke, even an old one," Elise responded, and her sisters laughed in agreement. Tweedie did like to sneak from the punch bowl.

And in the end, the promise of a lovely new dress and an evening with her family was too hard to resist. Elise agreed to go to the ball.

# CHAPTER TWENTY-THREE

*As the sun follows its course, may you follow me.*
IRISH BLESSING

Lord and Lady Woolfolk's ball was a crush. The coach carrying the Brogans and the Lanscarrs seemed to sit still for the better part of an hour before they were able to pull up to the front doors.

Once they did get inside, everyone seemed in excellent spirits. Soon, those who had country houses would adjourn to them to prepare for the hunting season, and those who didn't hoped for invitations to those houses. Friends who might not see each other for a while were happy for the opportunity to spend time with each other before they left Town.

Elise knew she looked well. Molly and Gwendolyn had both worked on her hair. "We need to set the rumors to rest that you were somehow unwell," Gwendolyn had said. "I also want you to outshine not only the Byrne sisters but all those jealous debutantes who had whispered mean things."

Surprisingly, Elise found she didn't care about the gossips.

Although, as she admired herself in the full-length glass, she would like Kit to see her this way. The gown her sisters had created for her was lovely. The skirts were of delicate layers of the light blue muslin; the low-cut bodice was of a marine velvet. Its short sleeves showed her shoulders off to perfection.

She chose to wear no adornment. Not even in her hair, which was piled on her head to fall to her shoulders in a cascade of curls. This simplicity made her feel as if she was signaling to one and all that she was not in search of a suitor. She had her man.

Of course, her sisters could not leave well enough alone. Gwendolyn wanted to pin flowers in Elise's hair. Dara wished to loan her a silver locket Michael had given her.

She refused both. She finished her outfit with her long white kid gloves. She didn't even bother with a fan, although the evening promised to be warm.

Once they had finally stepped across the threshold of the Woolfolk residence, Elise wished she could go right back outside. With all of the guests crowded in, the house retained the day's heat. The warmth mixed with the scent of human bodies wearing their favorite perfumes and colognes, the burning wax of the candles, and the aroma of the supper being prepared for later.

How she missed the green of the woods.

As she waited her turn in the receiving line, she caught a glimpse of envious looks being thrown toward her and Gwendolyn by other young women. The animosity was almost laughable when, really, none of them were guilty of anything more than trying to survive in Society.

She understood their fears. But her perspective had changed. Before she'd run away, she'd assumed this was how life *had* to be as they all vied for the same small circle of suitors.

Now she knew, there was a world of possibilities waiting beyond class and strictures. Titles and money were lovely things . . . but they couldn't make her feel whole, not the way Kit had.

She knew Dara understood. To a point. Dara had married well. Very well. Her sweet sister who dearly loved the rules of Society might not endorse the idea of Elise choosing a wanderer. A ruffian. A nobody.

Or would she?

Her glance strayed to where her sister and her husband stood talking to two loud, braying men with the air of politicians. The men had charged up to him the minute he'd walked through the door. Michael hadn't even started through the receiving line.

Elise noticed that Dara, the strongest of all of them, had covertly reached for her husband's hand.

With his attention on the gentlemen, his hand grasped hers.

Elise stared at that tenuous touch, and she knew how much it meant. She yearned for it.

At last, they were announced. They stepped forward to greet their host and hostess.

"Miss Lanscarr, I heard you have been ill," Lady Woolfolk said in greeting.

In answer, Elise smiled. She'd learned long ago that most people just wanted to talk *at* her. It didn't make any difference what she said because they didn't listen anyway. "Thank you for the invitation, my lady."

A mischievous expression crossed Lady Woolfolk's face. "We are glad you are with us. Of course, it is a pity you will not capture your duke this Season. At least, not the young one. Poor hunting for the Lanscarr sisters, eh? My friend Lady Pinwood said her daughter Alice has captured Winderton's attention. He may soon be off the market. Perhaps you will have better luck next Season. All the young women who didn't make a match the first time around usually do better the second time. They set their sights lower."

Elise realized she'd been insulted. She could inform their hostess she didn't want a duke. And how would that rumor sound?

Instead, Elise murmured something noncommittal and kept moving.

They all settled Tweedie with the other matrons and gave her a glass of orgeat. Tweedie frowned at the sweet drink but did not complain, although her gaze met Elise's in a meaningful way. Meaningful meant she expected Elise to purloin a forbidden glass of punch, or two.

Michael turned to his wife. "Do you mind if I speak to a few people?"

"Not at all," Dara said. "We shall be right here."

"Here" was beside one of the room's columns wrapped in peach-colored fabric, where they had an excellent view of the dance floor. The same fabric hung from the walls and covered chairs, although Elise doubted anyone noticed because the room was too crowded and everyone was busy trying to call attention to themselves.

Over the chatter of hundreds of guests, Lady Byrne's voice trilled out, "Good evening, Mrs. Brogan." She was gliding about with her daughters, Helen and Sophie, in her wake. Alongside them were two other mothers and their daughters, who Elise did not recognize.

"I see we have Miss Elise with us this evening," Lady Byrne announced loudly. "I'm so relieved. We feared you had come down with something fatal."

"If that was your hope, I am sorry to disappoint," Elise said with a little smile.

Gwendolyn and Dara had to look away quickly to stifle their laughter.

Lady Byrne did not take teasing well, and she

hated anyone who was a threat to her daughters' chances of making advantageous matches. She lifted her lorgnette, a new affectation for her, and eyed Elise from top to bottom. "You are dressed like some penitent."

Elise wanted to laugh. Her ladyship said this as if it was a bad thing to not wear jewelry. She slipped her hand around Dara's arm and then through Gwendolyn's. They stood as a united front. "Thank you, my lady," Elise responded pleasantly.

Her ladyship shook her head as if Elise hadn't known she was being insulted. And then, one of the other mothers, a woman who held her head in such a disapproving way it formed two extra chins against her neck, said to the daughters, "There is nothing like the promise of a duke's attendance to bring out the Lanscarr sisters."

Elise drew her sisters closer and said in the same sotto voce the woman had used, "I understand that this new duke is already promised to Lady Alice."

"*What?*" Any facade of politeness vanished from Lady Byrne's face. "I've heard nothing of the sort."

"I have this intelligence from Lady Woolfolk," Elise offered. "Perhaps you should ask her."

Lady Byrne rounded on her friends. She whispered furiously at them and they just as furiously replied. Without a word of farewell, the lot of them dove into the crowd.

"I detest that woman," Gwendolyn said. Dara nodded.

"She just wants to see her daughters launched," Elise explained.

Dara looked at her. "Hello, is this Elise? You could never abide her either."

"That was before," Elise admitted.

"Before what?"

"I realized how silly it all is." Her sisters looked puzzled. "We are all just trying to do the best we can," Elise explained. "Fortunately, I have the two of you in my life and not a mother like Lady Byrne. You will love me no matter who I am."

A looked passed between Gwendolyn and Dara. Dara said, "You've changed."

"In what way?"

"You used to be overly passionate about everything."

That was true. Elise now realized she'd been shrill and condemning, and then Kit had come along. Kit, who had listened to her. She didn't feel so invisible with him. Consequently, she no longer strived to be understood.

"We know it wasn't learning of Father's deception that brought this thoughtfulness out in you," Gwendolyn said.

Elise glanced away, uncertain what to say.

"I think it might have been that man who helped her after the coach wreck," Dara hazarded.

That caught Elise's attention. "What man?" she asked innocently.

Gwendolyn spoke. "Oh, please. Something happened, Elise, something that has given you a fresh perspective on life."

"It could be the danger of the crash," Dara suggested.

The oldest sister shook her head. "That does happen with some people. However, one doesn't sit at a window overlooking the street waiting for a wrecked coach."

"Waiting?" Elise queried.

Her sisters almost groaned.

"Any fool can tell that you miss him," Gwendolyn said.

"Well, not Michael," Dara said. "He was worried about Elise not going out. He feared you weren't well. I told him you were merely acting lovesick."

"Men don't understand," Gwendolyn said.

"Not unless they experience it themselves," Dara said. "But that is the way they are, isn't it—?"

Elise stepped between her sisters. "*Lovesick?*" Her first thought was her conversation with her great-aunt. "Did Tweedie—?"

"Tweedie said nothing," Gwendolyn cut in. "She didn't have to. We know you better than you know yourself. Who is he, Elise? Is he the one who helped you in the crash? We have been waiting for you to tell us on your own."

"You can trust us," Dara added.

"I do trust you . . . I just thought—" Elise broke off. She'd done it again. She'd discounted her sisters and their love for her. She pulled them into a tight circle, shutting out everyone in the ballroom. "He's not titled," she whispered. "Or wealthy. But he is the most wonderful, *noble* man alive. Even if he rarely shaves."

"Does he bathe?" Gwendolyn firmly believed in the efficacy of soap and water. She'd pushed her sisters to think the same.

"Of course," Elise answered. "I want you to meet him. He should be coming for me any day."

"Why hasn't he come yet?" Dara wanted to know.

So, Elise told them of Holbert and the vendetta . . . how Kit had saved her life again. All of the dangerous things she had left out of her earlier story.

They'd been so wrapped up in their discussion, they almost didn't realize that Lord and Lady Woolfolk had left the receiving line and were prepared to open the ball by leading the first dance.

Anything else Elise could have shared about Kit was interrupted by the arrival of a trio of young men racing to reach Elise and Gwendolyn before the others.

Viscount Morley begged Gwendolyn for the dance. Elise found herself agreeing to accompany young Lord Durbin and after that, there was a line for the following dances.

Elise understood her role. She could not attend a ball and refuse every offer for a dance. She smiled, she behaved, she danced, she was kind to the gentlemen.

However, her heart was light. Her sisters had seemed happy for her. Meanwhile, once again, she had underestimated their love for her.

Elise had just finished a dance with the Marquis of Combury. He gallantly escorted her back to her family. Michael had rejoined them. He stood at his wife's side. The marquis was thanking Elise for the honor of a dance just as there seemed to be a rush of whispers all around.

At first, Elise thought that the supper room must have opened. There was always an eagerness among the guests when that happened. Many would line up, crowding the door, except the hour was too early.

And then she realized the whisper was the pronouncement of a name. They were saying "Winderton." Repeating it over and over to each other until it sounded like a wind rustling through the guests.

She looked to the door. She wasn't the only one. Women immediately began preening as they turned toward the entrance. Men straightened as if preparing to be challenged for their women.

Dara squeezed her arm. "The eighth wonder of the world, a 'young' duke has arrived," she said with mock excitement, and they laughed.

A butler stepped forward. In loud sonorous tones, much louder and more sonorous than he had introduced Elise and her family, he said, "His Grace, the Duke of Winderton, and Her Grace, the Dowager Duchess of Winderton."

The duke had arrived.

Everyone around Elise seemed to be taking this arrival with a seriousness one would save for a king. Mothers pushed daughters forward. One almost tripped and fell.

Michael shook his head. "It is about time Winderton showed his face. He's been missing for months."

"Where has he been?" Dara asked.

"No one knows." Michael made a scoffing sound. "I met him over a year ago."

"And?" his wife prodded.

"He was another spoiled, petulant aristocrat who was not interested in helping with any bills before the Lords, including those on agriculture. He'd rather drink."

Dara made a disgusted sound. "Dukes are a disappointment."

"Some aren't," Michael answered. "*He* is."

Gwendolyn joined them from the dance floor. Her partner had rushed the niceties and hastily left her with her family so he could edge closer to the door. Perhaps he wished to be one of the first to greet the duke. "What in the world is happening?" she asked, confused.

"Winderton has arrived," Michael said with great drama, making his wife and her sisters laugh.

And then he was there. *The duke.*

Elise saw movement by the door, but she couldn't catch a glimpse of the special guest because so many others were welcoming him. Even the musicians slowed their playing. Apparently they, too, wished to see this mighty Winderton. However, after what Michael had said, Elise's interest had waned. That is, until a woman swooned.

Several arms caught her before she fell.

Gwendolyn sent a look to Elise. "Can you believe this?"

"I'm curious now," Elise had to admit. She stood on her tiptoes, trying to see over the crowd—

She caught a glimpse—but it was enough.

*Kit was here.* She saw him.

She started forward, forgetting her sisters, forgetting where she was. This duke meant nothing to her. The man she wanted, the one who was important, was in the crowd by the door. She'd seen Kit. *Her* Kit.

However, she didn't know if she could reach him. He was in the deep knot of guests welcoming the duke. She'd have to wend her way around them and she didn't know if it was possible.

Because everyone had shifted to the door, the space at the center of the dance floor was empty. She moved to it and waited. Kit would find her here. He would see her and come to her. She clasped her hands in anticipation.

And then the crowd seemed to part and Kit walked forward . . .

He had never appeared so fine. His hair had

been cut. She noticed that immediately. And he was clean-shaven. He wore black evening attire. His waistcoat was red brocade.

Those were the changes.

Everything else about him was exactly as she recalled. The loose-hipped walk. The crooked smile. Gray eyes full of humor, understanding . . . *and love.* So full of love. Elise launched herself toward that love. He caught her up in his arms as if he would never let her go.

Kit still carried the scent of the forests and the rain and adventure. She held him tight, reveling in the feel of his body against hers.

And then she looked up at him and noticed faint bruises. And his nose—

"He broke your nose," she said with concern.

"It is nothing," he assured her. "It is practically healed." He smiled down at her. "The things I do for you."

"*That* one was on you—" she started, ready to defend herself, but then a new thought intruded. "How are you here?"

He'd set her feet on the floor but she kept her hands on his shoulders, needing the solid feeling of him.

His hands were loosely around her waist. "Elise, I have something to confess."

She didn't like the hesitation in his voice. It warned her that she might not like this confession.

"My full name is Christopher Fitzhugh-Cox."

Elise gave a small shrug. Kit Cox. His name

came from there. He also acted as if she should recognize him by it. She didn't.

"I'm the Duke of Winderton."

She was uncertain she'd heard him correctly. Her initial euphoria at uniting with him was settling down. Awareness of her surroundings returned.

They were the center of attention. Instead of everyone being gathered around the duke in the doorway, they now circled the dance floor.

*Everyone.* Even her family.

And the musicians had stopped playing so that, into the stillness, they had all heard what he'd said about his name.

No one corrected him.

Elise glanced over to Gwendolyn and Dara. Tweedie stood beside them. The three of them appeared thunderstruck, and Elise didn't know what to do, what to think. Kit? A duke?

The *young* duke?

Her Kit had another identity.

He also seemed to grow aware of how exposed they were. He took action. He reached for her hand and, before she could protest, started toward the doors leading to the back garden.

Kit moved so swiftly she almost had to skip to keep up.

Outside, torches provided a flickering golden light. There was no one with them. Everyone in attendance had been inside to witness the arrival of the famed missing Duke of Winderton. Now they all packed around the doors as if they were watching the most entertaining of plays.

Thankfully, they stayed in the house, and if Elise turned her back to them, she could pretend that she and Kit were somewhat private.

"It is starting," he said.

"Starting?"

He combed a frustrated hand through his newly trimmed hair. "The attention, the gossips." He shrugged. "I'm sorry for this, Elise." He made an exasperated sound. "It is part of my life in London. You can see how my behaving badly would make me the focus of the wrong sort of attention. I entertained the gossips for months."

"And made you wish to escape like Prince Hal?"

He straightened his shoulders. "Not the most mature reaction," he admitted.

Although certainly an imaginative one. She studied him, trying to see him with new eyes . . . and yet, he was still Kit to her.

Or was he?

"Why didn't you tell me who you were?" she asked.

"Would you have believed me?" he countered.

Elise thought back to the handsome Ruffian, to the smell of liquor on his breath and the way he had dressed. "No."

"Would you believe anything I told you if you had known I was keeping my identity secret?"

His question surprised her. She hesitated. "I don't know." There was a pause between them.

She remembered his palm on her breast and how it felt to have him inside her. "Lady Woolfolk claimed the Duke of Winderton is interested in Lady Alice Pinwood."

He made a face. "Pinwood? I've never heard of her. There are mothers who will spread rumors. I have no control over their behavior. I'm not promised to anyone."

He placed his hand on her arm, almost as if he feared she'd reject him. "Holbert was very thorough with his fists. I came as quickly as I was able."

She swallowed. She'd feared he'd been in danger. But now, here he was in front of her. But was it him? Or was he now changed?

There was a beat, and then he said, "I knew you would be here."

"And so you chose this public place?"

"I could see you here or go running around the city tracking down Brogan's residence. This seemed quicker. Do you believe me? Do you trust me?"

*Trust.* He'd used that word. There had been a time Elise had trusted everyone. Even her father. She was not so naive any longer.

As if reading her mind, he sank down to his knees in front of her. His hand slid down her arm to her hand. "But here is the true reason I'm here tonight, Elise. I'm in love with you. I fell in love with you, well, perhaps from that hour you blackened my eye. I admire your spirit, your courage, and your audacity. I promised myself that once

I found you again, I'd not waste time in telling you what is in my heart. You are intelligent and generous and I need you in my life.

"I need someone to walk with me in this life who sees my shortcomings, my occasional silliness, and the things I do right, as well. Someone who can hold a mirror to me and help me be the person I am meant to be. Someone *I* can trust.

"That person is you, Elise. I need you. I need your honesty. I need your heart. I need your warmth and your fearlessness. I need you to serve as a conscience and prod me into action.

"Will you do me the honor of becoming my wife? And, yes, that means you will be my duchess. It is a weighty title, but together, we shall find the joy in it."

*He loved her.*

Elise lowered to her knees in front of him. They were equals. That was what he was offering. This man understood her, knew her, and loved her anyway.

Her heart filled with joy . . . because at last, she'd found where she belonged—with him whether he was a duke or a ditch digger. He was the one.

"I will be honored to be your wife. I love you to the deepest depths of my being." And then she added, because she must, "I might even listen to you if you are my husband."

He shook his head. "I'm not looking for an obedient wife but one who will challenge me, Elise."

"Then I am the woman for you," she promised and he laughed, as she knew he would.

And then, he kissed her. Right there in front of everyone in the polite world, and she kissed him back.

A cheer went up around them. The doors had opened and too many people had covertly moved outside and overheard the proposal, including her sisters and Tweedie. They were the first to surround her with well wishes, and to introduce themselves to the man who would soon be the newest member of their family.

Kit helped her stand, but he kept his hands lightly, protectively on her shoulders.

Lady Woolfolk was happily preening over the success of her ball, what with the Duke of Winderton proposing in front of the gathered company. She seemed to have forgotten her claims about Alice Pinwood, and Elise did as well.

"There is someone I wish you to meet," Kit said. He motioned for an older woman to join them. Elise knew immediately that this was Kit's mother. He favored her with his gray eyes and bearing.

The dowager smiled at Elise. "You have given me back my son. I don't know if I can thank you enough."

"Your Grace, I have done very little—" Elise started. The dowager cut her off.

"Nonsense. Love is the best tonic in the world. Love him, Miss Lanscarr. Pour love into him, and I pray he does the same for you. It is a gift to marry a man you can respect. Now, why don't the two of you lead the next dance?" She placed Elise's hand into Kit's and gave them a small nudge toward the doors.

And as Kit led her into the ballroom, they walked by the Byrne sisters and their mother. The look on their faces was pure spite, but it didn't matter.

Elise wasn't marrying a duke. She was marrying the man she loved. And she prayed the Byrne sisters would someday be as happy as she was.

❦

THE DUKE OF Winderton's public declaration to Elise made the Woolfolk ball the talk of the Season. Mayhap the decade. Many debutante hopes had been dashed by the loss of the "young" duke, but there were just as many people who could not wait to brag that they had been there.

Tweedie had been disappointed. She hadn't received a cup of punch. With all the uproar over the engagement, she hadn't been able to find anyone to slip one to her.

When Kit heard this, he sent a footman over with a cup of his family's secret punch recipe, just for her. She pronounced it quite tasty and then spent the rest of the afternoon sleeping it off.

The one person who wasn't particularly pleased with the betrothal was Michael.

However, Kit called upon Michael to formally request permission to marry Elise and to lay out his prospects. Kit confided to Elise that his uncle had suggested it, and wise advice it was.

Michael had choice words to share about a man paying attention to his responsibilities. He had shared his opinions with Elise the night before, so she was somewhat anxious.

However, after a little less than an hour, Michael and Kit emerged from the study as if they were the best of friends. Kit had won him over. Elise was also not surprised to learn that Michael expected support for several of the major pieces of legislation to be presented in the next Parliament.

Kit had been happy to oblige.

And so it was that, in the middle of August, Kit and Elise spoke their vows in front of the vicar of the Winderton private chapel at Smythson. Tamsyn was there with the family in a collar of summer wildflowers.

When it came time to drink to their health, Kit spoke of how blessed he was to marry into the Lanscarr family. How Elise's sisters and great-aunt were now his. He hoped they would consider Smythson their family home as much as it was his.

Later that evening, while everyone, including the servants, celebrated and danced in celebration of the duke and his new duchess, Kit took Elise's hand. "Come with me."

She was happy to be away from the guests. The house seemed overcrowded and all seemed too busy for peace. Or rest.

Kit led her down moonlit and shadowed paths. The sounds of music and laughter drifted away. Their walk reminded her of their travels, of there just being the two of them.

At last they came upon what seemed to be a smaller version of Smythson. It had the same red brick, the same graceful lines. Candlelight glowed welcomingly from the windows. Torches burned in the front yard and lamps by the open door. The path leading up to it had been strewn with rose petals. Their fragrance was released with each step she and Kit took toward the door.

"What is this?" Elise asked. She had only arrived at Smythson the day before and had not had time for a tour.

"Our personal haven." He kissed the back of her hand. "It's the Dower House. I had it prepared for just us. Mother will have to wait until she moves in."

"You are a clever man, Kit Cox."

"So they tell me," he agreed with a smile, and then turned serious. "Elise, I know you miss Wiltham, and I'm sorry it is lost to you. But I pray that Smythson will become as dear to you as your home in Ireland was. That is my hope."

She turned him around to face her. "It already

is. Wiltham represented a dream, an ideal . . . but without the people I love in it, well, it is just wood and stones. Smythson is my future. We shall raise our children here and their laughter will echo through its hallways."

"You make me a proud man, Elise Lanscarr."

"And why is that?"

"Because I had the good sense to marry you."

She laughed, her heart light and full of joy. This was how marriage should be—a meeting of two people whose love made them stronger when they were together.

And with that, Kit swept her up into his arms and carried her over the threshold and into a new life.

# AND SO . . .

*G*wendolyn needed something to read. She was desperate for it. Now that both of her sisters were married, life had become rather dull.

Dara and Michael were completely wrapped up in each other. Elise and Winderton had not returned from Smythson, and there was no word on when to expect them.

Even Tweedie seemed to be busy. A retired Colonel McNeil who had known one of her late husbands had begun calling.

So, there it was. Everyone was paired off save Gwendolyn. It wasn't as if she couldn't have a partner. Viscount Morley had made an offer only last week. He was one of many to ask for her hand. Gwendolyn had become very good at expressing just the right amount of gratitude for the honor of the offer, while *regretfully* saying she could not marry them.

Morley was one of those who had left insulted. Gwendolyn had come to learn she had no power to soften the rejection. She had always attempted to be as honest as she could; however, men were strange creatures. They read into a dance or her giving them a moment of her time, something she had never intended to convey.

Meanwhile, *her* problem was that most of the gentlemen she'd met bored her to tears. She couldn't imagine spending a week with one of them, let alone her life.

But what *was* she going to do? Because living under Michael and Dara's roof or visiting Smythson would grow old, and very quickly.

The truth was, of the three sisters, Gwendolyn longed for adventure. The night in Dublin when she had disguised herself and gambled to raise the money for her and her sisters' Season in London several months ago had been exciting.

There had been a moment when all could have gone wrong, but then Mr. Steele had been there.

Mr. Steele, who had almost kissed her that night, and who had come to her family's rescue when she'd asked him to save Elise.

How could any mere lord compete with the phantom who was Beckett Steele?

She'd not confided her infatuation to her sisters. They would worry for her. *She* worried for her.

Steele was not the sort of man a conventional young woman should admire. Or so Gwendolyn had told herself several times since arriving in London.

Even still, her gaze sought him out at every ball and soiree and on every street corner. Once, she'd felt his presence and she'd found him waiting for her in the hostess's garden. It was as if he'd been sending a message that only the two of them could hear.

Alas, that probably had been more a fancy of her imagination than anything factual, because she had tried to conjure him many times since without success.

A little bell jingled as Gwendolyn entered the lending library. She was well-known here. She left her maid Molly outside by the front door. She enjoyed asking the clerks to take different books from the shelves behind the counter for her to consider. She delighted in the feel of paper and the smell of glue and bindings. She did not need Molly's sighs of boredom to interfere with her pleasure.

"Hello, Mr. Peters," she said as he signaled her over to him. They were quite busy today. She glanced around and didn't notice anyone she knew.

"Miss Lanscarr, what a pleasure." Mr. Peters was around her age. He had prominent ears that turned bright pink whenever he was around her. Sometimes, to his great embarrassment, his voice cracked. "I was just thinking of sending you a note."

"Really? Why?"

"We have a book here with your name on it."
He held up a slip of paper. Her name was indeed
scribbled across it.

"I haven't requested a book in recent memory,"
she said, moving closer to the counter.

"Well, here it is. I can put it back on the shelf if
there is a mistake—"

"No, no, let me see it," Gwendolyn said, holding out her gloved hand. She delighted in a
mystery. "Perhaps I asked for something and
forgot. That is possible."

He started to hand the book to her, then
paused. He frowned. "I—I don't think this is
proper reading for you."

"What do you mean?"

He turned the slim volume over. "It is Dante's
*Inferno*."

"Is it in the original Italian?" she asked.

Mr. Peters appeared confused. He shook his
head. "It is the Boyd." He referred to the English
translation.

"I have not read that one."

"Have you read the Italian?"

Gwendolyn could not read Italian. She'd only
inquired because she was offended that the milk-
and-water Mr. Peters believed he should curate
her reading for her. "Of course." She waved her
hand, showing she expected the book.

His brow furrowed in concern, or as if she had
fallen a notch in his estimation. She hoped it was
the latter.

Reluctantly, he gave the book over and then, his back stiff, he busied himself behind the counter.

Gwendolyn didn't give a care. There were other clerks who could check the book out for her. Instead, she moved toward the center of the room.

When she opened the book, the pages fell to where a snowy white calling card had been placed between them. She picked it up. On one side was the engraved word *Steele*.

On the other was a handwritten message addressed to no one.

But meant for *her*.

*You will receive an invitation.*
*Accept it.*

*S*

Gwendolyn shut the book, and just like that, life had become exciting again.

# More from
# CATHY MAXWELL

**The Gambler's — Daughters —**

**The Logical Man's Guide — to Dangerous Women —**

**—The Spinster Heiress—**

**— Marrying the Duke —**

**—The Brides of Wishmore—**

**— The Chattan Novels —**

**— The Scandals and Seductions Novels —**

## The Cameron Sisters

## The Marriage Novels